DUCK AND COVER

DUCK AND COVER

A NOVEL

BRENDA PETERSON

HarperCollins*Publishers*

Chapter 1 originally appeared under the title "Duck and Cover" in ZZYVA magazine, Fall 1986, and was a PEN Syndicated Fiction Project, 1988–89.

Chapter 2 originally appeared under the title "Carpool" in Savvy magazine, July 1989.

FIRST EDITION

Designed by Alma Orenstein

Library of Congress Cataloging-in-Publication Data

Peterson, Brenda.
Duck and cover / Brenda Peterson.
p.   cm.
ISBN 0-06-016320-8
I. Title.
PS3566.E767D83 1991
813´ .54—dc20   90-56368

91 92 93 94 95 HC 10 9 8 7 6 5 4 3 2 1

for my family—Mother, Father,
Paula, Marla, Dana Mark

and for Flor, *curandera*

ACKNOWLEDGMENTS

The author gratefully acknowledges the Seattle Arts Commission Artist-in-Residence fiction fellowship for its support during the writing of this book. I am also deeply grateful to my agent, Beth Vesel, whose astute readings helped me shape this novel; to Susan Biskeborn, who met with me for five years over our authors' dinners for nurturance and "creative whining"; to Katherine Koberg, for her finishing editorial touches; to my brother Dana Mark, who lent me his expert aerial eye; and to my sister Paula, who sees me through every book with her critical kindness.

CONTENTS

All things are connected like the blood that unites one family.
All things are connected.

—CHIEF SEATTLE, 1854

1

DUCK AND COVER

Sydney, 1982

My family has practiced the end of the world more than most, because of the five members of my family, three have top-security clearance. Perhaps this accounts for the "emergency personality" that is triggered whenever all of us come together. We usually meet in foreign airports and throw ourselves into carpool caravans cross-country to arrive at some prearranged destination—or as my mother, who works for the CIA, might say, "drop-off point."

Last summer, in a rare gesture toward the traditional, we held our reunion at my mother's family home in a small Virginia hamlet outside Washington, D.C. It is our Stateside home—but my father's work in the Foreign Service and as a captain in the Naval Reserve ensured we never stayed long in it or any one country. In fact, we pride ourselves on having retractable roots, like the wheels on an airplane, or being actually rootless, like those rare tropical plants that live in midair, dangling with an unearthly delight. My baby brother Davy is a fighter pilot now stationed for a stint in Naval Intelligence at the Pentagon. My younger sister Therese, or Tia as we call her, is also usually on duty, not in the Cold War, but in a bloodier arena: she is a trauma scrub nurse married to a heart surgeon.

I arrived in D.C. on a red-eye and was glad to find myself that next bright and balmy afternoon lazing in a lawn chair surrounded by siblings, parents, and a gaggle of the next generation. We were remarkably quiet: I remember listening to the lawn sprinkler's rhythmic clink along its cool, green hose as it circled nearer and nearer. Every now and then we'd all rouse ourselves to ask for seconds of Mother's homemade peach ice cream.

I was just holding out my Dixie cup for more of those pretty, pale scoops of ice-cold peach when I felt the ground beneath my feet trembling. Surprised, I looked up just in time to hear a thundering boom from above. I had never heard anything like it. It was so loud, so earsplitting that my head felt hollow, soft as a summer melon. My eyes rolled up, and I hunched my shoulders and listened to the sky as if it were dark.

For an instant I wondered if my own skull had exploded. If so, I hoped my nurse sister might save me. But when I looked around, I saw everyone in my family hunched over, horrified. Again that noise rumbled up through our feet, then burst between our ears. Suddenly, there was perfect silence like the eerie stillness that I'd only heard once before, in the aftermath of Mount Saint Helens's eruption. I'd stood in my Seattle shade garden after the mountain exploded and watched the gray-white ash fall like sooted snow over my bright rhododendrons, my wisteria, my slack wind sock, my rusty lawn chair. The only noise that afternoon was the slow-motion drone of a bee as it struggled to fly with ash-laden wings. After awhile it simply sank to the earth, shrouded in white.

Now in my parents' lawn chair I felt this same heaviness in the quiet air as I watched another bumblebee drone slowly, unsteadily. I looked into the blazing blue sky and felt its terrible pressure, the liquid, water-on-the-brain swelling as before rain. But there was not a cloud in sight. I stared hard, looking for ash or rockets or some sign that would tell me from what I had to save us.

The military element in my family—my father, mother, and brother—stared not at the sky but at each other. They knew enough strategic secrets between them to gaze at us civilians with the true alarm of deep pity, much the way parents look at a child who cannot escape injury because the biological imperative is to be upright and walk on one's own.

"What do we do?" my sister cried. There were no red trauma phones ringing, no stretchers being wheeled down the halls, no IVs and tubes flying behind like the tin cans and old shoes on a newlyweds' car.

But we knew what was going on. My generation might as well be called the Baby Bombers. That apocalyptic moment was natural to us. Hadn't we been trained, as children, in civil defense drills? Hadn't we sometimes even longed for Armageddon? On that day when the world cracked open above our heads, we decided—of course—to act.

"I've got to go," my father said so softly that we had to lean toward him to hear, like plants to the light. Only seconds had passed since the sky had exploded, and in those seconds Father had remembered all his emergency procedures. Knowing the most national and international security secrets of us all, he had been trained by the State Department and Pentagon to evacuate himself immediately to an underground military facility, Mount Weather, buried in the Blue Ridge Mountains, forty-five minutes from our nation's capital. Each year, no one knows when, a training drill whisks my father away to practice civil defense war games in what he calls the Secret City.

After he gently placed his ice-cream dish on the grass, Father gave us a look of leave-taking so sweeping it reminded me of my grandfather dying in a hospital bed. It was an expression at once impersonal and blank with love.

"I'll go with you," my brother said, standing up, his aviator eyes scanning the skies. Davy had some idea what the sound was: a new kind of sonic boom, perhaps—or had New York been hit and we had minutes to...to do what?

Davy has borne the worst brunt of our family's emergency personality. He is the only one on hazardous duty every day; he is the male heir expected to fight the good fight. He is the one who will be sent to all those "hot spots" in the world where armed forces practice nuclear war. Even Davy's wedding was an emergency. One night we received word that we had exactly four days to assemble in San Diego: the wedding had been moved up because the Soviets had shot down that Korean jet and my brother's squadron had been put on special alert. Davy was ordered to ship out, perhaps never to be seen again. From every corner of the country, we squeaked into San Diego with moments to spare. At the wedding we waved good-bye to my brother with fear and trembling. Then, like war widows we waited for him during the crisis.

Now Davy stood, as tall as our father and as lean as he once had been, and said as another boom shook the sky, "I hate that sound." When the tremors again echoed up from the earth, pounding our feet like fists, he added, "I've always hated that sound."

"I'll get us into D.C.," Mother announced, jumping up. She has never possessed the family trait of terrible calm. Instead she displays the side of the emergency personality that the rest of us try to keep secret—sometimes even from ourselves. She absorbs the exuberant rush of adrenaline as if it were a welcome narcotic. She acted out the absurdity of our situation, rummaging in her purse for the codes or instructions or back roads—whatever it is that the CIA hands its employees to guarantee safety in case of nuclear attack.

As for me, I found myself grinning, like laughing at a funeral.

This was not just the day the world would end, this was Mother's Big Day! All those years she had been trapped in child-rearing, all those years of having to content herself with eavesdropping on her children's conversations over the in-house P.A. system or making extra keys to our diaries. All those years of having to track down the whereabouts of kids instead of Communists. When we finally left home, the CIA did at last open its wide arms, welcoming her cunning gifts. From then on we could rarely return home without finding a defector at our dinner table; for Christmas last year we all got copies of *Inside the KGB*.

"All right, Madeleine, you drive," my father said to Mother. Then he looked at us, stricken. "And we'll...and we'll find shelter for Sydney and Tia, too."

But Father knew better; so did we. The Secret City would only admit him. There would certainly be no room in my brother's EA-6B Prowler cockpit, and the CIA shelters only its own.

"Do you *really* think it's...?" I began, and my father met my eyes with a steady gaze.

"I think it is," Davy answered very quietly. "I think we have about fifteen minutes, maybe less." He turned to Mother, who was jangling a set of keys that would rival any janitor's.

Mother had also produced from nowhere a tiny radio, which she tuned to the emergency broadcast system. But there was no insistent squeal, no grim but reassuring "This is a test...." There was only an easy-listening selection: Mitch Miller playing "My Blue Heaven."

They say that time can stand still in the shadow of death. That moment when three of my family stood poised for action under an unstable sky and two of us remained very still in our chairs, ice-cream cups and spoons dangling from our hands— that was such a moment. All our defenses, both inner and worldly, all our lifetimes of duck-and-cover emergency drills, all our subtle strategies for acting out inner wars, did not help when there seemed to be nothing to do.

"Not enough time," Father finally said, "to do anything."

So we remained very still. Our eyes met and suddenly we knew we were not who we thought we were; we saw we were most afraid of one another, and yet it was for one another we were most lonely. It was a body-longing—every body longing for everybody. Then, like fists unclenching, we all physically unraveled. I leaned against my sister and she against my brother, and around and around. Our relaxation was so deep, it was frightening. Then I remembered: fear was obsolete.

"You know," Davy yawned, stretching, "we can do anything we want right now. What do you want to do?"

"Eat ice cream," Tia said, "really *blow* my diet!"

"Let her blow," I said.

Then we called the grandchildren, who were so absorbed in their game of basement Ping-Pong they'd ignored the booms above. They came and sat in our laps. As we waited for the end, my family ended up sitting around and adoring our little ones. We watched their every move as if they were newborns. And then we looked at the summer grass, the sheer blue sky, the small houses scattered around like so many brave shelters, like our bodies—and we saw how lavish, how lovely this world was. Had the earth always embraced us so completely, as if we simply belonged here? Right here?

After another twenty minutes we looked at each other, knowing that this had been a false alarm.

"A test," my brother murmured, and we all breathed together. "Just a test."

My mother later found out through her stealthy channels that the booms were made by just another squad of top-secret jets. But, ironically, we had been left with a tremendous sense of peace: when we witnessed each other as if for the last time, everything but the bond fell away. We discovered that our only civil defense was ourselves. We had not hidden, ducked, or covered. Right out in the open we had rested on one another in a way we'd never been able to do in our normal world.

For me, this simple, accepting calm, though brief, has now outweighed a lifetime of emergency training, and I have begun to wonder if there might be other teachers besides terror. Of course, we seldom speak these days about that afternoon. The love of hot spots dies hard. Just last winter Davy spent a prevacation week in the Philippines—during their election. My mother continues to keep Communists at bay, and at any minute my father might be called back to do drill in the Secret City. For Tia, there are ambulances and children who need her immediate attention.

But the pendulum, once moved, never swings back to its original position. These days—what Tia calls our "afterlives"— whenever my emergency personality grabs hold, I gently remind myself: in any life there are very few *real* emergencies. Perhaps, I tell myself, the best way to do is simply to be, the best way to defend is simply to let go.

Recently, my father looked at me across a quick cup of airport coffee while he was waiting for a plane to whisk him cross-continent. "You know," he said slowly, lighting his pipe, "I've always just assumed life would go on…people my age do. But you don't really believe that, do you, Sydney?"

I looked at him, veiled behind smoke. He seemed both very wise and very innocent. I didn't answer. I don't know that answer anymore. I only know that I want to give myself time to answer.

All I told my father then was that I wanted to grow old with him. That sometime I wanted to sit with my sister and brother on some nursing home front-porch swing and rock and rock. My father laughed. He said we'd probably all have moved to a nursing home on another planet by then.

No, I told him, here, right here.

And then I told my father something else, something I hadn't known myself until I said it: I have begun to imagine what I've never dared imagine before—the rest of my long, my very long life.

2

CARPOOL

Madeleine, 1982

If there's one thing I can count on, it's my carpool. Every A.M. Earl, Donald, Julia, and I drive from our Camelot suburb near Fairfax, Virginia, down the Beltway, across the 14th Street Bridge into Washington, D.C. Our first stop is the Government Printing Office, where Earl works as head of the typography department; then we zip on through the carpool/transit lanes to the Folger Shakespeare Library, where Julia works in Permissions. Finally, Donald drops me at a checkpoint (which I'm not at liberty to divulge here) where I pick up my shuttle van to Langley, before he goes to the national office of Woodward & Lothrop, a chain of department stores for which he does public relations.

Of course, I can't talk about my job at the CIA. Suffice it to say I have a high-security clearance, have successfully completed Clandestine Operations Course II, and am proficient in dead drops. My office is in a self-locking vault, right next to the lie-detector testing rooms. But enough—we don't allow shoptalk, as

Earl calls it, not in our carpool. Five years ago, when we first found one another through that ad in green computer lights over the Beltway—"Need a lift? Call P–O–O–L"—we made the firm rules of our carpool contract. Put simply, they are the Three R's of the Road: We don't talk about Religion, Relationships, or Revelations (of the personal kind). Every week we rotate who brings the stainless-steel carpool thermos of coffee—we all drink it black— and who drives. Julia, with her weak nerves, doesn't drive, so she pays for the Maxwell House and chips in on gas when I drive my red Dodge Dart.

We rarely listen to the radio, except for emergencies or the seven o'clock traffic report from the WPDC Flybird hovering overhead in his little yellow jacket of a helicopter. Not listening to the radio was my idea because we couldn't agree on music. Earl likes country western. Once when he picked me up, I caught him listening to a song that went:

You stepped on my heart, and you
squashed that sucker flat
You just kinda sorta stomped on my aorta.

Julia likes opera, and Donald, if he had a chance, would make us endure entire innings of the Baltimore Orioles, all the while driving his battered blue Mustang as if he were stealing bases for home. Of course, I like to listen to the gospel station, even though sometimes they sing my favorite hymns like punk rock. But I do love "The Miracle Hour," which is weekdays at 7:30 A.M. Pastor Gaylord Hurston only has to hit you smack on the forehead once with his lightning hand, shouting, "Come out, you nicotine demon!" and you quit smoking—not to mention other miracles.

We like to joke and say that our carpool was made in some commuter heaven because more than anything it's a constant in our lives. Sometimes I think if they dropped the bomb—and, of course, the Soviet Union is always aiming straight at our hearts here in the nation's capital—I'd like it to be when I'm riding in my carpool. Pasted to the inside of my glove compartment is my favorite postcard, a colorful 3-D painting of *The Rapture:* vehicles and buildings abandoned, the dead hurled to the ground by God's quick hand; but in His other hand He's lifting up a car, tiny as a toy. I like to believe, even though I know Donald worships the Antichrist Pope, even though Julia is Jewish and reads novels instead of the Old Testament, and Earl hasn't been near a church since his wife died—I believe that my faith might help them be caught up to meet God in midair, saved inside my little red Dart.

I guess you might think it's funny that I include Earl, Julia, and Donald in this way. After all, they're not family, hardly even friends. Maybe that's exactly why I want to save them. I've worked on my family and friends for decades, and it just seems hopeless. Maybe it's a little like a booster shot for polio—it either takes or it doesn't. You walk upright all your life, or you're a crippled child.

But our carpool gives me faith. We have survived Donald's divorce, Earl's change of career, and Julia's new marriage. We've stayed together like a little wandering band of Israelites. Why shouldn't we all enter the Promised Land together, too?

You can imagine, then, why I was so upset this past summer when suddenly things went wrong with my carpool—and, at first, it was my fault. It really began months ago when I missed several days' riding to go to San Diego for my son Davy's wedding. His navy squadron was on military alert because the Soviets had just blown all those jet passengers right out of the sky. The national emergency forced my son to behave like a Christian and a gentleman. At last he married his fiancée Mathilde and legitimized their two-year-old son. Can you imagine my chagrin as the mother at that wedding? Not only was my grandson Timothy the ring-bearer at his own parents' wedding, but half the people at the ceremony were Catholic nuns.

I'll tell you, it put me in a foul mood. Even though the ceremony saved my grandson from being a bastard, it broke my heart to think that the Pope, working through the vehicle of Mathilde, will have more control over Timothy's upbringing than the good Lord.

Thank heavens it wasn't a Catholic ceremony. Davy convinced Mathilde to let his navy chaplain marry them. Captain McCormick gave a rousing good sermon on God as commander in chief who is especially close to his navy boys in the sky. I almost saluted when he finished. But I had to keep an eye on my oldest daughter Sydney, who was in cahoots with her sister Tia—they ducked out of the sermon with some excuse about seeing to the reception punch.

Those two gals saw to the punch, all right. They spiked it! Things naturally deteriorated from then on. I don't drink, but that pineapple sherbet punch is my favorite. Somehow, when I was taking Super-8 home movies of the pile of gifts, I tripped over an extension cord and broke my ankle. While I was being rushed to the hospital, all heck broke out back at the reception. Instead of polite chitchat, my son-in-law Hawkins got himself into a huge argument over the Falkland Islands. Someone—maybe it was one of those pacifist nuns—punched Hawkins in the nose and bloodied his white tux. It was war, and I was missing in action.

Well, you can see why the wedding worked me up so much that I just *had* to talk about it when I came home to my carpool. It was a perfect June morning and my ankle cast was propped up, aching and itching, on the dashboard. Earl drove that heap of his too slowly, humming "Days of Wine and Roses." No one said a word to me. They barely listened about my broken ankle or the reception fistfight. Julia was reading South American poetry and Donald was fixated on a windsurfer skimming the Potomac.

I felt real sad, or maybe it was the painkillers. I wondered, did Donald, Julia, and Earl really care about me? Here I was so set on saving *their* souls and not one of them seemed to give a hoot whether I lived or died. It was like riding with foreigners. I just had to break the rules.

"The problem with most people..." I began, looking over at Earl who was now whistling a Brylcreem commercial, "is that they don't know what I know. What I know could've stopped the ruckus at my son's wedding. Imagine! Grown-ups having a fist-fight over nuclear submarines, as if we had a choice....Everyone knows the Russians are always sneaking around in our territorial waters like so many nasty bottom fish!"

Everyone in my carpool was staring at me in surprise, and I took this opportunity to press my point. "In my business we talk about world war in terms of a stoplight. Green, of course, is go; red was what we had when Khrushchev calmed things down awhile; and yellow...well, yellow is the most dangerous light. You never know what they'll do—slow down or run right through your red light. That's why we have to be gunning our motors all the time to defend ourselves against their first strike."

"Yellow means *prepare to stop,* Madeleine," Donald said from the backseat. "But your CIA has no intention of doing that. Look at El Salvador, those murdered nuns. And what are we doing about it? Covering up for the killers, as usual."

"You're just upset because you're Catholic," I said, and Donald almost spilled his coffee. He glared at me and was about to say something when Julia cleared her throat to signal we were breaking the rules.

"Anyone for more coffee?" Julia asked.

I held out my orange Tupperware cup, the kind that hooks over the armrest; I decided to just be quiet about all I'd been through at the wedding. But then I saw Donald positively glowering at me from the backseat. No wonder his wife divorced him, I suddenly thought.

"It's a lovely day, isn't it?" Julia went on hurriedly. She almost scalded my hand when she poured the last of the coffee into my cup. "But a little too humid for me."

It was humid. And I suppose I could blame our carpool's first big fight in five years on the weather, instead of myself. The ground fog was clammy and thick; the Potomac ran so sluggishly along the George Washington Parkway, it was like watching your own blood backing up in low places of your body. My ankle throbbed like another heartbeat.

Of all things, at that exact moment, Earl started whistling "Over There," and when he got to the rousing chorus he burst out under his breath, "Say the Yanks are comin', so prepare!"

I joined in, singing low harmony like I do in church choir. Julia's face was beginning to relax, when Donald struck the front seat with his fist.

"Stop it!" he said. "I *hate* that song! That song got my father blown up, that kind of song got me into uniform and a fucking POW camp in Korea. That song got my nephew blown up in a jungle he'd never heard of!"

Donald didn't know what he was doing. He jerked up the door handle and would have fallen right out on the freeway if it hadn't been for Julia, who was fast enough to lean over and lock his door. Donald kind of bounced once or twice in his seat, all red-faced and stunned. He looked exactly like one of my kids when they were teenagers throwing a tantrum.

We drove across the 14th Street Bridge in what I later explained to my husband as a "deadman's float" kind of quiet. Everything had blown up right there in our carpool, and it was like all this debris floating on the top while we played dead to one another.

Now, this is the part of the carpool fight where I think it ceases to be all my fault. As we crossed the bridge, Donald abruptly started in again, and all of Julia's shushings couldn't stop him.

"What's the matter with you!" he shouted at me. "You see reports on this stuff every day—governments overthrown, thousands shot in the back with our weapons—and you don't *feel* it? You don't feel like the whole world's gone mad? I mean, look at this bridge. A few weeks ago a goddamn plane crashes right into it. We could have been killed here, too, instead of stuck in traffic back on Braddock Road.

"Now, we drive blithely across the bridge as if nothing happened, as if we didn't almost die, as if everything's just fine and there aren't people who, egged on by us, think it's perfectly OK to kill priests and children and rape Our Holy Mother's sisters before putting a bullet through their heads!"

Well, I'll tell you, there were so many things in what Donald Broadstreet said that made me see red. Also, he took the Lord's name in vain and in that same breath expected me to respect all his Holy Mother stuff. I think that's plain sacrilege. Mary had nothing to do with being holy. She was just God's vehicle, the same way I believe my red Dodge Dart is God's vehicle. But I don't go around saying Our Holy Car and expect to be taken seriously, do I? You also don't see any plastic saints on my rearview mirror, swinging there like little hanged people.

So, I turned to Donald, who was lighting cigarette after cigarette, and said, "Listen, Donald, even though you're Catholic, I know you believe in God more than the Pope. And God doesn't want us to be weeping and wailing and carrying on about these wars and revolutions. It's all part of His plan. Every new war or famine, every earthquake or volcano—it's all a sign of what's just around the corner. The glorious countdown for the Second Coming has begun and I..."

"And you're nuts!" Donald said, right in front of everyone. "You're crazy to be so...so *cheerful* about things that should break your heart. If everybody at the CIA is as fanatical as you, no wonder the world is on the brink of total disaster. And as for your Second Coming, Madeleine, you aren't saving the world by ending it!"

Donald shoved his paper in front of his face, but now I was

really mad. Here he was a Catholic and divorced and all he knew about the world was what he read in the newspaper. I leaned over the front seat and spoke directly to Donald's little shield of the *Post*.

I began in a soft voice to quote, "'For you know perfectly that the day of the Lord so cometh as a thief in the night. For when they shall say, peace and safety; then sudden destruction cometh upon them, as travail upon a woman with child; and they shall not escape.'"

At that moment I was drowned out by Earl snapping on the radio. But instead of the expected WPDC traffic report, a woman, her voice cool as silk, was saying, "I'm Tracy Carlyle and this morning we'll be analyzing *your* dreams. Let's take the first caller..."

"Oh, isn't that interesting?" Julia said in a sweet, high voice. "Turn it up, will you, Earl?"

Earl turned up the volume real loud. I could feel Donald staring at the back of my head and knew he'd go along with sidestepping the whole issue. People will do anything to ignore the end of the world—even live in a dream world.

And so instead of finishing our argument, we had to hear about other people's problems. There was a whiny-voiced woman who kept dreaming that her cats turned into cougars at night and were nibbling away at her twin daughters; there was a kid who dreamed he lost his retainer and all his teeth shattered; there was a man who insisted that every night a fat woman sat on his chest until he couldn't breathe—and on and on.

What I wanted to know was why don't we dream anymore like they did in the Old Testament? Then, one man's dream had meaning for a whole people. You wouldn't catch Saint Paul fretting about his teeth or his pets. You wouldn't read about Saint John's marital problems. In the Bible people dreamed divinely, generously.

Then I began thinking. What if nowadays God *did* talk to us in dreams? What would we do? Analyze them away; hoard them? The minute I admitted this, I got a strange feeling. It was a prickling tickle all the way up and down my backbone. I trust that feeling—once it saved my life. I imagine that it's God's finger just kind of poking me. Of course, I would rather He use a burning bush to get my attention, but in this secular day we make do with a shiver up the spine.

Anyway, right there in the front seat of my carpool, I had a vision. I saw myself as a little child, kneeling by my bed and praying, not to God, but to the Sandman.

Please, Mr. Sandman, I prayed very hard when I was seven, *bring me a dream.* Right then and there I decided that God and the Sandman were one. God put everybody to sleep at night to talk with them about their day. This was because He couldn't count on us to talk to Him. So He had to kind of knock us out to get our attention. Funny, isn't it, but as a kid I figured God must be awful lonely to want to chat with every one of His children, every single night. That's when I decided that He didn't do it individually, like *Evenin', Madeleine, how're you doing?* but that it was as if dreams were God's frequency and He could tune us all in at once.

That's why I got so excited riding in my carpool with Dr. Carlyle and a radio station that listened to our dreams. It had made me remember this childhood belief, and I wasn't going to put it away again. So I really surprised everyone by leaning forward in the front seat and cranking up the volume even more.

"After all, we are the stuff dreams are made of," she was saying, wrapping things up. "This is Dr. Tracy Carlyle, saying good morning and sweet dreams!"

Dr. Carlyle became a fifth passenger in our carpool. Every morning, in the warm summer light and sweet air, we piled into our carpool like children off to summer camp. Dr. Carlyle had advised that we keep a dream journal. We even quit drinking coffee—it interfered with the early morning "aura," as she called it. Well, if you can imagine my little red Dart scooting along the Beltway, surrounded by a shimmering white halo, you'll have the perfect picture of our carpool those last summer days. We rode, morning after morning, bleary eyed without our Maxwell House, but smiling vaguely to ourselves as we listened to each other's dream journals; then we switched on Dr. Carlyle and heard what seemed like hundreds and hundreds of other dreams. It was like a fellowship of the believers—right there over the airways. Nothing was too secret to reveal, as long as it was in our dreams.

Julia told us about her love dreams—beautiful, tempestuous, as if she wrote little sonnets to her husband in her sleep. Donald's dreams were often sad, unfinished; they always left him right at the moment something happy was going to happen. Some of his dreams had Saint-this-or-that in it. I quit thinking of saints as little suicides hanging on the dashboard and began to see: Saint Lorenzo and his night of shooting stars when wishes come true; Saint Sabrinus, who knew the language of birds and preached to them, note by note; Saint Teresa of Avila, who was so righteous that in her raptures she had to grab hold of the altar rail to keep herself from floating upward. Earl had a lot of cowboy dreams with country-western soundtracks. My own dreams were mostly about my kids when they were children—tender dreams, really, so different from the grown-ups they are now.

Then one day everything changed. It was mid-September and frost was ruining my tomatoes. I dreamed we were wandering Israelites, Earl, Donald, Julia, and myself. We were camped in the desert and all of our kids were still little. They played in a dazzling desert campground while the adults kept watch for signs and miracles: a pillar of fire, water flowing from a rock.

Suddenly, amidst our tents, I saw soldiers fanning out everywhere. Their dark-green fatigues thwacked in the wind, machine guns swinging. Why were they chasing our children? First I thought it was a game, and then, right in front of me, my baby, Davy, ran into my arms. Almost smiling, I caught him up, then looked down and saw that the top of his head was dented, broken open by a rifle butt. I screamed. No sound. And then hundreds of other mothers were grabbing their children and running. Metal gagged and spluttered, and then I was running, too, clutching my son who was dead and so light it was like carrying a small bundle of hand-me-downs.

I woke screaming, but still no sound came from my mouth. My arms held my husband's pillow in a death grip. But he had already caught his carpool to work. I wandered down my hallway, looking inside every one of my children's empty, long-ago abandoned rooms. In the kitchen I drank the dregs of Sam's cold coffee. It was like I couldn't wake up. I didn't even hear Earl honking in the driveway. Julia had to come to the door. She rang and rang the bell; finally, she came into the kitchen and knelt down beside me.

"Are you sick, Madeleine?" she asked. Her small, dark eyes seemed especially kind. "Is something wrong? Maybe you better call the office and..."

At that exact moment the phone rang. It was my boss telling me that I better come prepared to work overtime tonight because the first reports of the Beirut massacre were coming in over the wire. *Tell nobody,* he said, *get here quick.*

I nodded numbly. I could hardly talk. My dream, I now knew, was prophecy. I had seen that Beirut slaughter in my sleep. And I had to tell, I couldn't keep that a secret. So I told Julia, who was sitting there holding my hand.

"Oh, no," she looked as if all the air had been knocked from her, "that can't be..."

Then we told Donald and Earl, who also couldn't believe it, the massacre and my dream. I don't know why but I couldn't keep from shaking and tears came out of my eyes like my body worked without me. I, who had been trained by the CIA. I, who had watched film after film of our covert operations. Why should I, of all people, tremble so?

Nobody in our carpool turned on Dr. Carlyle that morning. Maybe we were afraid to hear of the hundreds of other dreamers who had seen their own children dying. We all rode to work in silence, me slumped slightly against Julia's shoulder. Earl didn't even whistle. I imagined as we rode that our car was part of a long funeral parade, down the Beltway, across the 14th Street Bridge, fanning out into the Capitol—a mourning commute.

Then Donald surprised us all by turning around in the front seat and asking, "Anyone else need some coffee? I sure do. What say we stop at the Hot Shoppe next exit and get a bit of breakfast, too?"

"I'd like that," Julia said and squeezed my arm gently. "How about you, Madeleine?"

I opened my mouth to say *of course not, my boss has me on special assignment*—but what flew out of my mouth was "Yes!" I couldn't believe it. They'd broken the cardinal rule of our carpool contract: Never be late. Never wait for anyone. Now here they all were taking my part—like we'd all been in an accident or something and had to stay at the scene of the crime.

When we hit the Hot Shoppe, unsoldierly tears were sneaking out of my eyes. I could no longer trust myself. The others seemed almost as bewildered as I was as we filed in and found a booth in the corner. The place was humming, but nobody else looked like commuters. I felt we were doing something illegal, like playing hooky or being unfaithful.

Then I remembered with a jolt that I'd broken top-security clearance in telling them of the Beirut massacre. Just as I was about to swear Julia, Donald, and Earl to secrecy, the waitress arrived to take our orders.

Our food came and we ate quickly, all of us looking kind of sheepish and skittery. I realized that this was the first time we'd been together outside of an automobile. We hardly recognized each other without the front and back seats of our various cars.

"Hey, I've got an idea," Donald said. He pushed his plate back. "Let's call Dr. Carlyle and tell her about Madeleine's dream."

I sat bolt upright in the booth. "You do that, Donald Broadstreet, and you'll be violating national security!"

"You'll also get Madeleine fired," Julia said.

Nervously, Earl began whistling under his breath, the "Cowboy's Lament."

"You know, Madeleine," Donald playfully took my hand. This was the way he must have looked when he was divorcing his wife, I thought. He must have taken her hand tenderly like this, but in his eyes was that wild, bloodshot blue. "You know, we all have a lot of power over you right this minute, don't we, Madeleine? If we let it be known that you had broken security, that would be the end of your job, right? Kaput?"

I felt my heart fluttering again and those tears, but I fought them back this time—just as I had been trained by top security. Jerking my hand out of Donald's, I managed to say, "Don't you dare!"

Unfazed, Donald continued, staring directly at me, "It would be like the end of your own little world, losing your job, wouldn't it? Just like my divorce, losing my wife..." He leaned forward and grabbed for my hand again, but I wasn't giving it. "Don't you see, Madeleine." Now his expression changed. It was like he was begging—something I can't abide in a man. You'd never see anyone in the CIA beg and plead as Donald did that morning. "Don't you see," he went on, "you shouldn't wish the end of things on anybody. It's just plain mean, Madeleine." Donald was thoughtful a moment. "Like we'd be mean if we saved you from the CIA by getting you fired."

"But *I'm* going to save *you!*" My mouth blurted out my last secret. "Come the Rapture, I'm going to take you all up with me in my little Dodge Dart. I would never leave my carpool behind."

Donald jerked up and stared at me like I was one of those nuts who camp out over the street grates in D.C. *"What?"* he demanded.

He exchanged a look with Earl and Julia that worried me. It was as if they all stepped back from me the way those bad-breath commercials show everyone fading away when you open your mouth.

There was a very long silence that not even Earl dared to break. Then Donald said softly, "I don't think it's safe to let Madeleine drive—not with *that* kind of attitude."

"Not drive!" I said. "I'd sooner leave the carpool."

"Who are you, Donald, to tell us what to do, or who's to drive?" Earl asked.

"Obviously, I'm the only one who can see what she's up to," Donald retorted. "If Madeleine can't save our souls, she'll deep-six us. After all, the CIA does it all the time."

"Donald...," Julia began, but he would have none of her soothing.

"It's me or Madeleine," Donald said and stood up so fast the silverware clattered on the table. "You all choose."

Julia stared first at me and then at Donald. At last she said, "No, I won't choose between the two of you. Because no matter who wins, it'll destroy our carpool."

Earl nodded, lips pressed tightly together. "No, sir," he said to Donald. "And no, ma'am," he said to me. "We won't let you make what we got here with our carpool into a war."

Slowly Donald sank back into the booth. None of us looked at one another.

We drank our bottomless cups. I know what we were all thinking that moment. We were thinking of having to dial P–O–O–L again, of every morning riding with people who didn't care enough to make a carpool contract. There would be no Earl whistling in the front seat; there would be no Julia to sit dreamily thinking about her husband and Shakespeare. There would be nobody in charge of the gas fund. It would be the end of us.

After a long while Earl spoke up again. "I...I think we could stay together," he said and made a last stab at his cold eggs Benedict.

"We can let Madeleine keep on driving," Julia added, "*if* she slows down."

Donald gave me a long look. Slowly, as if he were swimming his way up to some surface as dark and slow-motion as the Potomac in summer, he said, "You wouldn't be happy, would you, Madeleine, even in heaven"—Donald paused, then took a big breath—"... not without us."

And then I understood what he meant. I knew he really didn't want me and my Dodge Dart to leave him. And maybe I didn't even want to go so badly anymore. We'd all lost enough, I guess. And then I knew that our carpool would go on as it always had—saved.

3

CHRISTMAS AT THE O.K. CORRAL

Mathilde, 1985

I

My estranged husband's entire family descended upon me that Saturday night with only four shopping days left until Christmas. It wasn't Davy's idea, but I hated him for it anyway. It was just like Davy to ring me up cross-country from his parents' home in D.C. and announce, "We're having an impromptu MacKenzie family Christmas in Seattle." He laughed nervously. "In other words, honey, I'm bringing a multitude home for dinner."

"Tonight?" I was too stunned for anger. "I don't believe this."

"They all especially want to see you, Mathilde," Davy's voice dropped into the intimate tones I haven't heard from him in half a year.

"You mean, they want to see us *together*," I told him. "Just because it's Christmas."

"Listen, honey," Davy began hesitantly. "I...I haven't told my folks yet that we're having...uh, troubles."

"What?" I demanded. "You've spent the past six months in D.C. riding in your mother's carpool every day and never once even mentioned that your stint at the Pentagon this time was really our trial separation?"

"Top secret." Davy tried to laugh, but the long-distance static made it sound like a cackle. "Of course my sisters know," Davy added as if in his defense. "They always know everything."

"Sydney knows because *I* told her," I reminded Davy. "And everything Sydney knows might as well be telepathically beamed cross-country to Tia. But, Davy, how in the world are we going to survive your whole family at Christmas if you and I can't even make it together?"

"We could pretend...," Davy suggested. "You know, honey, like a live nativity scene or a Christmas pageant."

"Or a passion play?" I sighed. While I was outraged that my husband would accept this holiday family reunion under such a pretense, some part of me was actually giddy with relief. Maybe it wasn't over yet between Davy and me. Maybe by pretending to his parents that we were still happily married, we might believe again ourselves. "Well...," I began slowly. "The nuns used to tell us in convent school that if we ever lost our faith, we should just go through the motions until belief came back to us. I suppose it wouldn't hurt to call a truce for Christmas."

"It'll be good for the kids," Davy said softly.

The softness in my husband's voice never fails to subdue me. He must have learned it from his sisters, this intimate shushing like nepenthe. That lulling in his low voice almost makes me forget his refusal to leave the navy for a normal job to be with his family more than half-time.

"Yes," I said slowly, under the influence of his narcotic tenderness. "Maybe our being together will be a good Christmas gift for the kids. It's what they want."

"It's what I want, too," Davy crooned.

Neither of us added the words *for now.*

"Some gift," Davy's older sister Sydney said when I immediately phoned her after her brother's call. "Kind of like those presents that explode in your face when you open them."

"Did you know they were all coming?" I asked Sydney. "Or are you playing top secret with me, too?"

Sydney was quiet a moment, then said, "There were signs, Mathilde, but I'd forgotten that most of my family takes planes the way others do Valium."

Then I remembered: Sydney has been threatening to boycott her parents' mandatory reunions; she and Tia are lobbying for their mother, Madeleine, to see a shrink. I've never liked Davy's mother, but she is someone to reckon with. Sydney and Tia, who've spent their entire lives fending off a banshee like Madeleine MacKenzie, should remember that even a mother who traditionally blows up every family holiday is still *there.* You may not be able to cozy up to Madeleine, but at least you can feel her. As an orphan, raised by the nuns, I had only the Virgin Mary; but the Mother of God doesn't have arms.

"I see your parental blockade isn't holding up," I told Sydney. "Did you try to say no?"

"I swore I wouldn't visit them." Sydney managed to laugh ruefully. "Then the folks got wind of Tia and Hawkins's driving out for Christmas here with me."

"Who leaked that secret?" I asked. "Dear Davy?"

Sydney hesitated. Even now she still protects her baby brother, though I must admit she's been very fair-handed with me. During this past year, when Davy's and my problems have deepened—or, as Davy says, "escalated"—Sydney has always seen my side. That's the therapist in her; the sister in her still shelters her own. Even though I am married to this MacKenzie family, their fold has never really embraced me.

"Davy doesn't tell our parents everything," Sydney said, but in a conciliatory tone. Like her father, the diplomat, Sydney was not defending another at my expense, she was simply stating a fact.

"Oh, Syd…" I suddenly found myself on the verge of tears. "Do you know Davy hasn't told your parents a thing about our separation?"

There was a long silence, during which I recognized that I'd shocked Sydney—something that doesn't happen often. Like a weatherwoman, she usually anticipates her family's storms way ahead of time.

"I'm sorry, Mathilde," she said simply. "Secrets in our family are a kind of false protection." Sydney dropped her voice, just the way Davy does. "Davy is protecting himself."

"From whom?" I asked. "From me, from his parents?"

"From himself," Sydney said quietly.

"Oh, stop it, Syd!" I blurted. "Stop sounding like a shrink. I want you to just be my sister-in-law and tell me what to do. Give me advice. I'm not saying I'll take it!"

"Well…" Sydney laughed. "I advised you against marrying into our family, Mathilde. And so did Davy."

"What about divorcing your family?" I asked, and those tears caught in my throat again.

Instead of comforting me like the nuns would, telling me divorce was a mortal sin, Sydney fell silent again. I could hear her adjusting herself to my pain. It's a subtle shift—but it's maddening to me, this reserve, as if she's stepped back from me slightly to see me better. Or to leave me to myself. Davy has the same habit, except there is rejection in his remove. Maybe it's a MacKenzie family trait, this skill at sidestepping the very people they love.

Suddenly Sydney startled me by saying, "Don't think I haven't thought about divorcing my family, too, Mathilde!"

She was talking about herself, not me. I hadn't expected that. Sydney usually keeps the focus away from her own problems. The MacKenzie family spotlight has a way of glaring down like a searchlight—especially if someone is attempting an escape. Her admission was a tonic to me. It made me feel like I was the older sister for once.

"Well, here's my advice, Sydney…" I laughed. "It's a secret only orphans know: a screwed-up family Christmas is better than nothing at all."

"That's why you're still in this marriage, Mathilde," Sydney said in her softest tones.

"And that's why you're letting your family come camping on your doorstep at a moment's notice," I countered.

Then we both had to laugh.

"Not exactly my doorstep," Sydney said. "I'll put them up at a B & B near the Space Needle. That way Mother will be near the amusement park's roller coaster, Dad can troop off with the grandchildren to the Science Center—and you and I and Tia can spend some time together."

"Yes," I said, and suddenly a glumness descended upon me, much the way the gray Seattle skies lower themselves when you had dearly hoped for sunshine. "Shopping and cooking. The whole week will be a blur of food, family, and fighting."

"The perfect family reunion," Sydney said. "Pray for sun."

"I guess I'm used to the fighting by now," I sighed. "I just wish you all didn't eat so much."

Sydney, like her sister Tia and my husband, is one of those people who can eat all day and never gain an ounce. Most of us would die for that metabolism. I knew exactly what the MacKenzies expected for dinner, even after devouring their airplane food right down to the plastic-molded airplane dessert: baked salmon with hollandaise sauce, russett potatoes slathered in butter and parsley, Madeleine's favorite wilted lettuce with special sweet 'n sour hot dressing, a truck farmer's helping of greens, and of course, homemade pie, crust and all. My failure as a hostess would betray to them my failure as a wife. Next, my motherhood would be suspect.

"We don't eat much, Mathilde," Sydney said.

"Not compared to a horde of locusts!"

Sydney burst out laughing. "Oh, honey," she said. "What can I tell you? Cook as little as you can. Don't get trapped into any religious debates with my mother. Don't let Davy sweet-talk you into anything you don't really want. Don't talk politics with my father or Hawkins. Don't even trust Tia or me if you think we're lost in the family *meshugge.*"

"What is *meshugge?*"

"Craziness."

"Do you think all families are crazy?"

Sydney did not hesitate. "Yes," she answered. "By definition. To be in a family is to be part of some kind of craziness...but all crazy families are not alike."

"I'll take comfort in that," I promised.

"Take comfort," Sydney said, "and *don't* cook. When I bring them by after dinner late tonight, let them eat cake."

"Just desserts?" I asked. "Thanks, Syd...," I added. "Thanks for being a pal."

"I'll always be your pal, Mathilde," Sydney said with that family tenderness in her voice. "Even if I'm no longer your sister-in-law."

Sydney is the only one in whom I've confided my secret: I am a supermarket phobic. It began right after Davy left for another assignment at the Pentagon. Trial separation, we called it. Trial and error. Perhaps the error was getting married in the first place. I'm just not cut out to be a navy pilot's wife—it's the same as being a single mother. So I gave Davy an ultimatum: either he leaves the navy, or he leaves me. "You divorce me and the kids every six months, anyway, to go running off to play war games with your squadron," I told him. "Why not make it official?"

Of course, he protested that just because he was gone, he never left me in his heart. "Gone is not dead," Davy argued. "If you'd had a real family you'd understand this. Look at my family, we're scattered all over the country, but we're always *there* for each other. Just a phone call away. Just a plane hop away."

"I'm sorry," I said. "I never got tuned into the family frequency. If you're not with me, Davy, you're not with me. I spent my whole childhood hosting tea parties for imaginary friends and family."

"Oh, great!" Davy snapped. "Now I'm an imaginary husband. Well, who sends you all those love letters and sings lullabies on tape for the kids?"

"Another woman I could understand, Davy," I finally ended the argument by breaking into tears. None of the MacKenzies will listen to anybody who is sobbing, except Sydney. She does it for a living. "But a tin can in the sky? You'd rather be with some hunk of junk than me?"

"She's *not* a hunk of junk, Mathilde!" Davy shouted. He'd broken the second MacKenzie family rule: Never shout. Say the most terrible things in a beautiful voice. Abruptly, Davy calmed himself. "You of all people should understand, Mathilde," he said. "You used to fly."

"Gymnasts stay on the earth." I dropped my voice the way Sydney does. "It's the other half of our act."

"Well," Davy sighed and tried to embrace me, "aren't I the other half of your act, too?"

"No," I said firmly. "Not when you're not around to break my falls…"

"You need a coach," Davy said and walked out, as he always does from our fights. "A spotter. Not a husband."

I knew where he was going. To call his sister. There is a phone booth at the corner of our street I call "Sydney's Stop," because that's where Davy goes to call her. And she always tells him the same thing: It's up to you, Flyboy—that's what she calls her brother—it's your call. You see, Sydney's smart enough never to tell him to stay with his family. He would rebel as he always did when his father grounded him—which was most of his teenage years, when Davy ran around with young communists in Panama or adolescent socialists in Costa Rica or wherever the MacKenzies were that year. Whoever thought a wild boy like that would grow up to be a U.S. Navy fighter pilot. It must be genetic, a patriotic chromosome that kicks in at times of national crisis. Or maybe it was the only way Davy's parents would approve of divorce—if it were routinely ordered by the government for national security reasons.

I wonder sometimes if Sydney ever tells anybody what to do. She won't tell her brother to stay with his family, and she won't tell me to stay out of the supermarket. All she says is to notice what goes on whenever I enter the gaping doors of our local Big Bear Giant Superstore. I'll tell you what goes on—I lose it.

Something about those towering walls of food. What if they topple like a Jericho of groceries? And me buried beneath the oozing, white lava of Yuletide eggnog? My hands sweat, I get light-headed. I start to meander down those wide aisles, driven only by the urgent chant of the Chipmunk's Christmas Muzak.

In Bulk Foods, bombarded by *bum-pa-pa-pum,* I can't make out the difference between bargain bins of breakfast crunchies or cat kibbles. In Fresh Produce, I stand beneath huge metal scales and hold a Granny Smith in my hands as if it were the whole wide world. All I can think of is that Catholic mystic the nuns taught me about. She said that true love would be if Eve, though starving, refused to eat that apple. Talk about disorienting shopping tips.

There I am, empty cart, empty stomach, when suddenly I veer off straight toward the Bermuda Triangle as if my grocery cart is scudding across a gigantic Ouija board. This Big Bear Baked Goods is practically an out-of-body experience. The divine smell of hot mincemeat pies, brandied fruitcake, frosted sugar cookies, and stollen, not to mention yule logs with swirls of mocha and chocolate like buttercream galaxies set in a whole universe of pastry. Oh, the pastry is light, transubstantial. Only a moment in the mouth, an instant of that heavenly body melting into mine. Then the pastry vanishes—as does all happiness.

That Saturday morning when I heard my in-laws were upon me, ignorant of Davy's and my marital mess or my supermarket phobia, I decided I had three options: to seek sanctuary in our local Lady of Perpetual Penitence confessional booth; to attempt another foray into the Big Bear and shop for eleven; or, to dash into the Seven-Eleven for some Sara Lee pound cake and frozen strawberries. I chose the shopping sprint over the Big Bear marathon and the sin of omission over the confessional.

By the time the hordes arrived at my house, I had a fairly respectable spread. I just hoped Davy's mother wouldn't snoop through my cupboards and discover them bare.

Sure enough, the first thing Madeleine did was make a bee-line to the refrigerator. She bypassed me on some pretext of being "parched" from not drinking enough water on the plane. Swinging open the refrigerator door, she exclaimed, "Why, Mathilde, no wonder you're so skinny. You can't live on dill pickles, cheese franks, and...," she rummaged in the vegetable bin with a grimace, "... and what's this? Something died in here!"

"Mother," Davy deftly led Madeleine into the dining room, where the rest of the family was devouring my desserts. I couldn't tell whether my husband was protecting me from his mother or himself from facing me after so many months' separation.

Davy looked thinner, even though I'm sure his mother made it a cause to force-feed him every night. He also looked happy to see me, but this family is so practiced at playacting that an outsider can never really tell. I took some satisfaction in the fact that my husband had lost weight while eating his mother's cooking— he's always held her recipes up to me as the gospel according to Saint Madeleine. I did not take satisfaction in the fact that the moment my husband walked back into my kitchen, I felt a stab of hunger.

David MacKenzie is not the most handsome man I've ever been with; but he is the one I've most desired. Add to that his fathering my children, his very features—delicate nose, long, chiseled hands, and those disconcerting gray eyes set off by black, curly hair—echoed in Izzie and Timo, and you see my dilemma: everyone I love, from my children, to my sister-in-law, to this crazy extended family, has Davy stamped into them. When I cry with Sydney and her gray gaze rests on me, I see Davy. When Timo throws his arm around me as I read him his favorite story-books, I feel Davy's lanky grace. When Izzie sobs at night and won't let me hold her because she says my "arms are too short," I smell Davy's insomniac night sweats. How can I divorce this man without losing everybody I hold dear?

As I stood pondering this, my spatula poised above the Cool Whip, Tia and Sydney ambled into the kitchen with their arms around each other. They mugged and sang a ragtime version of a song the MacKenzies made up themselves. Even though those two are always at odds with their mother, their interior sound-tracks must be full of Madeleine's music. They memorized the romantic top-ten hits of her postwar generation the way I did the Old Testament. While I was reciting Jeremiah's terrible visions, Tia and Sydney were singing harmony on "Chattanooga Choo Choo" or "Am I Blue?"

The only time this family stops fighting is when they sing together. Like angels, their voices blend in five-part harmony. It's seraphic really. They've all inherited their perfect pitch from Madeleine. But just when I close my eyes and am listening to my in-laws' choir the way, as a child, I used to listen to the orphanage sisters, one of the MacKenzies will stop everybody with some quibble over who is straying from what part. Suddenly all the singing angels fall down like so many black, squabbling starlings.

Move along, Let's move along!
That's our family's favorite song.
Ain't no heartache, ain't no care,
Ain't nobody who's so rare that
We can't just leave 'em there
And move along...

The sisters sang and swept me up in their embrace. Tia, who has always struck me as tidy, sprinkled a bit of salt on the linoleum and showed me their sidestepping shuffle. Before I knew it, Madeleine, who doesn't believe in dancing, was in sync with us.

"That's it, that's it, Mathilde!" Madeleine deftly twirled me around. "Why, you're a natural!"

It had been a long time since I'd done a back flip when I taught gymnastics, but that unexpected moment in my kitchen with these women spotting me, I felt my body arch eagerly as if I might fly backward from sheer physical happiness. Wouldn't Davy desire me again? Wouldn't his mother be impressed? Wouldn't all the children clap as if I were the centerpiece of their Christmas celebration?

"Oh, I'm so glad you have such a sweet tooth, Mathilde!" Madeleine shocked everybody by catching me up in an embrace that was welcome, if painful, as she smashed me against her chest. Her glasses still dangled there on a gold chain. Madeleine's hug was so hard, it bent her glasses and bruised my breastbone. "Let's all have seconds on cake and coffee."

"Not now, Mom." Davy held up his hands. "It's late. With all this sugar the kids are going to be bouncing off the walls. Let's check you and Dad into the hotel."

"It's not the kids who'll bounce off the walls," Tia suggested under her breath, but everybody heard her.

"I'm not budging one inch until I get another cup of Mathilde's coffee," Madeleine snapped. Her snap was like a German shepherd's. All her children instinctively flinched.

Suddenly Davy stood right next to me. I felt his body like heat lightning, elusive and electric. "My wife's coffee is even better in the morning," he told his mother. When he winked at me, his eyes lit up with their familiar luminosity, like underwater eyes. His whole family has them. These translucent, musing eyes first watched me perform in that gymnastics exhibition the night we met. As Davy possessively took my arm, even against his mother, I felt hunger growl again in my belly.

"Hup to, everybody!" Davy commanded in his best drill-instructor voice. "Let's move on out!"

As if under a magic spell, his entire family gathered raincoats, children, and not a little luggage. Without one word or any squabble at all, they all waited in the hallway to say good night. Sydney had her niece Daniella slung sleeping over her shoulder. Tia stood rocking Felicia in her arms so the baby wouldn't awake. Madeleine was rounding up her husband Sam and Tia's husband Hawkins, who were locked in deep silence over their chess game. For a moment all of us stood poised on the threshold of my house. I realized it was the first time, outside of a church prayer service, when we all were together and yet still. I don't know why, but I felt a holiness fall upon us, so hushed and attentive.

Everyone else must have mysteriously felt it, too, because without a cue, as if it occurred to all of us at once, we started singing. It wasn't a song, it was more a murmuring hum. Tia and Sydney swayed back and forth, each with a child on her shoulder, and took up a lullaby. I recognized it well, though I'd never sung it to my children. Davy is the singer, not I. Yet I joined in this family song that had been passed down among these MacKenzies for three generations:

Go to sleep, my little pickaninny
Br'er Fox'll catch you if you don't
Slumber on the bosom of your old Mammy Jenny

Mammy's gonna swat ya, if ya don't.
Lu La Lu La Lu La Lu La Lu Lu...

Still singing, each family member kissed me and moved out the door as if mesmerized. Of course, it was raining that December night, but no one seemed to mind the dark, midnight drizzle. Davy was the last out, and he kissed me full on the mouth. There was passion in his kiss and that terrible tenderness—against which I have not inherited the family immunity.

"Are you coming back...back home?" I whispered.

"Tonight?" he asked. It was a request.

"This is your home."

"Every sailor needs a home," he said. "I'll just settle the folks." Even in the dark his eyes shone.

It wasn't as dark when I saw Davy's eyes shining again as he leaned over our bed, gently shaking me from sleep. "Sorry it's so late, honey," he breathed and kissed my neck.

I had slept alone so many months that for a split second I almost cried out, as if he were a stranger in my bedroom. Then the habit of three years took over. I watched my husband's lithe, familiar silhouette move to the closet, neatly strip as his sisters and the navy had taught him, then disappear into the bathroom.

"What kept you?" I called.

"Sisters," he called back. I could hear him smiling in the dark to himself. "We got to singing and talking. You know how it is when we're together."

"No," I sat up in bed and snapped on the light. "No, I don't, Davy. We're never together."

"I meant..." He came out clad in his pajama bottoms, and they looked a size too big for him. With a pang I realized just how much weight he'd lost lately. "Oh, forget it. You're jealous of everything...the navy, now my sisters." Davy retreated into the bathroom. He was there for so long I almost lapsed into sleep. But when he returned to stand at the foot of our big bed, eyeing me appreciatively as he brushed his teeth, I felt unexpected warmth rush through my body.

It's an odd habit, his nightly ritual. When we were first married I was amused that he'd prefer to stand gazing at me instead of efficiently leaning over a bathroom sink as he brushed his teeth. "It's my form of worship," was how Davy explained it. Over the years I've grown so accustomed to his habit that I'd be bewildered now to find myself with a man who didn't honor me with this nightly sweet frothing-at-the-mouth.

The light snapped off in the bathroom, and I couldn't see Davy in the darkness until he cracked open the window and slipped into bed with me. I was about to remind him it was the middle of winter, that we'd made a deal to sleep with the window closed all during cold months because I chilled easily. Davy always slept hot no matter the temperature. But when I felt his naked body so warm against mine, I didn't protest. I even helped him unbutton my flannel nightgown. He kissed each breast, his teeth taking my nipples which stood up as if awakened from a long sleep.

"I've missed you, Mathilde," Davy said, and he might as well have sung me a lullaby, because my body relented; all the anger I'd held rigid in my bones fled somewhere else. Suddenly I felt as supple as any gymnast—as if my body were still elegant, aloft.

We sat interlocked on the bed, and I clasped my legs around him as we easily rocked. His mouth tasted of warm cinnamon. It was raining outside and the spray entered our bedroom, fell softly on our skin, a cool sprinkle like holy water as we rocked. He was humming still, that old lullaby from his granddaddy's mammy. And the hum vibrated along his tongue and into my jawbone, then reverberated inside my skull so that it seemed there was more space inside me.

My back arched as he eased himself up into me. I sat on his lap and rocked. Scissoring my legs around his waist, I planted my feet on his ass. I pushed him deeper into me, riding the waves of his arousal until my body found its own rhythm, its familiar, secret hollows which were wide open and willing. It's like water when he flows into me. If his body were a water witch, he would always find my hidden hot springs.

When we at last lay down together side by side on the bed, the rain eased into a mist that descended over our bodies. As if underwater, Davy's face wavered in diluted moonlight. He wrapped his body around my back, tucking my ass into his belly.

"You've lost…," he caught himself. "You're so light, Mathilde."

I turned quickly and shushed him with a kiss. "Sing to me, baby," I asked softly and fit myself against him, belly to belly, breast to breast. "Sing me to sleep."

And he did, just like I was family—no fighting now, just that granddaddy's lullaby as we rocked and left the window open for the rain and mist and dreams.

II

Davy found me early the next morning in our kitchen, cooking up his mother's favorite spaghetti-sauce recipe.

"There's enough sauce here for a whole squadron," Davy smiled and embraced me from behind. "Sydney's bringing dessert and Tia salad," Davy said.

"What about your parents?"

"We'll eat them for appetizers," Davy teased, but he seemed nervous. I could tell the way he kept washing the tomatoes as if reclaiming them from an oil slick. Then he added, "I rented a car for the folks…you know, in case things get intense."

"Of course things will get intense, Davy. Have you forgotten it's Sunday?"

"Oh, no…" Davy groaned and took to scrubbing the celery as if to shred it.

Sunday is prime time for a MacKenzie family debate—I call

them family holocausts—over whether Madeleine's grown kids will submit to going back to Sunday school with her. Madeleine always demands it as part of her visitation rights.

"Mathilde..." Davy left the vegetables for the coffee pot. "Maybe we should all just give in and go to church with my folks."

"Why not mass en masse?" I felt a familiar giddiness. It's the way I used to feel before performing a particularly dangerous routine on the uneven bars.

Agitated, Davy sipped his coffee; he'd forgotten cream. Then I remembered I didn't have any in the house. The rise I expected from Davy, over the cream or my comment, didn't come. Instead he lapsed into a fretful silence. For the first time I noticed that this morning his eyes were not clear; they were veiled. And he could hardly bring himself to look directly at me when I spoke.

"What's the matter, Davy?" I asked. "Do you anticipate another Sunday morning massacre?" Then I stopped and, on an instinct, asked, "Or do you have bad news for me? Like you're shipping out again tomorrow?"

"Actually, I can't tell you yet what the navy has planned for me."

"For *us*, you mean?" I took over chopping the celery, and Davy poured himself a cup of coffee.

"It's classified, Mathilde, you know I can't talk about it."

"And when your parents ask about our marriage, do you tell them that's classified, too?"

"They don't ask," Davy said quietly.

"I don't get it, Davy! Is every family like yours? Everywhere you turn, it's top secret! How can you call yourselves close-knit when all you do is hide out from one another?" I threw the celery like so much confetti into the bubbling sauce. "I mean, look at you all. You and your folks play secret war games for a living, then there's Sydney, who has a modern-day confessional and client confidentiality; Tia never really tells her own husband what she's up to, and you never tell me what part of the world you'll be in just in case, God forbid, your family might need you!"

"Everyone needs secrets, Mathilde!" Davy slammed down his coffee cup. "What about you? You've got your guilty little confessionals."

I was about to defend my faith, but the expression on my husband's face stopped me cold. He was miserable. I'd never seen Davy look so torn, certainly never when he was choosing between the navy and me. What could unhinge him so?

"I'm not feeling guilty." I felt a flat calm in my voice, but my belly rumbled. "Are you, Davy?"

He turned away as if I'd struck him full on the face. That one motion told me what only my belly had known until now.

"It's not the navy anymore, is it?" I asked. "It's someone else."

"No!" he said too quickly. Lamely, he added, "Not really..."

We stood in the center of our kitchen staring at one another. Davy's shoulders sagged and my arms hung loosely at my sides. "Tell me the truth, Davy." My voice trembled. "No more secrets."

For a moment Davy met my eyes and his filled with tears. At that moment the doorbell rang and I heard Timo racing to answer it. Davy snapped to attention and crossed to the stove. Awkwardly he dipped a wooden spoon into my sauce and held it up to me as if it were a peace offering. "Taste this, will you, honey?" he asked. "What's it need?"

"It's your mother's recipe," I fumed. "*You* figure it out!"

Davy stood there, dazed, the wooden spoon poised midair. His eyes cleared. "Mathilde...," he breathed, "I'm no good at this...being your husband or a full-time father. I'll never be what you want." With a look of blank despair, he took me by the shoulders and held me close, whispering, "I can't do this anymore. I just want out. Forgive me..."

I didn't explode inside. My whole body went numb. It was as if I wasn't there in his arms, in my kitchen. Instead, I floated above a woman and a man with a wooden spoon. I heard the woman say as she broke away, "That's why Catholics have confessionals. It's more civilized…"

"There's nothing civilized about Catholics," a loud woman interrupted the couple in the kitchen. "What about all those saints who are holy just because they get their breasts ripped off or their bodies burned at the stake? Baptists don't make much of martyrs, though we've certainly had our fair share!"

"Mom, please…" Davy turned to fend her off. "I'm talking to Mathilde."

His sister Tia made straight past her mother for the coffee pot. "It's Sunday morning, folks!" she announced.

"Yes," Davy's mother spoke up. "And wouldn't it be grand if we went together as a family to church?" Madeleine beamed as she took in the kitchen scene: Tia and all the grandchildren devouring donuts they'd brought from the Big Bear while Davy's father Sam and brother-in-law Hawkins broke out the chess board on the breakfast nook.

Unmoved, I watched them all as if I were behind glass. Davy had turned his back to me again and was stirring the spaghetti sauce round and round as if something were drowning in that bubbling red muck and he were trying to save it.

"Oh, Mathilde, dear!" Madeleine gave me another bone-crunching hug. "It smells like *my* recipe!" Madeleine stood next to her son, and like a robot he held the wooden spoon up for her to taste the sauce. In a blur, his mother moved from my spice shelf back to the stove, sprinkled oregano and thyme as if there were no tomorrow. "Now…that should do it!" She slapped Davy on the back, and he flinched.

If I could have felt anything right then I would have done a lot more than slap him. But I just stood there feeling too big and too obvious. Didn't they all see this chasm that had opened up in my kitchen with Davy and me on opposite sides? Weren't they afraid they might all fall in and never be seen again?

"So…" Madeleine glanced around in alarm, as if sensing

Davy's and my absence. "Who's going to Sunday school with me?"

"Well…" Davy's father crossed the kitchen for coffee. His tone was calculatedly casual, as if to make everyone sit down at a negotiating table. "Let's take a vote…after all, this is a democracy."

"Vote! Vote!" The grandchildren jumped up and down eagerly.

"Anyone under eighteen," Madeleine informed her grandchildren, "and your votes don't count. It'll be just me, Davy, and you, Sam, in favor of church. Tia and Sydney will oppose, as usual. But we'll win!"

"What about in-laws?" Hawkins yelled from the living room. "Don't Mathilde and I have any say?"

"You two can go to your mass," Madeleine snapped distractedly, her eyes riveted on her husband. "Besides, you're not family."

"Mother!" Tia protested.

But Davy surprised us all by turning from the stove with the spoon raised about his head like a blunt instrument. "We'll all stay home, dammit!" he shouted. "And have a nice Sunday supper!"

Whether it was his gray eyes, the color of gunmetal, or his navy drill-instructor manner—we all fell silent, watching him. In that stillness, the glass around me started to break, but slowly— the way a windshield crack will widen until one moment the whole window shatters in your face.

In one graceful movement, Sydney removed the wooden spatula from her brother's upraised hand. "Why, Davy, what a lovely invitation," she said.

Not to be outranked by his son, Sam ordered the grandchildren to set the table. "You see to that, Madeleine," he ordered his wife. "Tia and Sydney, what about rustling up a salad? Davy, carry on with that sauce."

There was much grumbling, but the entire family snapped to and went about their chores with a good naturedness that struck me as impossible. Then I realized they were all singing again, to themselves. But soon that private melody would meld into harmonies, as if no matter how far away they were from one another in my house, in this country, they were always alert to one another's parts. How could these MacKenzies blend together and yet be so at odds?

On my way to find my fine wedding silver for Davy's mother, I caught a glimpse of her leaning over the dining room table. She was hiding a tiny tape recorder under my poinsettia-and-holly centerpiece.

Watching Madeleine MacKenzie hum happily to herself as she prepared to tape her family's Christmas dinner, I felt a buzzing in my head that took me a moment to recognize as hatred. I hated this woman like I might have hated my own mother, if I'd had one. "You want to know a secret, Madeleine?" At the sound of my voice, she guiltily jumped back from the table. She was so startled she forgot to cover her tape recorder with the holly branch. "A top secret?"

Davy's mother glared at me as if any moment she might make a guilty pounce. "Well, Mathilde, what?"

In the face of her fierceness, I lost my ground and my voice. "Ask Davy..." was all I could say.

"That boy doesn't tell me anything about you two," Madeleine growled. "No one in this family tells me anything!"

"Why bother, Mom?" It was Sydney right behind me. Her voice was so cool I didn't recognize it. "You've probably got us all bugged by now."

"I can't believe this!" Tia burst into the dining room, her eyes riveted on the centerpiece. "You swore you'd never tape us again, Mother!"

Tia and Sydney surrounded their mother as if they'd planned this ambush. Madeleine backed away from the table, cornered by the low-hanging chandelier. "I was just going to play some Christmas carols at supper," Madeleine lied unconvincingly. Tia lunged across the table and grabbed the tape recorder, beating her mother to it by only a split second. Madeleine managed to knock over two of my Waterford crystal wine glasses.

"No matter," I said. "They were only wedding presents."

But no one paid any attention to me. As Sydney and Madeleine watched, Tia turned on the recorder, and we all listened.

"Christmas carols, Mother?" she said triumphantly. "That's why it's a *blank* tape."

"*We* were supposed to sing them," Madeleine insisted. "Like old times."

"Old times like when you made copies of the keys to all our diaries and read right along with us?"

"Hold it! What's all the feminine fireworks about?" Sam strode into the room carrying a bowl heaped high with noodles.

Tia turned to her father and closed her eyes tightly, clamping her arms by her side. She suddenly looked very young. Then she clicked her high heels together rapidly. "I wanna go home!" she shouted.

All the children picked up the chorus. "I wanna go home!" Then everybody but me burst out laughing. I thought it was most inappropriate, this hilarity right in the middle of a family feud.

"You *are* home, Dorothy," even Sydney chimed in, taking her familiar part as if programmed. "You're here with us...your very own family."

Tia glanced around in mock horror. "No, *this* is another hurricane!"

Sydney laughed and slung an arm around her sister, explaining, "You mean another tornado, Dorothy. They don't have hurricanes in Kansas...or Seattle."

"They do where I come from!" Slyly, Tia looked at her mother, who had barricaded herself behind the centerpiece and crystal at the end of the dining room table; then Tia gave her husband Hawk a meaningful wink.

I couldn't follow it, not any of it—the private family jokes, the faces smiling with hostility like those newspaper photos of polite politicians locked in a deadly debate. At that moment Davy walked in as if this were always his cue—too late to join the fight or fix it or comfort anybody. If he hadn't been carrying an essential part of our meal, I believe he would have fled from us all. The sight of Davy's stricken face over that bloody bowl of spaghetti sauce made my stomach turn. Suddenly I felt everything—pain, weariness, hunger. My body began shaking.

"What...?" I blurted out. "What's going on?"

"Oh, Mathilde," Tia said lightly and took my arm. "Didn't they ever let you watch *The Wizard of Oz* in convent school?"

I shrugged off my sister-in-law. "The Sisters censored scary, violent movies," I said and felt tears stream down my face.

Tia looked at me in wonder, which is her form of compassion. She shook her head. "So you had no preparation for family life..."

"No!" I screamed. "Not for *this* family. Not for families that fall apart."

Then Sydney was right by my side. "I've forgotten dessert, honey," she said softly, just a light touch of her hand on my shoulder. "Want to run to the Big Bear? There's a special on Pillsbury cinnamon-raisin danishes."

I hesitated. Why would Sydney send me to a place that scared me? Maybe she was saying that there was less terror in the supermarket than in family life. Maybe she meant my chances were greater at the Big Bear than with them. "I'll...I'll go," I said shakily.

"Thought you might." Sydney gave me a quick hug.

As I shut the front door, I tried to catch Davy's eye. Would he come with me? But he stared down at the table, his eyes blindly fixed. He didn't see me; he didn't see his family standing around in complete silence. Maybe he was looking at our crystal smashed, the centerpiece demolished, my poinsettia plant tilted crazily on its side. Poinsettia, the nuns taught us, first flower of the holy night.

III

The Big Bear was swarming. As I ran in I noticed that the neon sign above was broken so it flashed in fuchsia and orange capital letters, THE BIG _EAR. Today the whole store had a theme: "Christmas at the O.K. Corral." All the cashiers wore rodeo chaps over their Santa's Helper's red velvet skirts; they had candy canes stuck in their white cowboy boots like little ankle pistols; and their hats had buttons that showed Santa's lasso squeezed tight as a noose around a stagecoach of gifts with the slogan "Give yourself a present, pardner, giddyap for the savings!"

I am always so bewildered by the supermarket's zeal for these total-concept advertising stunts. It reminds me of Fridays in that junior high I went to when I left the convent school for my first foster family. They never fought at all, except behind closed doors. I didn't mind my foster parents so much, but I hated every Friday at Rolling Hills Junior High when we had our weekly themes: hillbilly days, pajama party, anchors aweigh, and so on. Why must supermarkets carry on this tradition of masquerade? I mean, what if CPAs or dentists or loan officers showed up every Friday with blacked-out teeth or baby-doll pajamas or lassos? It is hard enough to put your trust in people when they're just disguised as themselves.

As I ran up and down the Big Bear aisles, I felt my body's brittleness, how I jerked when I pushed my shopping cart, as if my limbs were attached to me by only the thinnest wires. It wasn't only Davy's request for a divorce that made me move as if I were one of those stop-action live mimes; it was also unnerving to see store clerks in Stetsons and spurs strut past me, toting their six-shooters like a lynch mob.

"Whoah there, Missy!" A sample man shoved a chocolate nativity scene my way. "A scrawny gal like you can afford to binge. How about you just take your pick?" On his tray were scattered assorted chocolate characters. All the animals and angels had been devoured, leaving a semisweet Joseph and malted-milk

Virgin Mary. The wise men were studded with pecans, and the Christ child looked crunchy.

Something in my chest caved in, and I found myself scooting along the aisles, fighting off panic. I was accosted by a Fred Flintstone vitamin salesman who also pushed purple Kool-Aid on me as if I were no more than a child. Among such commands, I did suddenly feel very small. Small enough to cry; small enough to not know how to feed myself.

In the Frozen Foods, I found myself leaning over the Weight Watchers section and sobbing.

"Are you lost?" someone asked me.

Slowly I straightened up to see two small children standing hand in hand, staring up at me. Through my blurred eyes they seemed to shimmer with a calming radiance, or maybe it was the fluorescent lights off the freezers. For one moment I wondered if they might be my guardian angels the nuns always promised me. I used to serve imaginary tea parties to those angels. Maybe I hadn't imagined them at all.

"Don't disappear again, Mommy," the boy said, and with a start I recognized him as my own son. "It's too scary."

I bent down and took Timo in my arms, trying to stop my tears. "Oh, Timo...," I said, midsob. "I'm...I'm sorry...it's just that I don't feel very good right now. My stomach hurts, that's all."

"But you haven't eaten anything." It was Daniella, Timo's cousin. She's the closest thing to heaven Timo can imagine. "How come you never eat, Aunt Mathilde?"

"Listen, Daniella," I tried to explain to her, "the first sin was eating." I told her all about it: how evil entered the world through Eve's appetite, how neither she nor Adam were ashamed by their bodies until they gobbled forbidden fruit, how we were forgiven only by the birth of a child who acted out with us our own mortality.

Daniella listened intently, then cast a quick glance at my son before she asked, "Do you stop being an orphan when you make your own family?"

I stared at her, open-mouthed. "I…I don't know," I answered. And I didn't.

Timo turned to his cousin and said hotly, "Of course, she does, silly! Otherwise we'd all be orphans, too."

Then each child took an elbow and flanked me as we passed through the Big Bear aisles. Their touch was so astonishingly warm; or maybe I'd held on to the frozen food bin too long.

"They make stores too big for one person," Daniella said sensibly.

"Sometimes we get lost," my son said as if there were no shame—no sin at all in being lost.

We floated down the vast aisles and a strange serenity settled over me. Or maybe it was simply surrender: my life would change, my marriage might end, everybody would still be hungry. Because only imaginary families can live on imaginary food.

As we meandered our way to the Baked Goods, I glanced up and noticed that everything around us seemed alive—from the giant jar of spiced holiday honey creme to the king-size Ken-L Ration Love Me Tender Chunks. Even my kids' favorite Ghostbuster breakfast cereal with its marshmallow ghosts was mildly shimmering. We stopped again at a glass freezer case, and Daniella let go of my hand to pull open the door and scoop out five packages of Pillsbury cinnamon-raisin danishes.

"These are on special today, ma'am," a sample woman said. If she noticed my mascara-streaked face, she didn't let on. Instead, she passed a fresh sweet roll to Daniella, who, without hesitation, took it.

"Eat, Auntie…," Daniella said softly as the sample woman handed me that light, fulfilling pastry drizzled with its warm flash of frosting. "Eat all of it."

And I did. I did eat.

4

THE SKY IS FULL OF PEOPLE

Timothy, 1988

Ever since Dad divorced us, we've lived on the third floor, apartment F—the same as I got on my schoolwork last year in second grade. Our apartment house is not as nice as our old Lake Washington house, but Mom says it's like living inside a *National Geographic* because every family known to man is here—and some unknown, she says.

Anyway, our apartment is sandwiched between the apartment of Mr. and Mrs. Ski—short for Mistovski—and Pepe Rodriguez's place. Pepe is from Cuba, a distant cousin of my Uncle Hawkins, who sent Pepe out to Seattle because Key West is too small for a wrestling champ like Pepe. My sister Izzie and I help Pepe train for his next big wrestling match with Killer Knudson; we slide-down the banister in the apartment lobby and land right on Pepe's tight, strong stomach. His stomach is Pepe's wrestling handle—"The Cast-Iron Cuban"—and even though my dad laughs at him, I know Pepe is the bravest.

For one thing, he doesn't leave his wife or little daughters, except to wrestle in Madison Square Garden with other giants like Macho Man, Backbreaking Bob, or the Hound of Hollywood. And he never flies anywhere. He stays on the ground with those big spatula-feet splayed out, barefoot even sometimes in winter. I've followed behind Pepe when he's out jogging and have seen the huge footprints he leaves in the Seattle mud as he runs—deep and solid as Bigfoot's marks. I can fit both my sneakers inside his mud-prints. Pepe drives or takes special World Wrestling Federation buses; he never leaves the earth.

Not like my father, who flies EA-6B Prowlers at Whidbey Island Naval Air Station and practices World War III. When Pepe heard what my father does for a living, he got me in a hammer-lock, his forearm right under my jaw like a mad dog, except he was laughing and tickling. "Mi hijo," he said to me in his Cuban accent which sounds like rough singing, "the sky is full of people. Never do they touch down. They think they too good for the earth, dese people. That's why we has to stay here. We keep dis world spinning." Then Pepe flipped me over his back in a somersault so fast, like an undertow in air, like the way he leg-locks and double-flips the Mean Meatcutter. The way he'll throw my father if Dad comes for us because of custody court.

Dad's taking my mother there to fight over us. So Izzie and I are looking out for ourselves, even though she is a girl and not much help. She cries, but she still goes flying with Dad on weekends, after he crashed with us once when his landing gear collapsed and five fire engines raced to our plane to help us out. Now on weekends I just sit in the Boeing Field hangar and read *War and Peace* while Dad and Izzie fly. I read Tolstoy because it's the biggest book I know and because Mr. Ski, who's Uzbek, lent it to me.

When Mr. Ski reads aloud to me, his eyes squint and his lips make little clicks like he's one of those bush people I read about in *National Geographic.* "Sometimes," he says, "history overwhelms you." His voice is old and raspy like a ricochet sounds on Dad's practice shooting range. But I'm not afraid of him, because he smells like red cabbage and Lucky Strikes and because when I come home after school from third grade (which is a lot better than second grade because my teacher, Mr. Lark, is a wrestling fan and loves world history), Mr. Ski sits with me on the lobby stairs until my mother comes home from her new job. She does product testing and sampling in supermarkets. She calls it "research surveys," but mainly she just gabs all day to housewives who are shopping.

"When history takes you," says Mr. Ski, "you are changed. In a moment. Like *that!*" He snaps his fingers, and every time it makes me jump. "Changed on the outside, yes. But on the inside…ah, that's a different story." And then he goes back to his big book.

So I'm reading his book, too—*War and Peace.* I'm at the part where Nikolay can't believe the soldiers really want to kill him, because his own mother and father love him so much he's invincible. I don't think Nikolay would go flying even if they had planes back then. He might wrestle. Wrestling is like being a soldier, but it's on the ground, even in the mud sometimes, and no one gets killed. Also it's just man-to-man combat. Sleeper-holds and double-whammy whackers—a dance on the ground, not a dogfight in the sky. Not someone inside a machine dropping bombs on regular people who live in villages or apartment houses like us.

They don't have wrestling in my school. The boys who don't play soccer or football play Pacman and Nintendo. They're video game freaks who think they're heroes because they have fast trigger fingers. These guys believe my father is a war hero. They ask me for photos of him in front of his Prowler jet and tell me they'll give me their desserts every day for two weeks if I steal one of his navy fighter-pilot patches or even some fatigues. Once, during show-and-tell when I wore my father's fighter-pilot jacket to school with all its colorful patches and insignias, someone tried to steal it from the coatroom. I was proud then, but that was second grade when I didn't know any better and before my father left us and went into the sky for good.

I don't mean he died; I just mean he didn't care enough to stay. He doesn't want us to stay either. Izzie says no, but I believe he'll kidnap us one weekend in his little Cessna and that will be that. A new identity, a new school, no Mr. Ski or Pepe to protect us, and my mother lost forever, like she was right after the divorce.

It's not that my dad dislikes my mother or where we've ended up living after the divorce. It's just that we're in a bad neighborhood, he says. When I told Pepe that, he laughed and spat something Spanish and then said, "*Sí. To your papa, most of dis world is a bad neighborhood.*"

I'm learning Spanish, too, along with a little Russian and Uzbek from Mr. Ski. My father hates the Russians, he and Grandmother MacKenzie, who also fights them daily from her desk in a vault at the CIA. "I'll go to the Soviet Union someday," I tell my dad and Grandmother MacKenzie. In school we have pen pals in our sister city Tashkent, and mine is named Ivan Yuldashev. In his last letter Ivan wrote to invite me to visit someday: "*Mehmonning rizgini xudo berar.*" Translated from Uzbek—he speaks that at home and Russian at school, he says—it means, "God provides for a guest." Mr. Ski is teaching me how to pronounce it, but it's much harder than Spanish. "Sure! Go to the Soviet Union! But go to Cuba first," my father says and shrugs like I don't know anything. "Go to a children's concentration camp there. Then decide. Besides, to go to the Soviet Union, you'll have to fly, won't you? And they don't give passports to scaredy-cats."

He talks like that sometimes—"scaredy-cat." A grown man. I would like him to just call me a coward, man to man, and then we could wrestle it out, with Pepe to referee. "Are you man enough to meet me in the mud, *señor*?" That's what I wrote across the 8" x 10" glossy of Pepe Rodriguez I sent to my father. It was last weekend after Dad took us to Boeing Field, flew with Izzie, and told her a secret: he'll get custody soon. He's sure of it, just a matter of tying up some legal loose ends. Besides, Mom can't support us and Dad has plans to transfer again on permanent assignment to the Pentagon, so we'll all live with my grandparents.

That's his plan. When I heard it from Izzie, I went into action. I may be a stay-on-the-ground coward, but I am very smart. Even if history overwhelms me, just as the U.S. Navy and my father conquer small unimportant countries because they happen to be part of a larger war, it doesn't mean I have to change on the inside. I will always speak languages my dad doesn't like. I will always wrestle instead of sneaking around in the air and attacking strangers. That's why I'm smarter than my dad. He thinks he's big as the sky. He never thinks he's just a little guy flying through space in his tin can of an airplane.

"I don't hate the Soviets," I told Mr. Ski. "I hate my dad."

Mr. Ski drew deeply on his Lucky Strike and let the smoke stream out his nose like an old dragon. "And why is this?" he asked, putting his big book down on the stairs.

I stared at the mist that always gathers under the rafters of the big apartment building. "Because he wants to take us away."

"And this *away*...," asks Mr. Ski, "do you want to go there, even a little? After all, it's you, isn't it, who wants to explore the world when you are big."

"On an *expedition*," I explained to him firmly, "not captured and held hostage in my grandparents' house." I told him my greatest secret: "I want to run away with you to the Soviet Union."

Mr. Ski laughed then and bent double, so his laugh sounded like a steam engine, huffing and puffing smoke. "Is it so terrible, then, our nation's capital and your grandparents? Maybe they make a spy of you, too, my Tim, and then you will travel anywhere you want. Yes, to Tashkent, even!" He laughed at his own joke, but there was a sadness now. I felt it, too. "That's what they ask of me," he said so low I could hardly hear.

"So you can go back?" I asked, happy that he was now part of my plan. "Then you can take me to Tashkent?"

Mr. Ski was thoughtful, then he gave me a look that made him resemble an old monkey, his eyes yellow and ringed with some other kind of color you don't usually see in humans. "Because of my work with radio telescopes, you know, our government would send me back to spy, and so then I could see my children, my parents. But that was long ago. And I never go back, because I cannot look at what I love with the eyes of a spy." He snubbed out his Lucky on the bottom of the steps and then tidily swept the ashes into his hand. He held the hot ashes there as if they were so precious. The way God, I read in the Bible, first made man in his hands from mud and ashes—from ordinary earth, everywhere underfoot, and magic.

"You are my first line of defense," I told Mr. Ski, "when my dad comes to kidnap us. You can talk to him. If he doesn't listen, Pepe will pin him down, so we can escape."

"Ah," he breathed, "I see. So I am your ambassador? And this little apartment house is your United Nations?" Mr. Ski drew me close, and I smelled the piroshki from his lunch that his wife makes for him on Saturdays—onions and that spicy ground meat. They never serve stuff like that at school, but Mrs. Ski saves piroshki for me when I come home. She's old, but she's a better cook than my mom, who doesn't much like food even though she gives out samples of it all day at the supermarket.

I could feel a gray misty gentleness coming from Mr. Ski and surrounding me like fog. Mr. Ski's arms feel different than my father's, who always used to grab me and throw me in the air. At the last moment—when I was afraid I'd fall—he caught me. It was always his favorite game. It was my fear of him that he loved.

"So if your father comes for you," asked Mr. Ski, "I am to make a treaty that denies him his own son?"

"Yes," I said, and my voice felt real small. Somehow my plan didn't seem so solid anymore.

"When does your father next come?" Mr. Ski asked, and my heart started beating fast. Maybe there was hope. On TV I'd seen Mr. Gorbachev and Mr. Reagan shaking hands at a summit table and sitting down to do tough negotiations. Now I imagined Mr. Ski offering my father a Lucky Strike as they both shook, man to man, not in combat (yet) but in agreement. I could be Mr. Ski's temporary son and stay in my apartment house until my father decided to settle down again with us. A good treaty. A treaty Tolstoy would make, too. Or maybe Prince Andrey.

"He's coming next weekend. I've...Pepe has...well, challenged him to a match."

"Pepe and your father?" Mr. Ski asked, laughing. He thought it was a joke. He didn't know about the glossy 8" x 10" mud challenge with the final forged words: "Señor, if you steal your son, I'll stomp on you!" I had written cursive with thick black Magic Marker, pretending I was an immigrant Cuban. I used all capital letters on the last line and signature because I wanted my dad to know that Pepe was yelling at him.

The only person we really ever heard Pepe yell at was his wife, Martha. She was not Cuban. Pepe would shout at her in Spanish, and she wouldn't answer until she had time to translate. Then she had to decide whether to be hurt or not, and then she had to figure out how to hurt him back. But it was too late. Pepe was yelling again and she had to start all over. His daughters were bilingual and chattered easily between themselves in a pidgin English that was so fast and furious, Izzie and I practiced our Pig Latin around them in retaliation. Besides, they had what we wanted and we were jealous. They had a bodyguard.

"They are going to fight for you?" Mr. Ski asked. "Pepe and your father?"

At 297 pounds—the wrestling-ring referee always called out Pepe's weight like an expensive price tag—Pepe is a match for my dad, who is lighter but so fast he can slip out of most hammerlocks. That's my dad's style—he should be called "The Escape Artist" or "The Human Fly."

"That's quite a match. I won't want to miss it." Mr. Ski was not laughing now. He was as serious as I was. "But don't you know, my Tim, that this Sunday is Pepe's big match against Killer Knudson? He won't even be here when your father comes for you."

My stomach dropped, just like it did when my dad threw me in the air. "What?" I yelled. "Pepe's big grudge match with Killer isn't until next month. We've been practicing on Pepe's stomach for weeks to train for…"

"They moved up the match," Mr. Ski announced. I could see he was as shaken up as I was. "Something about those men with the money."

"Sponsors," I said dully. All I could think was that those fat men with their fat cigars that weren't even Cuban were pushing Pepe around to make a match he wasn't ready for. Nowhere near ready. Why, Izzie and I hadn't slid off the banister onto Pepe's cast-iron stomach with sandbags in our arms yet. Even together we didn't equal Killer Knudson's 325-pound ring weight. I don't know who I was more worried about—Pepe with Killer, or me and Izzie with our dad after he got Pepe's photo-invitation to fight.

What happened next I remember in exact physical detail, the way you memorize instantly whatever smell, white noise, or pattern in the rug you are looking at at the moment someone gets hurt. I can still see the whole fight as clearly as if it were an experiment in earth science and we were using acid to etch into metal. Not the Pepe-Killer grudge match, but the fight between my mother and father. That happened the same night.

It was supposed to be what Izzie and I call "Normal Night." About once a month Dad comes for supper with Mom to pretend we are all back together again, at least for a meal. Dad usually helps cook, so we have an elaborate dinner with mostly Grandmother MacKenzie's recipes. Grandmother says that she's proud her son is a fighter pilot. But she's prouder still that he can handle her round-the-world recipes. She hates foreigners, but she gets hungry for their food. Grandmother MacKenzie boasts that she makes East Indian chicken so hot that even the Untouchables wouldn't eat it.

So it was "Normal Night" with Dad arriving in his leather pilot's jacket and throwing me up in the air. But then he did something not normal. Instead of catching me at the last moment and then putting me down like some sort of spinning top, he held onto me real rough at first. It took me a few minutes to recognize that it was Dad's try at a hammerlock. For a moment I was shocked. I could feel he was really there. Then he let me go and whipped out the glossy 8" x 10".

"Just practicing," he said, like it was a big joke between us. "By the way, where is my worthy opponent?"

"Gone," I murmured.

"Gone?" Dad laughed and his teeth were even, perfect. Izzie has his cavityless teeth, but not me. And I don't even like sweets. "But Rodriguez challenged me." My father threw up his hands. "What can I say? I hate to call him a coward...but what else does it look like?"

"Pepe's no coward!" I screamed then. My father was about three people taller than me, which is like the difference between being on the first story of our apartment building and being on the second. I probably see the upstairs neighbors as often as I see my father. "Pepe is fighting the most important match of his life tonight," I told my dad. "With that no-good muscle-crunching Killer Knudson."

"Timothy," my mother said and tried to soften it all, "you're beginning to sound like ringside. Come on and help us with supper. Forget the fight."

Me, forget the fight when I could feel anger all around me? Oh sure, we were pretending to be normal, but I could see my mother glare at Dad as he chopped the black walnuts Grandmother MacKenzie sent him specially from the South, and Mother tore apart the red cabbage with her bare hands. We were making borscht and plov—Grandmother MacKenzie's and Dad's favorite. It was an Uzbek recipe from a Russian defector who Grandmother took in for several months as part of her CIA job. Her plov substitutes weird nuts and capers, as hard and sour as pebbles, for white raisins.

"But Mom, you said we could watch Pepe's big match after supper," I reminded her.

"Sure," Dad said. "Let the kids go over to the Rodriguez's after we eat. I want to talk to you, anyway, Mathilde."

Dad talking—anytime—was not what used to happen on our Normal Nights. Mom's eyes dropped and she got lost in chopping the onions. Maybe that's why her eyes were full. No one spoke, but Mom's chopping got louder and Dad was smashing black-walnut shells open with his hammer. There was so much noise it was surprising we all heard Mother muttering under her breath, "Whoever heard of black walnuts in plov? Capers I can understand, but black walnuts don't belong in plov."

"It's the American version," snapped Dad. "And I like it better."

"Why cook foreign food if you're going to make it American? Why not add French fries and grits to the plov?"

"Look, I let you do the borscht your way, you let me do my plov!"

"It's your mother's plov, just like you swallow your mother's politics!" Mother grabbed a bunch of carrots and chopped four at a time with the cleaver. "All this playing soldier to prove you're a man...but you've never left your mother's house!" She whirled on him, cleaver held midchop. "That's why we never had a chance. That's why..."

"Shut up!"

"I suppose a new wife would just stud her plov with black walnuts. 'Yes dear, whatever you say...Mother knows best!'"

"That's it!" Dad yelled and threw his hammer on the counter. "I've put up with your slimy, runny borscht all these years without complaint, but you won't even try a new recipe for plov."

"Without complaint?" Mother demanded. She, too, dropped her cleaver on the counter. Both Izzie and I let go of the breaths we didn't know we were holding. "You left me! Isn't that kind of a complaint?"

"I left you because you hate the navy, which is the same as hating me."

"I don't hate you! I don't hate the navy! I only hate what it's done to you!"

"We owe everything to the navy!" Dad shouted. "Without the navy..."

"What does the United States Navy really have to do with anything important like raising children or staying with your wife? All you do is play war, like so many schoolyard bullies!"

"You're only a civilian," my father yelled as if he were calling her the worst name in his book. "And a naive one at that. Wake up, Mathilde! This is the twentieth century—the Cold War, the Nuclear Age—don't you remember? If we hadn't been protecting civilians, the whole world would have blown up by now!"

"Nuclear war!" Mother screamed and threw the entire skillet of plov into the sink. In a flash she flicked on the garbage disposal, and we watched our supper—rice, lamb, black walnuts, and all—dissolve down the sink like so much slop. "Always it's nuclear war. Well, what about your goddamned nuclear family? What about keeping *us* from blowing up?"

My dad got dead calm, like a pilot with his finger on the trigger of his throttle. His eyes clicked, calculating the distance, the time, the rocket trajectory, the hit. "Do you really want to escalate this, Mathilde?" he asked in his pilot's voice.

"Escalate!" My mother started laughing that high animal laugh. "I'm not escalating. I'm just trying to *talk* to you!" Suddenly she started crying. "Please, Davy, don't take the children...," and she started sobbing so hard the garbage disposal was a better sound.

"This discussion is over," my dad said coldly and at last snapped off the disposal. He turned smartly on his heel and dismissed himself and us. "Timothy, take your sister and run over to the Rodriguez's. You don't want to miss your big match."

"Come with us, Daddy," Izzie begged him.

He stooped over to give Izzie a brief hug. "Be a good little soldier," he told her, then turned to me. "I hope your man wins, Timo," he said, and his eyes held mine for a moment more.

In that moment I read his mind: the next time he came it would be for good. No more Normal Nights. He would come for us with bright, brand-new little flight bags, and he'd take us as hostages into the sky.

"See you soon, son," Dad said and gave me a purposeful salute.

At that moment I would rather he dropped a bomb on me and Izzie and Mom than make us survive his surprise attack when he comes to take us away. In world history, I read about schoolchildren in Hiroshima who got themselves etched into the sidewalk by the flash of that very first bomb. You can still see them there, little fallen shadows, not soldiers or heroes, but schoolkids, their silhouettes burned into the cement.

Then he was gone and Mother was crying, but she pretended to be cleaning the mess in the kitchen. "Go watch your match," she told us, "and when you come back we'll have your favorite TV dinners."

"Why can't we take our TV dinners over to watch TV?" Izzie asked sensibly.

This made my mother start laughing wildly. "You think of

everything, Izzie," Mom said, her face so white. "Run on, now, and come back when Pepe has smashed all opposition. I'll make cinnamon rolls for dessert."

So we went. The Rodriguez girls grudgingly let us come to watch their television. It had a huge screen, like a minimovie. Because they still had a dad, they still had credit—that's why their TV was so big and loud, almost like ringside.

Pepe's daughters ate corn nuts and red, rope-length licorice during the opening matches between midgets and women. Pepe's wife was studying a pamphlet called *Let's Go Spanish!* and eating a submarine sandwich as huge as the TV screen. At last it was time for the big grudge match between Pepe and Killer. In his corner, Killer was monstrous. At 325 pounds he was more than a match for Pepe, and when we saw him alive on the screen, growling and clambering over the referee to take a prematch swing at good-natured Pepe, we came the closest to despair that I ever remember. It was Izzie who distracted me in that bleak moment by asking what the little gold medallion was around Pepe's neck.

"Saint Jude," Mrs. Rodriguez replied, without looking up from her pamphlet. "Hope of the hopeless, help of the helpless."

I thought she was either very brave or very stupid. Pepe's daughters, too, pretended not to be afraid. Maybe they didn't know how just thinking about someone can protect him, if you do it right. I was thinking hard right then about Pepe.

"... to determine the *real* champion!" the "Wrestlemania" announcer was shouting live from the Tacoma Dome to a mob of waving, roaring people. I wondered if my teacher were there, taking a break from world history. I saw some ladies smoking little cigars and screaming. "Let's hope, ladies and gentlemen," the announcer lowered his voice to a hoarse whisper, "let's hope our upstart challenger Pepe Rodriguez really *does* have iron in him! If not, an ambulance is standing by..." The crowd went wild.

In his knee-laced white shoes and silver belt, Killer Knudson looked like a Roman gladiator from Bible times, and as he teetered atop the ropes, grinning down at Pepe stretched so defenselessly below, I wished I were Catholic and had my own medal to finger the way Pepe did his Saint Jude.

"Do you want a blindfold, Pepe?" the ring referee asked, and Pepe thought about this a minute while the crowd booed him. Then he laughed and looked straight into the TV camera and said, "No, *señor*, do *you*?"

The crowd cried out their approval as Killer bounced on the ropes, his arms as long as a full-grown baboon's. "Looks like there's going to be a whole world of hurt here tonight, folks," said the TV announcer.

"That's right, Jess," agreed his ringside sidekick. "I haven't seen so much hotheaded excitement since that match between the Iron Sheik and Hacksaw Jim Duggin!"

Now, as I watched Pepe lying in wait on the mat, I held my breath. Suddenly Killer Knudson spat down on Pepe. The crowd booed happily.

"Take a last look, *amigo*," Killer growled. "Look up at 325 pounds of the meanest revolutionary this side of Havana. I'm badder than ever, brother! So suck in that gut and say your Hail Marys because when I stomp that cast-iron stomach, you'll wish you was still back with the boat people!"

Like a true gentleman teaching Killer his manners, Pepe simply sat up and said, "You ain't no revolutionary, Señor Killer. I didn't get to be a tough guy, I didn't get to dis great country, playing Ping-Pong. I seen my people wrestle to the last dying breath, *señor*. I take Castro steel in my stomach, and I'm strong enough to take on a sissy boy *muchacha* like you lying down. So *jump*, Señor Killer, if you ain't too scared of cast-iron casts on your legs!"

The crowd screamed, then fell absolutely still. Killer and Pepe were glaring at one another as Pepe did his bellows-breath to pump up the rock-hard muscles in his stomach. Above, Killer bounced menacingly on the ropes.

Then the awful leap. Like Izzie and me in practice, Killer flew up first into midair, but now he was grabbing his knees like he was doing a cannonball off the high dive. He was falling forever, and in that slow-motion plunge, twisting his body around so that his knees pointed down like two shining, white bone hatchets.

Pepe didn't have a moment to move. You could see the whites of his eyes and then blood—it was so bright on the TV screen as it shot straight out of Pepe's mouth, as Killer drop-kicked him again in the throat. Then a full body slam and an elbow to Pepe's busted Adam's apple.

The referee tried to stop the fight. But Killer was grabbing Pepe's belly in his famous claw-hold that was like twisting a knife in Pepe's gut, and Pepe bent double, paralyzed with pain. "Killer's lost control, folks!" the announcer screamed as the referee at last pulled Killer off.

White-coated men ran in like cartoon people, stiff-legged, with their stretcher. I knew Pepe was dying. He didn't need strangers, he needed his family there, he needed us there beside him—not a ringside full of screaming strangers who wanted to watch him die.

I jumped up and ran for Mrs. Rodriguez. "Come on!" I pulled her arm. "My mom will take us all to the stadium and we'll help him."

Mrs. Rodriguez put down her *Let's Go* pamphlet and said something to me in Spanish. Then she laughed a low, amused chuckle. I couldn't believe it. Pepe's daughters were gibbering to one another in Spanish, too, and Izzie was just sitting, watching the commercial like she wasn't there.

"Some say there were no heroes in Vietnam," intoned Robert Stack in the commercial for Time-Life Books' *Combat Photographer: Volume I* of their Vietnam Experience Series. "Judge for yourself."

"You're all crazy!" I screamed and ran out into the hallway. I found my dad still there. He was sitting on the steps smoking a Lucky Strike, talking to Mr. Ski. I ran to him.

"Dad!" I cried. "Killer's broke all the rules. He jumped on Pepe's throat. Pepe's dying!"

"Timo, Timo...whoa, boy!" My father got me in his grip. Not a headlock, but tight just the same. "Don't you know it's not real? All this wrestling stuff. Hasn't Pepe told you they pay him just to pretend to fight? He's fine. He'll be home in a few hours screaming at his wife. That's your hero for you..."

I almost spit at my father. He'd spent too much time midair to know what was real anymore. He'd never seen blood or someone he loved bent double in death throes.

"You're crazy!" I screamed. "Pepe's dying and...and I've got to get to ringside. Maybe my teacher's there with him...maybe...just take me there, Dad. Please! I *promise* I'll go flying with you next time."

Dad sighed. "So much for a pleasant evening at home," he said to Mr. Ski, and this time I knew he would really leave. I didn't care. All I wanted was Pepe. I shot past my dad, but he grabbed me again and would have, I think, turned me upside down in a turnbuckle or flying camel if not for the sudden voice of a TV news bulletin coming loud from the Rodriguez's television.

"...in the Persian Gulf where the USS *Vincennes* shot down an Iran Air airbus carrying 290 passengers..."

"Turn it up! Turn it up!" commanded my father as he shoved me aside. He stood almost at attention before the television as it showed scenes of morgue workers laying out dead bodies in Bandar' Abbās—small bodies, burned and bloodied, some bent double like Pepe.

They were civilians, the news bulletin said, flying on a routine trip, on a routine flight. There were quick shots of U.S. soldiers staring into computer screens where radar blips hypnotized them. The soldiers looked like my friends playing real-life video.

"What choice did he have?" my father said in a low, savage voice to my mother who had somehow appeared, with Mr. Ski shaking his head slowly behind her. "Look what happened to the *Stark*! We lost a lotta guys and the captain lost his command."

"You're going to stand in front of our children and say we did the right thing shooting down those innocent Iranians!" Mother's face was white with fury. I was glad they'd left their cleaver and hammer at home.

"No Iranian is really innocent anymore!" my dad shouted, but he was backing out the door as the news bulletin continued.

"Since the *Stark* incident, the tensions in the Persian Gulf have reached a hair-trigger state of..."

"Under the rules of engagement, the captain had to..." My dad was backing out the door, and then my mother did something wild. She grabbed my dad's shirt so hard a button popped, and she snarled, "You don't have a chance with that custody judge. Who would give children to a fighter pilot?"

Dad took her hand in his and held it tightly. They were fist to fist, like dancing or wrestling. "You did," Dad said softly. "You gave me children."

Then he was through the door in a flash. Mom collapsed before the TV and we all watched the news bulletin. Except I wasn't seeing the navy chief of staff with his precise pointer and map. I was seeing Hacksaw hitting the Iron Sheik with his two-by-four, and Killer clawing Pepe's gut. Then everybody wrestling on the ground looked up to see the sky raining people—brightly colored, broken bodies falling from the sky as if world history had finally gunned down all the angels circling the earth. Satellites were falling, too, and airplanes bound to Soviet sister cities were exploding, and missiles were zigzagging crazily off course until the sky was full of so many dead people and bright bombs, it looked just like the earth upside down.

I don't remember how I got back to my room. All I remember is sitting all night looking at my 8" x 10" glossy of Pepe Rodriguez. He'd scrawled in big, block print across his oiled thighs: "*A mi amigo, Timo,* your good neighbor, Pepe." Finally, I think I cried a little, but not much. Izzie sobbed in the other twin bed and prayed for God to hold Pepe in an everlasting bear hug.

The next morning I woke to a familiar voice, and it was some time before I realized that Pepe was screaming at his wife to get him his coffee. Next thing I heard was the regular slap of Pepe's bare feet in the mud outside my window. I didn't know whether to be happy or mad. But by the time I put on my clothes and ran into the lobby, I was really angry. How dare Pepe pretend to fight the way my dad always pretends he's in World War III? How dare Pepe make us cry for him? He didn't fall from the sky.

Mr. Ski sat smoking as if nothing had happened the night before, but he watched me closely and nodded when he saw my hands clenched in fists. "No one loves you when you surrender" was all he said.

"He's a fake!" I yelled. "A loser! He's just like my father!"

"When you've already lost your country," said Mr. Ski softly, "you also lose interest in all the fighting."

"And when Dad comes to steal me and Izzie, you won't really fight him either, will you, Mr. Ski?" I demanded. "You'll give us up, just the way Pepe gave up."

"Yes, my Tim," he said. "I will let you go. I have learned to let go of what I love. It is my most terrible lesson. It is what history has taught me."

I hated Mr. Ski, I hated Pepe, I hated them all. That's why I had to cry out loud. Mr. Ski put his hand just a little on my shoulder. "Do you know that now Pepe can go back to the Canary Islands, where his grandparents emigrated from to Cuba?" he said. "There is some land there still in his name. The money from this match means he can end his exile here."

"Blood money," I said. But even though I hated Pepe, I didn't want him to leave us.

"And do you know why Marya and I came to this country?"

"No," I said and wanted to add "and I don't care" but didn't.

"An earthquake in Tashkent...destroyed most of my city..."

Mr. Ski stopped. "Oh, my Tim, I felt so betrayed by this earth moving, I leave my country. I am so angry. I am as angry at the earth then as you are now at the sky and your father." Mr. Ski scraped a match across his shoe and said softly, "Remember your young Nikolay on the battlefield, my Tim."

"Yeah? Well, he got shot."

"Even though his mama and papa truly love him. He is wounded anyway, because, you see, the soldiers don't love him. They don't even know him—that's why they can kill."

"That's why the navy can shoot down kids, just because they're in the wrong place, in the enemy sky…"

"Your navy has lost faith in the heavens as I once lost faith in the earth…and as you now give up your faith in your father, or Pepe, or me…" Mr. Ski took his hand off my shoulder. "No more heroes, Tim. Because now they're killing us."

The next week my dad came to kidnap us, picking us up as we walked home from school, with two brand-new flight bags filled with new clothes from Grandmother MacKenzie. In her sneaky CIA way, she'd bought the clothes and shipped them specially on a military hop from D.C. At Boeing Field I wrote Ivan Yuldashev a last letter from his sister city Seattle:

Dear Ivan,

    Mr. Ski tells me that once your city was almost destroyed by an earthquake. I am glad your parents stayed to rebuild Tashkent so that someday I can come visit and be your guest.

    You've probably heard about how our navy shot down all those regular people from Iran. It was not my father's aircraft carrier or fighter plane, but he thinks we did right. When the Soviets shot down all those Koreans, did you think it was right?

    I think I am sorry for all those people dying. They didn't know they were in a war and made good targets.

They didn't know they were enemies. You are not my enemy, Ivan Yuldashev. You are my pen pal.

Yours sincerely,

Timo

P.S. My dad has captured us, but I will sneak you another letter from Washington, D.C.

Now I will have two more pen pals, and right now as the plane takes off into the scary sky, I'm going to write both of them—Pepe in the Canary Islands, and Mr. Ski, who I know will make sure my mother gets enough piroshki until Izzie and I can escape and find our way home. Because I swear I will not be held hostage long, even though I'm trapped in this tin can in the sky and soon in Grandmother MacKenzie's house under lock and key like a Soviet defector.

Even though history has a hammerlock on me, I won't be pinned down for the count. I didn't get to be a tough guy playing video games. I'm in my parents' war now. Besides, even when we get back down on the ground, even in the nation's capital, God provides for a guest.

"Dear Pepe," I wrote on the free American Airlines in-flight postcard (it's a photo of a giant 747 before it blows up): "You are right. The sky is full of people. I'm up here now, too. But it's not as scary if I know you're still down there keeping the world spinning. Your good neighbor, Timo."

Then I wrote Mr. Ski. I told him I want to come back home. I will come back, even if I have to look at what I love with the eyes of a spy.

5

CONCH BOILER

Therese, 1989

I

We live in the only house in Key West with a basement boiler. Here in Conchtown, the other charmingly restored Bahamian-and-Spanish-style wooden white houses with Victorian verandas and widow's walks, have no heat. There is no need on this coral island that has never seen frost. What we really need in the basement of this old firetrap of a mansion my Cuban husband Hawkins inherited as a third-generation Conch boy is a generator to give us back the electricity that quits our house at every suggestion of a tropical storm.

"It's just like you, Tia," Hawkins always tells me, "to put your faith in something invisible like electricity, instead of something you can touch, that gives a body heat."

"I've got you for that, baby," I soothe him. "But maybe now

after a century of that ridiculous family antique, we can tear the boiler into scrap metal and afford central air conditioning?"

"Fans are fine for my family...always were, always will be," Hawkins reminds me. "You know that refrigerated air isn't healthy."

What my husband won't say, what his mainland medical education hasn't shaken, is his grandmother's conviction that air is a pure element that must not be meddled with, certainly not married in unholy union with the gaseous world of man-made Freon. No, the air must be free so that it can whirl itself into hurricanes that haunt us islanders. Secretly, I believe Hawkins's grandmother was half in love with hurricanes; it was how she rid herself of sailing captain husbands every decade or so, except for her last man, Hawkins's grandfather, who in his dotage was the only father Hawkins ever knew.

Hawkins was raised by his grandmother, Felicia Costarella, here in this family house. Of course, Felicia died during a hurricane. A *curandera* from Old Cuba—whose healers don't wear starched white jackets like me or her grandson, but instead call upon the spirits of trees and sea and air to graciously absorb human sickness—Felicia gazed out the shuttered window of her upstairs bedroom (which is now Hawkins and my bedroom, too). She clasped her hands and quite calmly said, "*¡Que bonito!* It's so beautiful...all this wind will carry me away. When it is still, I'll be in another world." And she was.

I've always disliked weather; it's not dependable. I like the lush life—royal palms whispering against my windowpanes like lazy whisk brooms; the warm, startling turquoise salt water only a slightly lower temperature than my own skin; the dense, intimate humidity. I don't like to wear clothes. I don't like to be cold for one instant.

But here it's simple: from November to August we enjoy varying shades of sun, humidity, some rain. Of course, there's a catch for this paradisiacal climate. Of course, there's a sacrifice for win-

ter days when we balmy islanders indulge in our Christmas pic-
nics of conch fritters, Key lime pie, and smoked alligator spread,
while the radio describes New Yorkers huddled like Nean-
derthals, driven along stone canyons by icy river winds. In the
Keys, it's like hearing the news via satellite from frozen Neptune.
Still, the price we pay for blithely ignoring weather reports most
of the year is hurricane season.

This fall it was Hugo—a hulking, 125 mph maelstrom of
wind, tidal waves, and wanton weather. Such natural recklessness
confirms my suspicions about Mother Nature. She is as head-
strong and violently willful as my own mother. The only difference is that she isn't backed by the CIA—at least, not yet.

My mother is a fanatic, pure and simple, as single-minded as
hurricane winds. For Mother, the most direct path between two
points may be so straight and narrow that she simply has to oblit-
erate towns or people to get where she's going. A soul unsaved, a
country in the grip of that Red Devil communism, a daughter
unrepentant—no matter the method, the devastation, my mother
must wage war to wrest them her way. I have been battling my
mother for thirty-six years. It's a fight that makes the Cold War
seem cool.

My siblings are some help, though my older sister Sydney
tends toward bliss. She meditates herself into other states, not
only cross-country, but light years and lifetimes away from our
parents. Once she told me she'd remembered other lives in which
she was well mothered. Sometimes she dreams of the many dark
and light shifting faces of these more benevolent madonnas. I told
her, thank you very much, but one mother and one lifetime is
enough for me.

Then Sydney said, "All right then, Tia. Comfort yourself; you
have no mother. Give up."

"What do you mean, give up? We should *surrender* to Mother? Then we'd really be in danger."

"Give *her* up," Sydney said in that soft voice of hers. We both used to sing lullabies in this lilting, southern voice; we'd lull our brother Davy to sleep while Mother raged downstairs, throwing things around the house. I know hurricane season. I know the boarded-up windows, the drawn shades, the shattering glass as we waited for Mother's moods to break like a storm over our shallow island. I know that there is really no hiding place when a hurricane is headed your way. That's why I sing to my children during hurricanes—sweet, silly ditties while the winds shake our beds, claw off our roofs, and waves engulf whole villages. I sing. And my own children, as my little brother did long ago, achieve a miracle of innocence: they sleep.

Maybe Sydney and I shouldn't have sung Davy to sleep during Mother's rages. Our lullabies were like nepenthe, for now he has yielded to Mother's religion, as well as her politics. It's as if he's forgotten her hurricane season, dreamed it away, remembering from Mother's storms only how to build shelters of church and conservatism. Perhaps Davy believes this is real protection, since it is all Mother respects. Perhaps he hopes she will not come howling down upon him if he hides inside God's house or the U.S. Navy barracks. But deep down, we all know the truth. Mother is, as one radio commentator described Hugo last fall, "an equal-opportunity destroyer." When she hits, families like ours should be declared natural disaster areas.

Our childhood has left Sydney and me with a knack of intuiting not only our mother's storms, but also Mother Nature's. We are particularly sensitive to earthquakes, like those small forest animals who, twenty-four hours before any quake, run shrieking through the woods in terror. Sydney and I have anticipated most every major earthquake in the past ten years. The problem is, at the time the dread hits us, we can't tell whether it's really a seizure of the earth or one of Mother's attacks. That's why in the shadow of Hugo, I was also on guard against Mother.

Our neighbor Carlos, who owns the downstairs apartment in this old converted gingerbread mansion, is a ham radio operator.

Monitoring Hugo, he minded his obscure, crackling static and deciphered reports from the Caribbean: Virgin Islands hit bad, 90 percent of their crops and shelters lost on Saint Croix, police joining in the looting; and Puerto Rico mangled by winds and tidal waves. Carlos told me he heard a story of a dead stranger on one island; no one could figure out who he was—seems he was blown there from another island.

Sure enough, Mother struck, too. It was one of her famous poison-pen letters. Her note was on CIA interdepartmental memoranda:

1200 hours

9/19/89

Dear Therese,

   Things are hot in the Middle East, but I'm stealing a moment to remind you that in 1976 you bought Grandfather's old Pontiac for $1000, of which to date you've only paid $250. I know you were broke before you married Hawkins, but now that he's finished his surgery Fellowship and you'll be moving to a bigger (salary and) hospital for his cardiac practice, why not make good that old debt? After all, Grandmother is going into a nursing home and needs a new wheelchair.

   By the way, Davy is headed down to Key West on a secret mission there at Boca Chica Naval Air Station—you can guess what it is! We'll win that war on those Colombian drug lords. Thank God, none of my kids ever got into dope—although I still pray every day that you and Sydney will join Davy and sometime return to Sunday school.

   Got to go. You have no idea how close we are to war in some places I can't name right now.

Lovingly,

Your Mom

The signature was a red rubber stamp Mother delights in using. Davy gave it to her for Mother's Day one year. He dotes on her as he does his first drill instructor. There are times when I get angry enough to betray my brother and set the record straight: to tell Mother, for example, that her angel with jet pilot's wings was dropping acid at thirteen and threw a homemade Molotov cocktail into the baptistry. She thought it was Catholic El Salvadoran terrorists.

When Davy arrived at the height of Hugo hysteria, I showed him Mother's letter. To his credit, he did not take her side.

"Oh, Tia, sometimes Ma does go too far." He shook his head and gave my arm a small, though somewhat militaristic squeeze. Because of his brief masculine grip, I could tell he hadn't slept with a woman in a long time, that he'd only touched men lately. Underneath his military manners, Davy has always been very loving toward his older sisters. It didn't help him in his marriage with Mathilde, but it may well someday. After all, the navy has only had my brother for eight years; his sisters had him first and for twice as long. "I'm sorry, Sis," Davy said. "Ma's just gone off again. That's the way she is. Accept it."

"You don't just accept a Soviet jet in your own airspace, do you Davy?" I demanded. "When a hurricane like Mother is headed your way, you don't just shrug and say there's no defense."

"Listen..." Davy would not be dragged in. He laughed, and his amusement was as frustrating as Sydney's transcendence. "Listen, Big Sister. I fight what I can win. And there's no winning with women or weather. I'm not coming between you and Mother, especially in a hurricane. No, sir!"

For a moment I considered a low blow about his marriage and how perhaps if he'd fought with Mathilde instead of flying into the great beyond, he might still be with his wife and kids instead of visiting them every blue moon at the folks' house in Virginia. Izzie and Timothy are miserable with Mom and Dad—everybody knows it, including Mathilde, who is suing for custody and accusing Davy of kidnapping. I was silent, listening to the wind strip our French shutters so that they hung, gap-toothed in a weird, wooden smile. I decided Davy had enough on his hands, and my fight was really not with him. Besides, I had a hurricane and a husband on their way.

At that moment Hawkins strode through the door. He greeted Davy as if he always lived with us. "Hi, Flyboy, how's the rocket man? You gonna take on this World War III weather?"

"Naw, Hawk, I'd rather wrestle me an alligator."

"There she is," Hawk pointed at me with a laugh, then embraced me fondly, a masculine mauling that I didn't mind since I hadn't seen my husband in two days. We were working opposite OR shifts, and I hardly ever had more than two words with him. One week we'd been so desperate we stole a kiss over the anesthetized body of Mrs. Hernandez, in for a high-risk triple by-pass surgery. There was really nothing we could do for her anyway, and perhaps a deep kiss over her ancient body was as much healing as we could offer.

"I'll never understand why the two of you boys—bred in schools and not some backwoods swamps—talk redneck the minute you meet." I smiled. It was good to have my men around, especially with a hurricane coming.

"It's male bonding, darlin'," Hawk said. "We don't like all that goo you girls gunk on one another. It's messy, slows a man down. Speaking of which…" Hawk fixed on my brother. "Rocket Man, check out the shoes."

Dutifully, Davy looked down at Hawk's deeply polished, dark oxfords. "Spit shine?" Davy asked.

"No," Hawk said. "Blood. Nothing shines shoes better than blood."

"I'll tell my squadron." Davy laughed and let himself be dragged off to the basement.

I had no idea what Hawk was really about in the basement. As his contribution to hurricane precautions he'd made noises about firing up our old boiler to see if it still worked. But I figured he was really fashioning an anniversary present. Our tenth was coming up at the height of this hurricane season. Every year Hawk makes me a symbolic present to siphon off the full fury of his possessiveness.

His jealousy—still fierce, forbidding, and I confess, at times, unsettling—is not really funny. We've dealt with it most successfully by assigning him these intricate anniversary presents which, with his work schedule, take him half a year to complete. One year he made me a mock chastity belt from scrap iron. Another year he built a wooden bed that folds up into our bedroom wall. If he ever discovers me with another lover, he'll simply thrust his hand-built bed back into its coffinlike berth—crushing the guilty without retribution. The judge would call it a malfunction, the Latin jury would believe it justifiable revenge, the islanders who remember Hawk's grandmother's Old Cuba family as one of the original Key West settlers, would forgive their native son.

So that night when Hawk and Davy descended to the boiler—I call it the Barracuda because it looks like a vertical version of the mounted fishing trophies Hawk has hung in our condo like a deep-sea mausoleum—I never suspected that Hawk would really lay hands on that old behemoth. It is one of the things that really frightens him.

Our boiler frightens my husband because it killed his uncle. This boiler, imported piecemeal from London by Hawk's grandfather—a ragingly senile scion of an island salvaging family's fortune whom natives simply called the Captain—was only fired up once. That was in 1945 when Hawkins was two and living with his mother and grandparents while his father was at war. Hawkins well remembers the two events that shaped his life that year: that winter the Captain's boiler blew, shooting a geyser of scalding water and Hawk's uncle through the roof; that summer we dropped the bomb and Hawk's father was one of the Americans killed in a POW camp near Nagasaki. At the loss of both sons, the Captain declared that his basement boiler, like the bomb, must never be used again. He even asked in his will that the boiler be dismantled, but everyone, including Hawkins, was too afraid of it.

I suspect my husband is not really frightened by our boiler so much as by what it changed in his family. After the explosions in Hawk's home and Nagasaki, Hawk's mother ran off with a sailor whose main attraction was that he managed to make it home after the war. Crazed with grief, disoriented, a civilian instead of a sur- vivor—these were the descriptive phrases tagged to Hawk's way- ward mother. Sometimes I wonder if they might also apply to Hawkins himself.

Both Hawk and I believe in being prepared, rather than frightened. That's why with Hugo about to hit I could sit on our upstairs veranda with my husband and brother drinking rum by way of keeping hurricane watch while the warm winds shud- dered floorboards and rain lashed our bare feet. We were already prepared with emergency batteries, food, and blankets in our basement. God knows we had enough medical supplies for a small island. As long as the winds didn't wreck our home, we would survive just fine.

Nevertheless, it wasn't what you'd call a relaxing evening, with fishtail palm trees bowed to pound against our roof and the hurricane winds hitting 70 mph.

"Let's go inside now, boys," I suggested to Hawk and Davy. "Even conchs don't wait on their porches to greet a hurricane."

"No," Hawk insisted. "I like it out here. Do you realize that this may be the last night of our lives? Who knows where Hugo will hit? Right now she's out there, gathering power, headed right for us. As Davy here would say, we're one minute to midnight. Now…," Hawk sighed, and it sounded almost sexual, "now we can surrender to her."

"That her's a him, Hawk," Davy remarked good-naturedly. "You know, it was the air force and navy boys who first gave the weather service feds the idea to name hurricanes after women."

"Spanish named them after saints," Hawkins mused and poured rum all around. "Used to be we called a hurricane by whatever saint's feast day was nearest when it struck. "Let's see…this would be…" He fell silent.

"Don't remember your saints' days?" I teased him.

"Not many saints around to jog my memory." Hawk laughed. He glanced over at Davy. "What you brooding about, boy? The last saint you slept with?"

I could see my brother was shocked; he dislikes ex-Catholics as much as my mother does. But he's still Mother's holy boy when it comes to sin and sex. Sometimes it's hard to believe my brother is in the navy. I try to imagine him in stark, green locker rooms swatting his fellow jet pilots' naked bodies with skimpy towels. And I sometimes wonder what kind of lover he is. Mathilde said he was unexpectedly shy, romantic, stripping off his jet-pilot role as he did his uniform. I imagined my brother naked now, but all I could visualize was his body when I gave him baby baths. My mind censored me, either from some deep incest taboo or because it was unsafe even to imagine a naked brother I loved when Hawkins was so near. What if my imagination suddenly bleeped on Hawk's radar? He has a sixth sense, perhaps honed by his jealousy.

Just last month I received a bouquet of three dozen roses, anonymously. I knew they were from Hawk. That night we scrubbed together on a heart murmur. Hawk was sewing up that boy's chest with tiny, perfect stitches that would have made his Grandmother Felicia, with her Cuban convent-bred skill of sewing lace, quite proud.

"Anything special happen today, darlin'?" Hawk asked, and the sweetness in his tone was an ambush.

"No, baby," I smiled and slapped an eleven-blade between his thumb and forefinger. We've operated together for so many years that I often catch myself smartly smacking the catsup bottle into his surgeon's grip at the dinner table. "Why do you ask?"

I watched the dark blush begin in his throat, turning his skin even darker. *Negrito,* his mother called him when she saw her Cuban blood mirrored in his skin. I felt that momentary thrill Hawk's jealousy aroused in me. But lately I've been wondering about my excitement. Long ago, when I told Sydney about my first date with Hawkins, she was too quiet. I told her that at our first dinner I suddenly found myself unable to breathe. Excusing myself for the ladies' room, I looked in the mirror, saw my flushed face, my chest heaving shallowly, and clasped my hand to my heart. *I've never been this aroused by anyone,* I said to my reflection. Hawk and I became lovers that night. Of course, Sydney had to kill the mood completely by suggesting in her soft voice, "Maybe that wasn't arousal, Tia. Maybe it was fear."

Anyway, that night when Hawk thought for a spilt second that I was accustomed to receiving lavish bouquets from a secret lover, I did feel a little frightened. "*Nothing* happened today?" he'd demanded. He held my eyes fiercely, his bloody needle held mid-stitch. It was as if he'd discovered me in another's arms and was considering his next move.

"Nothing...oh, except that you sent me flowers, my darling." I smiled innocently. "Now, are you going to close up this boy or will I, even though I flunked sewing in home ec.?" Hawk dutifully went back to his stitches. But his smile was strained.

"Romantic love is sure death," Hawk was telling my brother as if teaching him the facts of life. The hurricane winds howled through our old banyan tree, its many rooted limbs trembling. "We're talking passion, son. Passionate love is sure death. AIDS just shows up the simple truth of this: you love someone, you gotta be prepared to lose your own life."

Davy was awkwardly silent. He believed Hawk was betraying an unmanly vulnerability. He didn't realize it was Hawk's own peculiar bravado. I've heard it for so many years, it hardly phases me. "Listen, Hawkins," Davy insisted, "a guy can love a lot of women in his life. You're saying that because Mathilde and I didn't make it, I'm as good as dead?"

"Do you love Mathilde more than your life?" Hawkins leaned over, his face near my brother's. It was as if I were not there at all, just the wind, the rum, the men. They might as well have been in the trenches.

"Of course not!" Davy exploded.

"Do you love flying more than your life?" Hawkins had my brother in the palm of his hand, those surgeon's hands that were exact, that sliced open skin with complete precision. "And did you love flying more than Mathilde?"

Davy squirmed and I intervened. "Stop it, Hawk. Let him be."

"Save the children?" Hawk demanded, and I was astonished to see the glint of steel in his eyes. He was jealous, even of my little brother. I stood up, unsteadied more by the realization than by the rum.

"Let's go to bed," I said, hoping to distract Hawkins, soften him.

"You can't keep protecting your little brother here from life," Hawkins muttered, but his tone said he'd dropped it. With a particularly hard thump on the back, Hawkins put one arm around Davy and the other around me. As if protecting us both from the hurricane which had picked up gale-force winds, he led us inside. Calmly, as if he did this every night, Hawkins then nailed two-by-fours across our wooden shutters. He showered, kissed our daughters as they slept, and came to bed, wrapping me tightly in his big arms.

Fresh from his midnight shower, Hawk's muscled, masculine embrace was belied by the baby powder smell of his dark skin. And for a moment I was confused—after all, my little brother slept in the next room, just as we had as children.

"Come here," Hawkins breathed.

He is as skilled a lover as he is a surgeon. I would never be afraid of Hawkins's hands, remarkable really for their deft, sure touch. Sometimes I wonder if all the generations of *curanderas* in Hawk's grandmother's blood haven't come through in his hands. Times like this, I'm glad Grandmother Felicia raised Hawkins. Felicia must have taught him how to touch a woman, though Hawk rarely talks of her. He talks more about the mother he doesn't remember.

That night as the wind howled like a living thing outside our boarded windows, Hawk made love to me so passionately it took my breath away. But as we rose up, our stomachs slapping against one another's, he suddenly pulled himself away from me and stood, still erect, above the bed.

"Say there's no one else," he demanded.

"You know there isn't," I answered, panting, somehow more urgently aroused by his parting. "Come back…" In my belly I felt a hunger that was old, deep, compelling.

"It's the wind…," Hawk murmured. "Too loud. I can't hear our hearts beating." And then I remembered something he'd told me long ago about listening to both our hearts pounding when we made love, how this *lub-lub-lub* growing louder drowned out all his fears of the dark, of me, of himself.

"Mi dulce corazón," I whispered and held out my arms, opening my legs.

Hawkins turned his back to me, and I thought for one bewildering minute that he was crying. Then he switched on the television, turned down the sound, and snapped on the stereo. As he came back to bed, entering me with a wildness that peaked just as my own was subsiding, he wept. I lay confused, comforting him, my hand gently patting his wide back from the long-ago habit I had of soothing my siblings. I tenderly coiled Hawk's hair around my fingers and asked, "Baby, what's wrong?"

He said nothing. His eyes flickered in sync with the silent television screen as he watched one of those maddening hurricane specials they broadcast throughout south Florida. It's supposed to inform residents of impending hurricane danger. But the effect is to scare us silly. This show, called "Hurricane: The Dark Side of Nature," boasted old footage of the 1935 hurricane that leveled the Flagler Railroad, killing scores of Great Depression construction workers and flattening the Keys. Hawk's eyes glazed over as he watched photo after photo of jagged railroad tracks poking upward in the wind like steel fangs.

"What is it, Hawk?" I asked in my softest voice. I wondered if he would let me sing him a lullaby.

"*El viento fuerte trae cambios,*" Hawk answered as if mesmerized, his voice as soft as mine.

A chill ran through me as a particularly nasty blast of wind rammed against our bedroom window. I thought of my brother sleeping next door. What if I lost them all, Hawkins and Davy and my children?

Gripping Hawk with all my strength, I demanded, "What? What are you saying?"

"The strong wind brings change," he answered in a singsong tone. It was a litany he must have learned long ago because he repeated it with the exact and credulous tone of a child. "It changes everything."

"Not us," I said and held him tightly until at last he slept.

It was because I did not sleep that we survived. Right before dawn and above the din and holler of the wind, which sounded like lions and tigers clawing outside our window, I heard another sound. It was not natural; it was a metallic clucking that changed to a steady, sonorous whir, then a mechanical mewling. It was a sound I almost recognized. After about an hour, I suddenly realized all the clanking was coming from *inside* our house. Then I remembered: this was the sound of heat! Hot water boiling up through copper pipes. Our Barracuda was alive and spiraling its scalding water upward through our walls.

"Hawkins!" I shook him awake.

But before I could say *boiler,* it began its bellowing rumble below.

Years of all-night stints in the operating room, and yet Hawk was slow to wake. As I desperately jabbed my knees into his back, he groaned and turned to me in a deep embrace. He pinned me in his arms as I yelled, "Move! Move! We've got to..." Then I remembered my brother next door. "Davy!" I screamed above the howl of the hurricane winds. "The children!"

I heard my brother's feet hit the floor. But he wasn't headed for safety. He thundered toward our room. I bit Hawk's hand and let out an animal roar.

"Stay still!" he said in a voice so commanding I realized he hadn't really been asleep at all. "It's better this way."

Now I heard it, the boiler's high whine, like an airplane engine taking off. "But it's going to...!"

"When it blows," Hawk said calmly, his face radiant in the dark, "we'll be in another world." He held my hands in his fists, his eyes fixed mine.

"No, Hawk...," I began.

"If we try to run, one of us might not make it," he explained as if reasoning with a child. "We don't want to live without one another."

His eyes were so familiar and luminous in the dark. I struggled a moment against his greater body, then yielded. And that acquiescence was the most terrifying thing yet. "Yes," I heard myself say as if in a trance. He was right; how could we give each other up? I was sinking deeper into the center of the storm, the hurricane's exact eye, where all is calm and perfect.

Then I remembered. "Davy!" I screamed. "The girls!" I wrestled with Hawk, fingernails clawing his chest. "Let me *go!*"

Still Hawkins held me as I screamed. Then suddenly we were both flying by our feet as Davy dragged us out of our shuddering room. Who knows where Davy got the strength? But my brother carried us as if Hawk and I were huge twins being born breech— down the hallway and into the bathroom where the girls cowered in the big tub, swaddled in their bedclothes.

"Duck!" Davy commanded, his military voice booming around the small bathroom. We all did, we five in the fetal position as the boiler churned up, exploding with the metallic sound of twisting steel. Water and wooden shingles whizzed everywhere. Then the hurricane winds took what the boiler had left of our roof.

II

This anniversary Hawk did not give me one of his usual presents. He built me a new roof. And as an act of love or contrition, he took a week off from the hospital to clean out our basement. The Barracuda had exploded upward two floors, demolishing our bedroom and private bath. You could say that along with my brother, Hugo saved us; it carried aloft the roof rubble that might have buried us alive. Two days later, however, Hugo proved himself not such a savior as he hit Charleston with screaming 135 mph winds and walls of water surging six feet high. As we cleared out our own boiler-blast debris, we watched citizens of Charleston digging out from under their storm, and looters in Saint Croix at last chased off the streets by U.S. troops. It seemed the whole world was gingerly checking themselves and their shelters to see if they still survived.

We have recovered—for the most part. Hawkins and I never speak of that suicide pact he tried to make with me the night our boiler blew. At some deep, unconscious level I wonder if my husband believes I am a deserter because I struggled not to die beside him. Sometimes I catch Hawk gazing at me with the eyes of a wounded, furious child. And I am afraid of what he will do. But I know his dark mood will pass. I understand that his family boiler's exploding again would trigger Hawk's early trauma of losing both father and mother. But there's something different in him, something I don't understand.

There's also something I don't quite understand about myself;

and it frightens me. Every now and then when Hawk and I make love, I feel hot energy burst in my belly. I imagine hurling my husband off me, high into the air, straight up through our new roof. Instead of trembling with pleasure under Hawk's hands, my body shakes with anger, my abdominals vibrating like muscular ropes snapping, no longer holding me down. This recurring murderous image confuses me. After all, Hawkins is the violent one. In my worst moments, I wonder if Hawk unknowingly set me up: What if in his idle tinkerings with the Barracuda, he intended it to explode, to again test my love, my loyalty to him? What if Hawk wanted to make absolutely sure his family never left him by controlling when and at what time we would all die together? Surgeons are used to holding life and death in their hands, but never the fate of their own family.

I don't like to think about these things. Unlike Sydney, who lives and breathes people's dark sides in her daily work, I am uncomfortable in the world of what if's. Recently I've noticed that Sydney says nothing about the boiler explosion, even when I bring it up. It's as if she's forgotten it or doesn't realize what a huge difference it's made in our lives. This surprises me, Sydney's silence. If I were the psychologist, I'd say it was a downright denial. Whenever I confide in Sydney my fears about Hawk's boiler behavior, she says quietly, "I have to give up being your bodyguard now, honey. It's too dangerous doing it cross-country. You'll have to be on guard with just yourself." And I am. I never let my husband see the anger that suddenly erupts right in the middle of our bed. Besides, he's got enough anger for both of us. Lately it's been bordering on paranoia.

One weekend when some of my brother's navy buddies from Key West came over to help Davy and Hawkins reshingle our roof, they got to talking about the end of the world. Some of the navy guys belong to a hush-hush quasi-military group called SONS—Survivors of Nuclear Strike. Hawk refuses to call his SONS comrades "survivalists"; he refers to their monthly meetings as "crisis relocation planning." The SONS remind me of my mother's End-Time Bible studies or Rapture prayer meetings, except Hawk's fellowship of the believers doesn't leave anything to God or chance.

I've tried to listen to Hawk's midnight lectures as we lie in our new waterbed, our bodies undulating lightly. I wish I could say this waterbed was Hawk's offering to our erotic life; but it, like so much else he tries to give me these days, is simply a precaution against fire, hurricane, or nuclear attack. I don't understand the logic, especially since my biggest fear is drowning. And since Hawk is home less and less often these nights, sleeping over often in the OR or away on his SONS' overnights, I am set adrift, alone in a bed that sloshes me back and forth like so much flotsam.

I suppose SONS is Hawk's way of reenlisting in the military, SONS being a kind of drill-happy reserve. Even though his own father died in nuclear war on Nagasaki, Hawk is still attracted to the military. Sometimes he even harks back to his brief navy doctor stint in Panama as one might a happy childhood. "Happy and poor," I remind him, "they don't go together."

Hawk's survivalist mood makes me worry about the children. Daniella's teacher sent home one of her recent drawings: a vivid orange-red painting of the Barracuda blowing up our condo. But in the midnight-blue sky overhead are missiles exploding with that same angry orange-rouge phosphorescent glow. There was a note from the school counselor in perfect cursive: "Dear Mrs. Costarella: Daniella seems deeply affected by the boiler episode. Perhaps we might meet and talk about ways to calm her fears?" How could I tell her it wasn't so much the boiler anymore as the stories Hawk tells the girls at bedtime? Hawk has sworn me and his SONS' clandestine activities to secrecy. But children don't keep secrets.

How can a child keep still when her father tells her that we now have enough nuclear firepower for one million Nagasakis? That the missiles will strike our island at twenty times the speed of sound, and World War III will last only half an hour? How can my girls or anybody fathom that at Ground Zero our bodies, being mostly water, will simply evaporate like so much mist? Though they are children, they no longer have my generation's assurance as we dutifully practiced our duck-and-cover drills. My girls now have the scant comfort of terrible foresight. The other night, I walked in to hear Hawk confiding his SONS' gospel to the girls—his eyes held the same fervor as my mother when she used to read us the Old Testament as if it were a proper bedtime story. Hawk was reading about a man in Utah who built condos underground, complete with outdoor scenes lavishly painted on the buried windows.

"I could paint the ocean in our underground condo," Daniella offered brightly. She has always been Hawk's favorite and has taken it as her job these days to cheer a father who seems far away in his doomsday fantasies.

"Now, remember, girls," Hawk instructed, "if I can't get to you, what do you do?"

"Dig a hole, cover ourselves with wood or metal, then lots of dirt," they repeated the SONS' catechism in that memorized, chirping voice I used when my mother made me recite Bible verses.

"Don't bury them alive, Hawkins!" I flew into the room, tucking my babies in. "Come to bed," I said. It was not a request.

When we crawled into our bed, Hawk embraced me and we both rocked on a wave like surfers caught in an undertow. He held me very close.

"You can't keep scaring the girls like this," I told Hawk and wriggled out of his clasp.

"I want to tell you the SONS' plan...for the children's sake."

"Sydney's right," I sighed. "I did marry my mother."

"So what else does Sydney say?" Hawkins baited me. He tried to raise himself up on one elbow to glare at me, but he simply sunk into the waterbed.

"She suggests that we're in shock after the boiler explosion and should..."

"See a shrink?" Hawkins rose up and down in bed as if caught in a riptide. "It's enough I pay for all your long-distance phone calls to Sydney. If you want to have your head examined here, I'll pay for that, too."

"Oh, I see," I grabbed hold of the headboard like a raft to steady myself on this damned drifting bed. "It's all *my* problem! Even though it was your family and your stupid boiler that blew up, it's I who need help." I stared straight at Hawkins and saw his green eyes widen. Was it fear or fury? I didn't care. "What I don't understand," I leaned close to him, "is if you're so willing to die for love, like you bragged to my brother, why are you a survivalist?"

Hawkins recoiled as if I'd struck him. For a long moment he said nothing, simply stared, without really seeing me. What flashed across his face? Some shadow, some grief that I recognized had little to do with me. I wondered if my husband's longing for death was so strong it could only be balanced by fiercely seizing life—the way I'd often seen Hawkins grip his scalpel as he slit a chest from sternum to navel. If I loved his passion for saving life, must I also love his draw toward death? Must I be married to it?

Hawkins startled me from my thoughts with his softest tones. "Tia," he began and met my eyes with a tenderness I'd almost forgotten in him. Hawkins took my hand in hands that were large and knowing. "I'm preparing myself and my family to survive a first strike just like you're always protecting yourself and us from your mother. We're alike, Tia."

"No," I protested. "We're not anything alike. You and my mother are...you're terrorists."

"Oh, darlin'"—Hawk shook his head ruefully—"isn't it terror you learned to love first? You're used to knowing that at any time it might all blow up—your family, our marriage, our family. That way, you don't have to feel trapped. You can imagine just moving on without me like I was no more than one of those unimportant

Latin countries your father was temporarily posted at. Everything is temporary for you, Tia. Your family always lived on the edge of everyday explosions—leaving everything you loved." Hawkins dropped my hand and seemed to float away from me on our waterbed. "You've never been left, darlin'. Your family is an underground mine, but it never really blew. It's still intact. You don't know what it's like to have people die in the explosion, to survive them...to have to live on by yourself."

I was silent. A strange wave of sorrow washed over me. Hawk and I seemed then like two shipwreck survivors afloat, searching for some island that might again give us common ground.

We were too far away to comfort one another. At last I said, "All right, Hawkins. Do what you need to feel safe, to survive. But spare telling the children."

"I tell them because *you* won't listen," Hawk confessed, his expression hurt, confused.

I rolled farther away from him on my own little wave. Between us the water rose and fell in a small tempest. *"Díme tú,"* I offered one of the few Spanish phrases I could remember. Spanish calms Hawkins; it is the voice of his lost family. "I'm listening."

"OK, here's the plan..." Hawkins brightened. Did he know how alone we were together? Did he sense that now I was lonelier with him than if he were away? "At the first sign of nuclear strike—we have connections with a Pentagon early-warning system—I'll beep you if we're not together. You grab the girls and take your flat-skiff to this uninhabited key..." He pulled a map from the nightstand drawer and pointed out a speck several miles from our backyard beach. "Remember? We saw it spear fishing last summer?"

"But it's nothing except a glob of floating mangrove roots, hardly an island. How are we going to survive there?"

"That's just the check-out point," Hawk rushed on, exhilarated at last to confide in me. "I've already built a little fishing shack on that key, stocked with minimum supplies. But here's the really great part…"

"Do tell, darling."

"Well, SONS survivors will come from all over the Keys. We have check-out points on hundreds of the uninhabited islands— only smugglers usually go there. They don't mind us. Anyway, you could get lost forever in those backwater keys if you don't memorize ours right."

"I know the place you mean," I assured him sleepily.

"I've bought a motorboat, small but seaworthy enough to get us the seventy miles down to our SONS' survival headquarters."

"And where's that?" I asked. "Cuba?"

"Close," he laughed proudly. "Fort Jefferson."

I sat up in bed, rocking back and forth. Fort Jefferson—a ghostly old garrison in the Dry Tortugas so remote that when Hawkins took me there as part of our honeymoon tour of the Keys and my new home, I'd shuddered to come upon the six-sided, blood-red, brick-walled fortress. The nineteenth-century monstrosity gobbles up its entire red-sand coral key. To Fort Jefferson, everything outside its thick walls is a moat. By seaplane Hawk and I visited this outpost which never saw military action. Swooping like gulls, we looked down on the Dry Tortugas; they resembled the broken string of a bright native necklace. Waterless, these tortoise-shaped islands lead off into nowhere.

"But Fort Jefferson is so…such a grim prison place," I protested.

"'Let's you and I away to prison,'" Hawk smiled sweetly. "'There we shall sing like birds and…'"

"Why couldn't we just survive a strike with the smugglers on some little key of our own?"

"Because all the other SONS will be at Fort Jefferson," Hawk explained.

For a moment I had the wild idea that he saw Fort Jefferson as some kind of end-of-the-world military ball. Images of my mother's hail-hail-the-gang's-all-here vision of heaven after Armageddon came to mind.

"I don't want to know any more," I said and eased out of the bed to leave Hawk floating alone.

"We chose Fort Jefferson," he called after me as I holed up in the bathroom, "because it's isolated, it's got months of supplies—food, water, medicine—and there are only five park guards. We'll convince them to join us or..."

"Or what?" I asked, coming back into the bedroom. I noticed that though the bedroom walls were new, the humidity was already peeling at the plaster. Our bedroom felt close, boarded up, like before a hurricane.

"Or...take them out," Hawkins said firmly and folded his map.

"Take them out! Take no survivors?" I yelled. "And you, Hawk, a doctor? This isn't spear fishing, you know."

"I've killed plenty of people," Hawk commented drily. "On the table and not on purpose. I'm used to taking responsibility for my own and other people's lives."

"Well, not mine," I started crying. "And not my children."

"*My* children, too," he said, and his voice was cold as surgical steel.

I thought of my brother stealing his children from Mathilde. I swore at that moment that my girls would not be kidnapped by Hawk, to be shanghaied off to his Cuban cousins on God knows what other island, as remote and walled off as Fort Jefferson. But unlike Hawkins, I had no plan of how to save them.

III

Hawkins has begun rebuilding our boiler. It's too early to start another anniversary present. Besides, I would not accept such a gift. Evenings when he disappears into our basement, I listen to his clankings and feel that it is I who might explode. Sometimes his SONS cronies help him out. I come down with dark rum, and in the guise of offering refreshments, I eavesdrop on their plans. But they whisper and cover their talk with clanging hammers as they rebuild their Buddha of steel. Sometimes I think they worship this boiler. Sometimes I am confused as to whether they're referring to their boiler repair, their bomb preparations, or Fort Jefferson reconnaissance. I think they get it all confused, too. Once when I demanded that Hawkins dismantle the antique and be done with it, he snarled and called me a "peace nut."

"It has nothing to do with peace or nuclear preparation," I tell Hawk, but I despair. Maybe I am surrendering to him; maybe I might have to give him up. "It has to do with spending every moment and all this money to build something we don't need here."

"We need it just in case," Hawk always responds in that calm doctor's voice, detached from any pain he might need to cause in the name of a cure. "Just in case we need the heat."

I've been avoiding my husband at home and at the hospital. It's easy; he's always in the basement or with his SONS comrades. At the hospital here, he's now only part-time, spending most of his days doing cardiac surgery up in Miami. Sometimes I wonder if he has a mistress on the mainland. That might be easier to accept than his love affair with an antique whose temperament is like a living land mine or his weekend rendezvous with his survivalists. How can I even hope to compete against these dates with death?

It was during one of Hawk's secret dates that I wandered into Mrs. Hernandez's hospital room one day. The evening was still balmy, a tropical winter day while the rest of the country was weathering blizzards. I was surprised to find that the woman, who is dying slowly and without complaint, was not alone. Sitting very near her on the bed was the new male nurse our hospital administrator hired—a local boy, Gabriel Alvarez. He was doing something strange with his hands flat on Mrs. Hernandez's belly. It didn't seem sexual and it didn't appear very scientific. The slight, dark-haired man sat absolutely still, his black eyes holding Mrs. Hernandez's own as if they carried on a conversation at such depth there were no words. The only time I've ever felt that kind of complete, wordless bonding is between myself and my baby girls, especially Daniella. Long before she talked, Daniella communicated with me by the great, black Spanish eyes passed to her from her Grandmother Felicia through her green-eyed son with the intensity of a recessive gene that dominates against all odds. I'd gaze into my baby's dark eyes and imagine I saw pictures there—what she wanted, what she needed, and what she wondered. Daniella read my mind, too. Still seems to sometimes. I can be standing in the kitchen remembering a winter picnic Hawk and I had with the girls before the boiler blew up our bedroom and our lives. Daniella will run in from her play and offer softly, "We could have a picnic without Daddy. We could take the skiff and go to our secret key and spend the night in our fishing shack even without a nuclear bomb."

I take this telepathy between myself and Daniella as simply a mother-child phenomenon; but that afternoon when I came upon Gabriel and Mrs. Hernandez gazing so profoundly into one another's eyes, I recognized at once that anybody could be a mother, even a man. I was so struck by Gabriel's maternal attentiveness that I began to back out the door as if I'd stumbled into some sanctuary. It was then I noticed the tiny wooden carving of Saint Teresa of Avila tucked into Mrs. Hernandez's green, metal nightstand.

Maybe Gabriel Alvarez was a priest as well as a trained nurse. But he didn't have that piety and detachment I see in the priesthood. Long schooled in celibacy, their touch is sometimes as non-physical as a bird wing or a leaf falling. Gabriel's fingers poised on the old woman's belly were somehow sensual. And yet it was obvious that his intent was only to arouse something in herself toward herself; it had nothing to do with him. Oh, let them be, I thought and quietly stepped out of the room backward. Let the dear old woman find healing wherever she may. It was then, in my retreat, that Gabriel raised his eyes and rested them on mine.

There is a light in my family's eyes that is pale and brilliant like electricity. These blue-gray beacons that I've looked into all my life are sometimes too bright, like the sea dazzled by sunlight. I've had to turn away from my siblings and my own mirror to rest from these eyes. But here were dark eyes with the same incandescence, but a calm—like the ocean at night solaced by moonlight. Gabriel's eyes shone on me with this darker luminosity, and I suddenly felt very sleepy. Like a somnambulist, I walked back into Mrs. Hernandez's room.

"*Gracias,*" he said. "Thank you for staying. I need you to please hold the back of her head now while I hold her feet." With a start I realized he was appealing to me as another nurse, as well as on a deeper level I couldn't explain but recognized. I accepted without hesitation.

Leaning on the bed, I cupped Mrs. Hernandez's wizened head in my hands, feeling for her delicate occipital ridge. How many times had I held my girls this way when they had headaches? But this was not an ache that would go away. The woman was dying. It was strange I hadn't recognized the signs the moment I walked in. Her critical state had been belied by how deeply engaged she was with the living.

Now she closed her eyes, and I felt her pulse in those precious cranial points in the back of the skull; it fluttered.

"We are sorry to see you go," Gabriel whispered softly and the old woman nodded almost imperceptibly. In my hands small tufts of hair came off. I felt I held a tiny bird's nest made of down, feathers, twigs, and refuse in my hands. "We will miss you, Gregorita," Gabriel continued in the same lulling singsong voice Sydney and I had used long ago. "We'll be sad when you are not here with us."

"*Sí*," she said, "*triste*." It seemed to comfort her, our sorrow, so that she might then let go of her own. In my fingers, her pulse throbbed strongly and only once, then was silent. She slipped away like so much vapor.

No one had ever died while I held them so tenderly, like family. I was shocked to find myself weeping. Gabriel did not come to comfort me. He kept holding Mrs. Hernandez's feet, though they were now cooling, as was her head. Because he did not comfort me, I could cry.

But as I did, I realized that this man at the opposite end of the bed was somehow holding me. Though he did not touch me, I felt his embrace. He was so still I felt I had all the room in the world, all the time I needed. And then I realized, as I at last looked up from my hands to meet his gaze, that it was simply his presence that held me. Was this the union Hawkins so desired when he wrapped his great arms around me too tightly?

"Someone else?" he asked quietly. "Someone else who is leaving you?"

I nodded. "Yes, in a way…"

He said simply, "I cried like that when I left Cuba and my grandmother." His accent was so lyrical, like masculine music. In one graceful movement he covered Mrs. Hernandez with the sheet, and her small face was outlined sharply in the starched cotton. Gabriel crossed to the sink, ran a hospital washcloth in hot water, soaped it into a luxurious lather, and then returned to the bed. As if this were part of his job, he began washing the old woman's feet.

I did not interrupt his chore, though I was charge nurse this shift. I did not question his ritual, because looking at his black, long-lashed eyes, his mouth slightly downturned in concentration, he was more Cuban than nurse. "Did your grandmother teach you this?" I asked softly.

"Yes," he answered. "She was a *curandera total* and I was the one she chose to carry on her work." He sighed and slowly dried

Mrs. Hernandez's small feet. "But I am here and my grandmother died alone in Cuba. She would not leave and I could not stay."

"What happened?" I asked. *"Díme tú."*

And then Gabriel Alvarez told me about his childhood. How he was taken from his grandmother and parents and their large, wealthy tribe who owned the island's largest sugarcane plantation. At the age of eleven, Gabriel found himself in the *escuela al campo,* no more than a concentration camp for children. From dawn to evening, he worked with other children in the sugarcane fields, before some little schooling late at night. Then the children collapsed into their hammocks for the few hours' sleep allowed them. Their diet was imported Russian canned beef and rotten rice, which explained Gabriel's delicate bones and smallness, despite his coming from a family of tall men and women. He rarely saw his family and survived by playing chess in tournaments for extra rations. He told me all of this in a calm voice, but in his eyes was a fierceness I'd not seen before. Yes, I recognized, he knew all about growing up with hatred that often felt too big for a small child to contain.

"Do you hate Castro?" I asked.

He paused, then nodded slowly. "I hate the system that stole my childhood and kept my grandmother in a prison until she died. You see," he said proudly, "she was the most powerful *curandera* on the island." His eyes flamed. "If my grandmother wanted to, she could raise a revolution by lifting one of her hands."

"Why didn't she?" I asked. "Why didn't you and she fight Castro's communism? My brother and mother and father do."

"If I stayed," Gabriel began, "I would be a guerrilla, killing or dying. My grandmother forbid me this. She said my hands are meant for healing only..." He gave me a troubled look. "The real war, she said, is always on the inside." Gabriel Alvarez fell quiet for a long time.

Sadness washed over me and I sighed, "Inside every home and every person."

"Yes." Gabriel met my eyes. He smiled, and I saw that the top of his mouth remained downward. This was the way his mouth was shaped as if permanently pursed in some private sorrow.

"Why were you chosen, Gabriel?" I asked on an impulse. Perhaps it was to distract myself from his mouth, which was the same dark magenta shade of Hawkins's mouth, but wider.

"By my grandmother, you mean?" His laugh was soft, self-effacing. "She's the only one that ever really has chosen me."

I held back the desire to remark that there were others, many others who might do so.

"In Cuba, they say when a baby cries in the womb, it is God's sign of a healer. That's why my grandmother chose me."

"Why did you cry before you were born?" I asked.

"Maybe I didn't want to be here," Gabriel answered. He gave me a grave look. "Maybe I was afraid to stay."

"But you did stay here," I said. "Maybe that's also why your grandmother chose you to continue her healing."

"I stayed," he said softly, "to heal myself."

We stood there side by side in our nurse's uniforms listening to the chink and bleep of life-support systems from the intensive care unit next door. Sometimes all the noise sounds like night crickets ratcheting away, a seesaw mechanical murmur of whirring computers helping people live on. This was a machine sound I could love; I'd heard it for so many years, it seemed almost human, another language, another lullaby. And that night with Gabriel Alvarez I was overwhelmed with tenderness for this machine music during our long night shift, this machine that human hands have made to heal, to help us stay here.

"May I help you wash Mrs. Hernandez's body?" I asked. Gabriel's face was familiar to me now, as if I'd met Hawk's brother.

"*Gracias,* Señora Costarella," Gabriel said. Briefly I touched his hand and nodded. Then we turned to tend the old woman's abandoned body as if she were our mother.

IV

When it came, I was not prepared. It was early evening, an ordinary October day with news of the Midwest digging out from under an early blizzard. But in the Keys it was so humid, I had to turn up the central air in the hospital. One coma patient was even sweating. As I stood over yet another "murder-cycle" victim, as Hawk calls them, I had the most unexpected shock. I bent double with a sharp cramp of pain, dizziness spun before my eyes. *It's over, it's all over!* I knew with perfect dread and certainty that the world was coming to an end. Without planning, I followed Hawk's plan.

At exactly 7:17, I swung into my girls' ballet class and collected them, using some excuse about a family emergency.

"Our world is over, isn't it?" Daniella demanded, seeing the pictures in my mind. "Will you beep Daddy?"

"Of course," I said and then was horrified to find I'd left my beeper by the coma patient's bedside.

I skidded to a stop at the Conch-on-Inn Motel and slammed myself inside the glass phone booth. I made three calls: Hawk's Miami service, Sydney's answering machine in Seattle, and Davy's officers' quarters in Key West. I assumed that my mother would be secure in her CIA shelter, and Dad was probably speeding his way right now toward the Secret City. I wished I could call everyone I loved—all my friends and even some of my old lovers. It even crossed my mind to alert Gabriel Alvarez, but there was no time.

At 8:30 we landed on our secret key. Clambering over the red mangrove roots, slipping often, we secured the skiff in its iron shed and ran for the fishing shack. I was shocked to see how sturdy it was. Expertly welded steel plates surrounded every side of this once ramshackle place. Instead of wooden stilts, the shack rested on iron pilings, no doubt sunk straight into concrete. Inside the place was a miniature fortress with an entire wall of blue distilled-water bottles, enough canned goods for an army, flashlights, radio, walkie-talkies, candles, and even a battered Parcheesi game I recognized as the only possession Hawkins kept from his childhood summers in Cuba.

The shack was the most complete fallout shelter I'd ever seen. Hawk must have spent a fortune here. Now I understood that all those weekends Hawk deserted us was his way of keeping us together and making sure we survived as a family.

I would have wept, but the girls were already donning their black snorkeling masks and scuba tanks. I realized with a shock that they'd been here before, perhaps several times.

"We drilled with Daddy," Daniella explained. "It was secret. Put on your gear, Mommy," she said. "We only have five more minutes."

Suddenly there was a sound. I ran to unbolt the steel door thinking it might be a local smuggler hailing us. "Anybody can help now," I told the children.

But it was not anybody; it was Hawkins. How had he gotten here so quickly from Miami? Was Hawkins at last tuned in to my telepathy?

"Hawkins?" I said. "How in the world did you…?"

"Where is he?" Hawkins demanded, pushing me aside as if I were no more than the maid to this little iron stronghold.

Then I realized—Hawkins must have been following me. He tracked us here expecting to surprise me with another man. How many other days when he'd said he was in Miami had Hawkins really been shadowing me? In my disgust, I forgot all about my end-of-the-world premonition. "How dare you, Hawkins Costarella…!"

But he glared at me, his fists clenched. And as always, his fury squelched mine. "One day, Therese, I swear I'll…!" He took a threatening step toward me but kept his hands clamped by his sides.

"One day will never come!" I said. "I'm here because I followed your stupid plan." Hawkins jerked back as if I'd slapped him. Now it was safe to raise my voice. "I expected the missiles to hit...not my own husband!"

"Didn't you want to save me, too?" he demanded. But I could see his pain. He reached into a metal box on the storage shelf and took out a portable phone. Looking straight into my eyes, he punched in the numbers of his answering service. As he listened, his eyes closed and he let out a long sigh, chagrined. "I'm sorry, Tia...sorry..." Then he reached for me, but I stepped back from his embrace. He acknowledged my reprimand with a rueful smile as he went over to very gently help the girls off with their scuba gear. "It's not a nuclear war, Tia," he called softly to me. "It was an earthquake you picked up on your family radar. Sydney called on the car phone. San Francisco...6.9 on the Richter scale, maybe more. Part of the Bay Bridge is down. She's OK, of course. Sends love."

"What's a Richter scale, Daddy?" Daniella asked.

"As long as we're all here," Hawkins said, "let's spend the night. We can have a picnic and play Parcheesi. All right?" The girls agreed. "All right?" he gazed at me, penitent.

That night as we each lay in our separate sleeping bag cocoons, I listened to the police radio Hawkins always keeps on at night. Between static, cops chatted about the quake, quoting body counts and survivors as if it were sort of the World Series. I was far from sleep and lay, eyes wide open, scanning the shelves of stockpiled food, the spear-guns and rifles, the pile of iron oxygen tanks. My breath was shallow, as if I were not inside this steel-fortified fishing shack but in an oldfangled iron lung or suffocating coffin. Glancing over at the girls, I saw that Daniella was awake, shining her small flashlight on a pamphlet entitled *Mom, Dad...What Is Nuclear War?* Hawkins had filed it neatly in the shack's tiny bookshelf next to the *PDR* and dog-eared *Survivalist's Handbook.*

"Oh, honey..." I tried to keep despair from my voice. "Can't you close your eyes and dream?"

I closed my eyes, too. But I did not dream. Instead I watched images float across my mind: I was lying on a white hospital bed, but not quietly like Mrs. Hernandez. I was struggling with all my might, legs grinding down against metal stirrups as Hawkins braced me from behind, his voice soothing. During the thirty-six-hour labor with Daniella, Hawkins sang Spanish to me. He sobbed when my OB told him the baby was traumatized, perhaps brain-damaged from all those hours banging her head against my pubic bone. The C-section saved her from the dead-end tunnel of my birth canal. At delivery, Daniella's face was as black-and-blue as a tiny prizefighter's—and she wasn't breathing.

Beside himself, Hawkins reached to slap her bottom and make Daniella breathe. But my OB calmly stepped back. Cradling our newborn, my doctor opened that miniature mouth to clear the mucus. Then he sprinkled a few drops of cold water on top of Daniella's soft head. First she opened her eyes, then her lungs. But there was no wail. Only a deep draw of breath that sounded like a small snorkeler's.

"There are other ways to stimulate breathing, Dr. Costarella," my OB told Hawkins. Carefully he lay Daniella across my belly and leisurely snipped the cord. "As you know, through the adrenals. But I prefer to stimulate the pineal gland or perhaps simply clear the nasal passages. There's already so much adrenaline in the mother's blood because of labor—why make the baby take her first breath in terror? Let her respond instead to the light, the warmth, the welcome."

Did Daniella feel welcome in this world Hawkins and I had made for her? A world we practiced ending, where we picnicked in fallout shelters? I remembered Daniella's drawings—the gray missiles like dolphins diving into the sea.

I fell into a fitful sleep. In my dream I was kissing a dark-skinned, slight man whose lips were the exact color of Hawk's, except downturning. Suddenly Hawkins burst in through the door, an eleven-blade in his plastic-gloved hand. He was head-to-

toe in his blue scrubs, still splattered with blood from the OR. I grabbed the surgical steel scissors from a nearby instrument tray and sprang on him like a swamp wildcat. And though he struggled, his surprise at my rage sent him into physical shock. So he simply lay there, his green eyes glowing as I expertly opened him—everywhere it mattered.

I awoke in a dead sweat with my sleeping bag twisted around my body. My flashlight was clenched in my hand like a blunt weapon. I was so alarmed, I checked Hawkins to make sure it was just a dream. Then I leaned over the girls to make sure they, too, survived my nightmare. My whole body was shaking as I slipped on my clothes and, still carrying the flashlight, ran out to the dock. Without thinking, I slid my flat-skiff into the water and then fired up the outboard. The roar of the motor neither drowned out my despair nor stopped my rage.

It was such a strong feeling, this fury, and unfamiliar. I had spent so many years monitoring first my mother's, then Hawkins's anger, I had no idea of the parameters of my own. I might do anything! As my boat sped across the dark ocean, as my own neighborhood beach came into sight, I was more afraid of myself than of Hawkins or nuclear war or hurricanes or even my mother.

Knowing this didn't stop my shaking. I slipped into the house without turning on the lights. In the bedroom, I took a cold shower and tried to lie down. But as I tossed and turned, that damned waterbed churned into a tempest of little tidal waves. A growling noise came from my throat. With a cry I hardly recognized as my own, I leapt from the bed, opened the night drawer, and took out Hawk's Swiss army knife. With one slash, I cleaved the bed in two. A sonorous blub-blub, as the warm, heavy plastic ballooned up, then split apart—a slit not wide enough to flood but certain to make sure I never slept here, seasick, again.

I stood panting. That Swiss army knife felt too small, silly in my hand. I needed something bigger. And then I remembered the Barracuda. How I hated that metal monster sitting like a fat octopus that gripped us in its tentacles. Was I going to spend the rest of my life in this boiler stranglehold?

No! No more—not in my home, not in my heart. It was the simplest thing I've ever done. In the basement I hefted Hawk's sledgehammer; it felt as light as those rubber hammers we use in the OR to break noses. My first great clang rang out like a bass gong. Then I struck its metal belly and the little door sprang open, falling off its hinges with a clunk. I made metal music enough to menace any punk-rock group as I banged this big steel drum, singing at the top of my lungs:

If (clang) they (clang) could (clang) see (clang-clang)
me (clang) now (clang) that (clang) little (clang-clang)
gang (clang) bang (clang) of mine! (clang-clang-clang)!

I played that big, fat steel boiler like a one-woman band until the lights went on and the house came down. I mean, our downstairs apartment neighbors came running to the basement, dreading another explosion because the noise I made was just the same as before the boiler blew last time. When I turned to them, my sledgehammer raised high above my head like a master's violin, their faces were shocked. But then Carlos whistled between his teeth and started clapping. His wife laughed. "*Gracias,* Tia!" she laughed and cried at the same time. "We got enough heat here."

Then another neighbor brought down espresso and hot, homemade mango tarts. With the food, my body at last stopped trembling. After everyone left to go about their daily business, I sat cross-legged on the cement floor and surveyed my damage. Our family boiler looked like it had been unhinged by a hurricane. I noticed for the first time then that it was a rather remarkable creation—like a steel sculpture. Did I suddenly feel this appreciation because I'd made this monster of round, tangled steel? I found myself wondering, how exactly had it worked? Did the water boil there and then shoot up those long arms like great tree branches to embrace the house? What fueled the boiler? And just how did those perfect little nuts thread into the metal holes—clockwise, counterclockwise?

On a hunch, I reached for a Phillips screwdriver. It was several hours later—when I heard my own stomach growling and mistook it for signs of life again in the boiler—that I was startled by the shadow of someone's presence.

Hawkins stood in the basement, keeping his distance from me and my dented steel creature. The girls stood behind him, peeping out from behind his arms. They were not afraid. I could see Daniella smiling broadly, and Felicia could hardly keep from jumping up and down as if denied a chance to join in the grown-up play.

"What do you think you're doing?" Hawkins demanded. But his voice was soft.

"Like it?" I yelled and began to laugh, a deep rumbling in my belly. "Call it...call it personal disarmament."

Hawkins noticed my sturdiness, the screwdriver in one hand, monkey wrench in the other. "You left me...me and the girls," he began.

"That's an option," I shot back. "You never reckoned on that, did you, Hawkins? On me leaving alone so you couldn't use the girls as hostages to keep me." I gave him a long, level look. Something was exchanged between us in that second, something deeper than that death pact we'd made the night our boiler blew.

"I can leave you, Hawkins," I said. "I can now."

He was still, his eyes pale in so dark a face. "I know, Therese," he said.

And then I saw it, not his rage, not his jealousy, not his fierceness. I saw his fear. And I realized he had always been afraid of me. He stood there looking down at his shoes which were dull, still wet from the boat. I saw him as he must have looked standing in this same house forty-five years ago when he beheld another boiler in pieces and knew his father was dead, his mother would leave him. What love I had left for Hawkins went to that despairing child in him. And what fear I had of Hawkins now belonged to me. Who knew what I might do, might destroy, might survive?

6

MY NUCLEAR FAMILY

Daniella, 1989

I

My mother is like an elephant. She can hear the rumbles of earthquakes the way elephants talk so low humans can't hear. It's called infrasound and I'm writing a report on it for my science class. Only terrible weather, volcanoes, earthquakes, wind, ocean waves, finback, blue whales, and elephants can make these really deep murmurings. But elephants and whales can talk it to one another.

It's not that my mother is fat, but then elephants aren't really fat, either; they're just big. That's what they're supposed to be. Big and beautiful. My father says my mother is beautiful. Too beautiful for her own good. He's afraid she'll leave him because that's what beautiful women do if their husbands don't make enough money. I think my father is paying for my mother on the installment plan. Even though he's got more money than any of my friends' fathers—especially now that he's moving to Miami and a bigger hospital, I know he's worried about making all his monthly payments. He doesn't have to buy us two girls, not unless we divorce him and he has to add us to his monthly payments.

My mother used to be afraid my father would leave her, although he's not beautiful, just good-looking. But now that he's always leaving us to work up in the Miami hospital, she's not so afraid anymore. She's more afraid of being poor. Dad says until she moves us to Miami with him, he's cut off all her credit cards, so it's hard for her to stay here supporting us just by being a night nurse. But I think she's more afraid to leave Key West than of anything else—even losing Dad, even losing her allowance.

My mom and dad are living apart a lot right now because of Dad's new job. When my cousin Timothy—I call him Timo like everybody else—wrote me from my grandparents' house in Virginia, he asked me if we were divorced yet like him so we cousins could maybe all live together. He hates Nana and Nanpa, but he likes living near the giant statues of Abraham Lincoln and the one you climb so high up six hundred steps it's like flying without leaving the ground.

I sent him back my drawing of two elephants who still love each other but keep a desert between them so they can each have their own watering holes. Water is very precious in those African deserts; and think about this, I told him, even though sometimes elephants go for days without water, they still cry, which means they give up what matters to them most—water. I told Timo that it's natural for mother and father elephants to live separately; they can still talk across the miles in their lower-than-human language. They can hear each other, I said, even though we can't.

I overheard Mom telling Aunt Sydney that she's afraid she'll lose her new friend Gabriel Alvarez even though he's not married to her or anybody else. I think he's too poor to afford a wife or children, that's why he's alone. Well, not totally alone. He has

Mother at nights when they nurse together, and he has his dolphins down by the saltwater bay. Every Saturday Gabriel swims with the autistic children—you know, the ones who are locked into their own worlds so they can't get out into ours. I think maybe those autistic children just might have another language we can't hear. It might be low, secret rumbles like elephants or earthquakes.

You know when elephants are singing to each other in infrasound because the air around their trunks trembles like seeing heat waves or hearing thunder far-off. If my mother can hear earthquakes, then she can hear her mate calling her from Miami. The thing is, it's mostly the mother elephants who call the males to them. Sometimes just one mother elephant is followed by ten males all wanting to be fathers. My mother doesn't have a whole herd of males around her, just Daddy and Gabriel Alvarez.

Mom doesn't think I know about her dolphin man; but Gabriel Alvarez is always in her mind. And I see him there sometimes more than I see my Dad. But there's a lot more on my mother's mind than mates. She thinks about me a lot, and my sister. Felicia is so little, Mom doesn't worry about her as much. But there are all sorts of terrible pictures in her mind and dreams about me. She even saw me one night with my stomach all bloated like African children who die every day without food or water. Her dream woke me up and I went and crawled into her bed. It's small now and not full of water like her and Daddy's wavy bed before. I curled up in the crook of her arm and sent her a picture of a mama elephant wrapping its long, strong trunk around its calf while all around gray aunt elephants stand guard against poachers so they can't tear her ivory tusks out of her mouth and take her away from her baby. Ivory is worth a lot of money, and both mother and father elephants have tusks, so they're both worth the same amount of money. But only if they're dead.

And then I discovered that night while my mother dreamed that I could make a noise lower than human sound that she could hear. And it helps her. I kind of hum without noise like wind or ocean waves. The minute I made my infrasound, Mom relaxed and her dream changed to a picture of snorkeling off Pennekamp coral reef, our favorite place in the whole Keys. Dad and Mom used to take us there all the time.

Early the next morning I sneaked back to my bed. Mom came in with a strange look on her face.

"I dreamed about us all snorkeling the Pennekamp," she said. "And this morning a tanker ran aground there…"

"Did it bleed blackness onto everything?" I asked. "Like in Alaska?" I'd seen those pictures everywhere—the oily otters who froze to death in the water that was their home, the birds whose wings were too heavy to stay in the air so they fell to be eaten by grizzly bears who will die, too.

"No, honey," my mother said and sat down on my bed, holding my feet the way I like her to do. "No spill. The ship just really shook up our little reef." She didn't say any more. But later, when we bought Gummi bears at the store, I saw the headline: "Damaged Reefs Take Centuries to Recover."

That means I will be dead many times over before our reef will ever be alive again as it was when my family swam there and in my mother's dreams. I know I'll be around to see the reef heal hundreds of years from now—but not as myself, as a bird or blowfish maybe. But it won't be the same.

I did my third-grade science project last year on coral reefs like our Keys. Reefs are alive like us, built over centuries by tiny soft animals called coral polyps. It's their skeletons that harden into reefs, but the polyps are always building, even though we walk on their bones, all their ancestors. Mom and Dad taught us never to touch the coral reef with our flippers or hands when we're snorkeling, just to look. So we swim—me, Dad, Mom, and Felicia—holding hands like a family chain, and whoever is on each end uses her free hand to point out mysterious blue holes or pretty pink brain coral or a barracuda or my favorite, the yellowtail damselfish, which have shiny blue twinkles all over their silver bodies, with yellow tails and eyes. Swimming through a whole school of them is like floating at night through the stars.

We've seen so many mysteries underwater, our family just floating, like dreaming except you're awake and everyone is in the same dream. Our family has a secret life there under the sea. Actually we all get along better underwater—there are no arguments, we have to stick together, we've learned to listen and talk with our hands, and there's no sound except all of us breathing. Sometimes when we're snorkeling together even Dad can see the pictures Mom, Felicia, and I send in our minds.

Dad calls our snorkeling trips "visiting our relatives," since he says we all came from the sea anyway. He calls me his monkey-fish, although that's a make-believe creature. Sometimes he teases me and calls me *Clown Wrasse, Puddingwife,* or his little *Spanish hogfish.* I call him *Doctorfish, Night Sargeant,* and Mom is that shine-in-the-dark turquoise, midnight blue, and incandescent yellow *Queen Angelfish.* I call Felicia *Flameback Cherubfish, Highhat,* or sometimes just *Chub.*

But we're really more like mammals than fishes. In the sea there are a lot of animals who decided long ago to go back to the ocean after living on land—giant turtles, otters, dolphins and whales, walruses, seals, and sea lions. They breathe both air and water. I think that's neat. You don't see any of us on land also breathing water except preemies who breathe liquid oxygen in my mom's hospital's intensive care unit. Liquid oxygen is slower and easier on little lungs, as if those babies are still inside their mothers, breathing the ocean. I wonder if when the preemies grow up they'll be able to live on land and sea because they'll remember how to breathe water after they're born. I saw a *National Geographic* special on deep-sea divers who are also using liquid oxygen to stay on the bottom of the ocean longer. Maybe when I grow up, I'll become a deep-sea diving scientist and spend half my life on the bottom of the ocean like Mrs. Manatee.

Mrs. Manatee lives in Dad's backyard canal with her calf I call Yammer. Yammer's still inside Mrs. Manatee's belly. Mrs. Manatee is under Dad's protection now, but it wasn't always that way. At Thanksgiving, when Mom and Felicia and I drove to Miami to Dad's condo on the canal, he took us spear fishing. We've never had turkey—that's for landlubbers, Dad says, unless the turkey is wild and he shoots it himself. We usually have lobster, pompano, grouper, and sometimes swordfish or shark steaks. This year Dad and Mom were hunting our Thanksgiving supper while we stayed above in Dad's motorboat. Mom uses scuba gear, Dad just dives holding his breath.

I've inherited Dad's big lungs and I can dive deep, too, but he wouldn't let me swim in those dangerous open waters. I'm more afraid of jellyfish than sharks. Jellyfish don't think; they just sting whatever they bump into. Sharks are so smart. They can't see through you like a dolphin, but they wouldn't eat anyone unless they were starving. Maybe I'd do the same if I were that hungry.

I've seen my father pet a shark or a barracuda. Those are the ones he doesn't kill. He has a rule: If a shark allows him to come near and stroke it, he will never harm it. I think that's fair. And most sharks are smart enough to figure this out about my father, which is why we hardly ever have shark for Thanksgiving supper.

This Thanksgiving morning Felicia and I were just dangling our legs off the boat ladder waiting for Mom and Dad. Our babysitter, Anita, was talking to her boyfriend in Spanish over the boat radio. I've known Spanish since I was born. My Greatnana Felicia taught me Spanish first, and Dad still talks it to me like our own elephant language.

Suddenly a huge explosion of air shot up out of the water at about 100 mph. A giant sea monster, gray and big as an elephant, rose up out of the water and looked at me with her small black eyes. But it was as though she couldn't see me too well because she wasn't scared. Or maybe we were invisible to her. I'd never seen a creature like this one—so round and chubby with white barnacles on her wrinkly forehead and a snout full of whiskers. She looked like a big gray world globe floating with flippers. Then I saw them, the toenails on her flippers, just like an elephant's foot. Felicia jumped up and down but I stood very still, the way elephants freeze to listen to their secret language. Then very slowly I began making my own elephant song, like I do when I crawl into my mother's nightmares.

I hummed my infrasound song and it worked on this sea elephant the way it did on Mom. Then I saw the sea creature's back as she raised up to hear me better. Oh, it was so cut up—crisscrossed with bloody stripes like a sword fight on her skin.

"She's dying, that big fish!" Felicia screamed. "We'll never eat her all up for Thanksgiving."

"We'll never eat her at all, stupid!" I told her. "She's an elephant underwater."

I held out my hand and the sea elephant kind of bumped into me very gently. She was shy, but she let me stroke her big head. It was all kind of smushed-up and funny-looking like a giant Pekinese face. Her skin was soft like rubber, but loose and crinkly. I kept up my elephant infrasound song, and the creature closed her eyes and nostrils and sighed.

I didn't hear him because my father doesn't splash like most swimmers, but Dad surfaced, his spear raised above his head.

"No, Daddy!" I yelled. "You can't! She's hurt already...and she let me stroke her first, so you can't kill her!"

"Shhhhh," my dad shushed me, and his voice was gentle.

The sea elephant turned to him, and then he saw her bleeding, crisscrossed back. Dad forgot he was spear fishing and became a surgeon as he ran a very light hand over her sad back.

"Boat propeller," Dad said, completely absorbed in the wound.

"Is she going to die, Daddy?" Felicia demanded. "Is she for Thanksgiving?"

"No, honey," Dad said firmly, and I remembered then how

much I loved him. I don't like to think about it much because he's always gone. "This is a manatee. They're almost extinct nowadays so you hardly ever see one. And they're awful shy...when they're not so hurt." He turned to the manatee. "I wish I could stitch you up, old girl, but you'd never stand for it. I can do something...Daniella, fetch me the first aid kit."

I did. And do you know that Mrs. Manatee, as I named her, let my father rub salve on her back and give her an antibiotic shot. She must've been in shock to let him touch her. But I think she knew Dad was a doctor more than a hunter.

"Now, big girl," Dad slowly swam her off from the boat. "Stay away from us people and you'll heal."

As Mrs. Manatee inhaled a big breath and dove back to the bottom of the ocean, my mother surfaced. Mom and Dad bobbed about in the ocean like they belonged there. Dad was even laughing. "Well...what'd ya get us to eat?"

"*Nada*, Señor Costarella," Mom shrugged and her scuba gear clanked.

"Me, neither," Dad smiled. "Except a shark." Since he was empty-handed, we knew the shark had been smart.

"Looks like we'll have to try again," Mom said and splashed Dad with her flippers.

"You know, baby," my dad called to me, "manatees were the first mermaids."

"They're too ugly!" Felicia squealed.

"Not if you're a lonely sailor on the sea." My dad laughed and dove down after Mother.

Soon after, they surfaced, both carrying a thirty-five-pound red grouper for Thanksgiving. Neither Mom nor Dad saw that Mrs. Manatee was trailing them. And I didn't say a word. I just kept singing my infrasound and hoped that our elephant-mermaid who lives in both worlds of air and water would follow us to Dad's home.

There Mrs. Manatee has stayed in the backyard canal ever

since. In her way, Mrs. Manatee is married to my dad, and now I'll have a kind of half-sister in the sea because Mrs. Manatee is going to have Baby Yammer next Christmas.

I don't tell Dad or Nanpa that I think of Mrs. Manatee's baby coming into the world like a miracle baby. Or that I'm working on a nativity scene drawing for my grandparents; it's called *Key West Christmas* and it's got all underwater creatures: A manatee miracle calf to save his kind from extinction lies on a manger made of seaweed. Yellow angelfish float around the baby manatee like bright little halos. Dolphins and purple whales sing a Christmas cantata of clicks and bleeps that mean "Welcome to the world!" There are sea bass as shepherds, three old white sea turtles for wise men, Joseph is a sleek sea lion, and Mary is Mrs. Manatee, so big and shining and round she's like the whole world, but underwater.

I know Nana and Nanpa will like my Christmas-present drawing because Nana drives her small red car that has fish stickers all over the bumper. When I asked her why she had fish swimming on her car, she said, "Because I'm a Christian, darlin', and you could be, too, if your parents ever took you to Sunday school." Then she told me how the first Christians were fishes. I told her that my parents took me snorkeling most Sundays and there were a lot more schools of fishes under the sea than in church.

She didn't listen. Nana's kind of like my fourth-grade teacher, Mrs. Moray. I try to explain things to Mrs. Moray, but she doesn't really hear me. Her eyes are always darting back and forth like it's time for a cigarette. And she strains to hear the recess bell even more than we do. That's why it's hard for her to hear us. Or maybe some adults can't hear children because we speak lower than grown-ups in our infrasound language of wind and elephants. I don't know. Anyway, Mrs. Moray decided our whole class would do Christmas drawings of our families to put up for Parents' Night.

I drew our entire family: There was Mom swimming with her

dolphin man and his autistic children who were each in their own little blue bubble. Then there was Felicia and me holding hands with Mrs. Manatee, who had polished her sea-elephant toenails with my mother's Caribbean Coral orange-glow nail polish; we were all holding our breaths in a big blue hole inside our coral reef that stretched like a rainbow over us. My daddy stroked a long, striped hammerhead shark. Nana and Nanpa swam by as big balloonfish, and above everybody stood a mother and father elephant on land deciding to live in both worlds and breathe water and air.

"What are all these animals doing here?" Mrs. Moray said, holding up my drawing in front of the class. Everybody who didn't like me giggled.

"They're part of us," I explained. I always talk very slowly to Mrs. Moray because she is so busy listening for the bell. "That's Africa up there where the elephants began it all by..."

"I didn't ask for Noah's ark, Daniella," Mrs. Moray snapped. "I asked you to draw your nuclear family."

I don't know why Mrs. Moray has changed so much this year. About Thanksgiving she started smoking again—we smell it like she's got a bad climate about her. She used to be kinder, though she's always been strict with us. But lately she seems like she's not even here. My mother says it's because her marriage is on the rocks like everybody else's. But I think it's something else—a secret maybe even from herself.

Our class has learned in the past few months that Mrs. Moray will become like her old self again if you ask her science questions. Then she kind of snaps to attention like my Uncle Davy in the military and gives her own science reports. So when she hated my drawing I asked her, "What is a nuclear family, Mrs. Moray?"

She started in about a nucleus—how an amoeba has one in its one-celled self. The nucleus helps it grow and reproduce itself, pass on genetic traits. We have nuclei in our brains and so do atoms, comets, water, and ice. "So you see, class, when I say *nuclear* I mean that central part, the core, about which everything else is grouped." She looked around, glanced at the big clock.

We saw by her sudden attentiveness that it must be moments before the bell. So she could smile.

But I shouldn't have smiled back when I asked a nonscientific question, "Are all nuclear families related to the nuclear bomb?"

Mrs. Moray prickled like a porcupine and said, "You children certainly don't have the sophistication to understand the atom bomb—some small *countries* don't yet understand it. Suffice it to say that it takes a nuclear family to live in our nuclear age." She gave me a hard look, "And by family, I don't mean any animal or creature you can dream up."

Then the bell rang and she bolted for the door. She was so sick of us, I could see. She didn't want us around her; she wanted something secret, like smoke.

Later that day I got a nasty note from Chuck Lagree, who has been stupid since the first grade. It said: *Your mother was a Big Bang.*

I didn't feel so well that night. How was I going to tell my mother that of all the kids in the class we would be the only family not represented on the walls for Parents' Night? Dad never goes to that stuff, but Mom does, and it would make her sad to see us as an invisible family. The more I thought about it, the more my head hurt. By the time midnight came, it felt like hot steel gurgled inside my chest, and I sweat through my sheets.

I don't know what happened next, but I woke up in my mother's hospital. She held my hand; a small man was beside her. The air around them shimmered like the heat waves near elephants when they're rumbling low. There was secret thunder everywhere. I closed my eyes, and they sunk so far into my head I couldn't open them again—not for the world.

I was in a cave inside my own skull, floating. Very clearly I saw Mrs. Moray giving a science lecture. She drew a picture on the board of a big brain floating in water. I realized I must have shrunk so tiny I was inside the hidden ocean that floats my brain. It was OK because the water was warm and I knew there were no sharks. My brain was big and full of pink knobs like giant brain coral as I snorkeled all by myself inside my skull. A blazing butterfly fish floated by, but except for that I was lonely. Now I knew what my dad meant when he said those sailors were so sad and alone they'd believe even a sweet, rumpled face full of whiskers was a mermaid.

I called out for Mrs. Manatee to come with her bright elephant toenails and big, round belly. But it was not Mrs. Manatee who swam toward me; it was my Greatnana Felicia, who is dead. I guess I disturbed her because she's buried in my brain as well as the ocean. Since they could not bury Greatnana in Cuba, her home, she asked that her body be burnt up and the ashes scattered in the sea. My daddy carried her in an urn on his motorboat all by himself as far south as Americans can go before the water turns Cuban, with patrol boats and aircraft. That's where he buried Greatnana, where her ashes would float free and find their way back to her home without anyone knowing. They couldn't keep her away if she were fish food—that's exactly what she said in her will. So when my Nana MacKenzie talks about people who love God being fishes, I know my Greatnana Felicia is in heaven even though it's underwater and not in the sky.

Well, Greatnana swam toward me and she was smiling. She didn't look old at all, and her body was back together although it was kind of see-through, like fishes had nibbled a lot of her. But it didn't bother Greatnana a bit. She told me she'd missed me, but she'd never been far away, just as close as the ocean in my own body. I liked that, discovering that the sea was inside me and I could snorkel there anytime, without waiting for my family to get itself back together and hold hands.

"*Te sientes sola aquí?*" I asked Greatnana in the first language she taught me.

She said, no, she wasn't lonely. This ocean was full of others. I just couldn't see them yet, the way some people couldn't hear elephants or ocean waves talk.

"*Enséñeme!*" I begged her. More than anything, I wanted to stay and swim with Greatnana and the invisible others. I could almost hear them, now that she told me how quiet they talk…just a whoosh like waves underwater, like holding your breath.

I held my breath so hard, my pink brain coral began spinning. No, Greatnana said, not yet. But already I was whirling round and round like an undertow, and then I heard it—the singing. It wasn't infrasound or secret anymore. It was full, the most beautiful voices I've ever heard—like mermaids, so many of them in an underwater choir. And then the mermen chimed in with their foghorn voices. I wanted to sing, too.

I opened my mouth and the salt water rushed in. But it didn't scare me; it was so warm and familiar. And then I remembered, not only how to sing underwater with the mermaids, but to breathe water again. It filled me with its liquid warmth, and there was brightness, too; but it was inside. And then I saw that I was my own small sun now, like those fishes at the very bottom of the ocean who shine in the darkest dark because just by being alive they give off light.

Just settling down on the sea bottom in my own shining skin, I had to laugh, thinking that Mrs. Moray might really like this science project. But then I'd have to go back up to the surface to get to the school. So maybe I'd just stay down here and drift with Greatnana and all the others. Yes, that's exactly what I would do.

"*Regreza, mi niña.*" It was my first language but not my greatnana's voice. "*Te necesitamos.*"

No, I would not come back, no matter how much they needed me. There was nothing I could do to make our family not invisible; there was no one up there who spoke my language or sang infrasound except in secret; and there was no science report that I could ever do that would be good enough to bring Mrs. Moray back to herself or us.

So I sat with my arms across my chest because it still ached a bit and breathed water. Greatnana Felicia was near me again, I knew, but she was completely nibbled away now and nearly invisible. Still I heard her. She wasn't speaking to me but to that other voice; and they didn't speak Spanish or any language I understood. It was high-pitched, maybe above my hearing. And then suddenly I recognized it. Dolphin talk. Sure enough, here they came—a whole school of them.

And there were other children swimming with them, but not in bubbles. They held onto dorsal fins, sometimes two dolphins at a time carrying those kids. They called out to me to join them; but they were heading to the bright surface again to breathe air. I knew that would hurt my chest even more, so I hid in a piece of my brain coral like a blue hole. I guess some part of me hoped someone would come because one of the dolphins stayed behind, even though it was time for him to breathe above.

He called me with his high ultrasound, and I answered in elephant talk. I threatened him—*don't come near.* But he did, and his long dolphin beak fit perfectly into the coral tunnel where I hid.

You're not a fish yet, the dolphin smiled. *If you were, I might just eat you. But I'd rather swim with you.* His eyes were dark like Greatnana's; for just a moment I thought it was her, changed. I reached out and saw I still had my hands. Whoosh! That dolphin slipped under my arm and pulled me up so fast, I swallowed a gulp of water that had something else in it—oh, it was air again.

You can live in both worlds, the dolphin said as I sputtered. *I do.*

My mouth and my eyes opened wide. It felt like all the water in my brain just rushed out my eyes, my ears, my mouth in a little flood. Through the waves I saw a small man, his eyes black and familiar, his hands flat on my chest. I knew he wasn't my father, but he looked like he belonged in our family because even though he was small he had features like my dad and Greatnana Felicia.

Then I recognized him. It was the dolphin man. And he

wasn't in the ocean floating around my brain or my mother's mind—he was in a too-bright room with machines all around. I tried to move, but there was something stuck up my nose. It hurt more than air.

"We'll take it out," the man said and gently pulled the long plastic thing from my nose. Then he said real low, "Thank you for coming back, little one."

"Did you see my Greatnana, too?" I demanded and tried to sit up, but I was too tired. So I just flopped back like a fish.

"Did you?" he asked.

"Oh, yes," I said, and then my mouth yawned and the world went watery again. But then I heard my mother's voice.

"Darling…," she whispered, her hands on my chest, too. "You had pleurisy, fluid in your lungs. But you'll be fine, thank God."

And thank Greatnana Felicia and all the fishes and dolphins, I wanted to tell her but again yawned. It was like I was a guppy and couldn't stop flapping my mouth open and shut. But my chest did feel warm and soft again, not like steel.

"I'm right here, Daniella…," my mother said. Her voice was far away, but her hands weren't.

So I decided to sleep with all those hands helping my chest breathe. And then they turned off some of those loud machines and the louder lights.

Maybe it was a day later. Maybe it was more, I don't know. But it was still nighttime, and I woke up because Mom and the dolphin man were talking just in normal human-range. I didn't open my eyes because my chest was open again and that was enough.

"I really think her teacher is having a nervous breakdown," my mom was saying softly. "Maybe if I take Daniella out of school for the holidays and go away…" She stopped like she was waiting for the dolphin man to say something.

"Christmas is for children and families," he said finally. But it was kind of sad the way he said it.

"We'll have other Christmases," my mother made a promise.

"I'll be here when you come home," he said.

"Gabriel," she said his name at last, and I sighed because it all made sense. "I'm not going to Miami for Christmas. I'll go…I'll go home. The kids can see their cousins. Maybe Davy and I together can fend off my parents."

There was quiet. I liked the idea of seeing Timo again; even though he is a boy, he's my favorite. I almost opened my eyes and shouted *yes!* but there was too much quiet in the room. Then Mom and Gabriel spoke in voices too low for even my hearing, but I heard my father's name more than once. For the first time I wondered where he was. Later I found out that he and Mom had a fight about keeping me in the small intensive care unit in this Key West hospital. Dad wanted to move me to Miami, and when Mom said no, he started yelling like a surgeon, then cried like my daddy, then left.

"I'll miss you, *mi amada*," Gabriel said sadly.

"Maybe not…" my mom laughed, but it wasn't a real laugh. "I'm such a mess lately…and now this with Daniella…"

They were both quiet a long time; I could feel for the first time that they were both in their own little bubbles like those autistic children. "Will you come back to me?" Gabriel asked, his voice was very low, as if he were wondering out loud.

"I won't let you go," my mother promised him, but somehow that didn't sound real, either. Then she got kind of weepy. "I don't know anymore. I expected anything but Hawkins letting me go. It's like the villain in my little love story is just *not* doing his dastardly deeds."

Gabriel laughed, but only a little. "What a villain."

"*You're* the one I'm really afraid of," my mother said suddenly.

I opened my eyes then and saw Gabriel give my mom a long look, like he had all the time in the world or like he was just listening to the earthquake talk inside her. "No," he finally said, real soft. "Not me."

"Damn you," my mom made a curse real low like an animal. It wasn't a purr, it was a warning. "Damn your eyes!"

He raised his eyebrows the way foreign people do when they want a translation. I think he even smiled though his mouth stayed turned down.

"It's a song," my mother sighed and shook her head. "It means damn you, Gabriel Alvarez...damn you for seeing me."

I saw them both but didn't want my eyes to get damned, so I stayed in pretend sleep. And by the time I woke up, it was just Mom and Dad there sitting on opposite sides of my bed, each holding a hand.

It was kind of like we were all snorkeling there in the hospital room, but it really wasn't the same—just like our reef hasn't been the same since that oil tank wrecked on it.

"How would you like to go up to Virginia and see Cousin Timo, Izzie, and Uncle Davy for Christmas?" my mother asked.

I looked first at my dad. He was bigger than I remember; or maybe it was just that the dolphin man is so much smaller. "What about Mrs. Manatee, Daddy?" I asked him. "Will she stay with you for Christmas?"

My dad smiled at me and squeezed my hand. "She's not going to have her baby until next Christmas," he said. "And we'll all be there to see it."

Then I felt better, even though in my other hand that Mom held, I felt a little jolt of electricity.

II

Like our family snorkeling, like our Pennekamp coral reef, Christmas was not the same. For one thing, it was *cold*. Mom had to buy us winter clothes, since we don't really own any. And sometimes the heat in my grandparents' house was so intense it felt like every night some troll came and vacuumed us out so that by morning our mouths were dry and sore.

Nana and Nanpa, even Timo and Izzie must have been used to the heat up there because they didn't notice things like the weather. They were too busy with history.

"This is where history happens," Nanpa says all the time. He promised to take us all sight-seeing while the grown-ups go Christmas shopping. But it was hard to have history happening to me when I was so distracted by the outside cold and the inside heat.

All of my mother's nuclear family was there, except Aunt ShiShi, who stayed in Seattle because she's boycotting my grandparents until Nana agrees to see a psychiatrist. Uncle Davy says Aunt ShiShi will have to wait until hell freezes over for that to happen. But if hell is as cold as Virginia, that might happen anytime.

When we arrived, Uncle Davy took just Mom out to dinner and left us cousins with a babysitter, even though Nana MacKenzie was home, too. Uncle Davy kept talking to my mother in French, which is their secret language. When he and Mom and Aunt ShiShi were my age, they studied French in school so they could talk together in their bedrooms without Nana listening in over the house intercom, like she was still at her CIA work instead of in her own home. I would have spoken Spanish with Timo and Izzie, but they only have one language. So I taught Timo infrasound humming to make sure Nana didn't spy on our conversations.

Izzie was wearing a sling made out of a pretty holiday napkin with Christmas-tree patterns. She looked like a little angel because she has that bright halo hair. Felicia and I are dark as pirates—that's what Uncle Davy says. And he should know since his navy is always fighting them. No one knows exactly how Izzie dislocated her arm. She told me Nana hugged her so hard it popped out her little elbow.

The first time Mom ever took us to meet Nana and Nanpa MacKenzie, I was almost five and Felicia was just learning to walk. Aunt ShiShi traveled with us and we met Aunt Mathilde and Uncle Davy in Union Station. We all stood on the train plat-form waiting for Uncle Davy to return with Nana and Nanpa. I was excited because I'd never known Daddy's parents, since they left the world before I was born. We had our Greatnana Felicia, of course, but the Captain was long gone. So grandparents were new to us. I remember looking hard to see Uncle Davy in his military whites and shiny shoes swing out through the big train station doors with our two bundled-up grandparents. From far away, they looked really small, but then one of them broke into a run.

"Oh, no...," Aunt ShiShi said to Mom. "Batten down the babies!" My aunts put the stroller belts on Izzie and Felicia. Mom firmly took my hand and Aunt Mathilde pulled Timo to her side, clamping him there. Then Aunt ShiShi stepped right in front of the strollers and held her arms out wide.

I was surprised by all the commotion. But when I looked up to see Nana barreling down on us faster than a train, I under-stood. It was like Nana had no brakes because she ran straight into Aunt ShiShi's open arms, knocked her down, fell on top of her, and hugged her, shouting, "I'm so happy to see you, Sydney. All my family together at last!"

Uncle Davy lifted Nana up and kept holding onto one of her arms as she grabbed for each grandchild with a squeal. Later I found out that Nana's always like that when she's excited. Too happy, I mean. Like in stories some grown-ups tell that are too cheerful in the places where they should be sad. Nana also gets too sad sometimes. I've seen it. First she gets speeded-up like a train that can't slow down even for the station. Then she realizes she's missed her stop. Then she starts crying like she's been pun-ished and has to travel alone.

So this Christmas when we heard how Izzie got her arm dis-located, we knew to just kind of duck out whenever Nana got in the hugging or too-happy mood. And I guess that's why Uncle Davy hired a babysitter to stay with Nana and us, too. Nanpa was at a meeting for his diplomat work. He was really busy because of the Berlin Wall falling down and he was on call to fly off at a minute's notice in case that wall came down so fast it made Communists in other countries crazy.

Timo and I kept our eye on Izzie and Felicia, but mostly we watched Nana. If you stay on your toes, she is more fun to watch than a video. That night she was in the kitchen making about a thousand cupcakes for the church social after her choir's big cantata. Nana is the church organist and she plays the piano better than anyone. Uncle Davy says she's half-black when her hands hit the keys because no better boogie was ever played in a white Southern Baptist church.

That night before her cantata, Nana took our breath away with her magic hands. In the kitchen, she rolled up her sleeves, shoved her hands into a paper bag full of flour, shook the bag with her arms inside. "Ta da!" she said and held up arms that were white from fingernail to elbow. She threw some flour on the linoleum floor, did a shuffle while she sang "I'ma coming...I'ma coming...," and then we watched those cupcakes fly together.

First she tossed Timo a big baking bowl, then me two muffin tins, then a wooden spoon upped and swooshed into her white hand like that man I've seen on TV who moves things across the room with his mind. On went the oven, around and round went the wooden spoon, the flour got sifted over everything, including a dab on each of our heads for fun, then before we knew it, big dollops of dough the size of Izzie's fist dropped into the metal muffin tins. Nana let us put whatever food coloring we wanted for frosting. I made my cupcakes rainbow-colored; Timo's turned green and some red. Izzie's went all pink, and Felicia mixed green and blue so hers got kind of like big bruises. But Nana said that was OK—the family could eat them.

She set the timer and then gave us a bright look. Her face is really long and pale, but sometimes it shines like it did that night.

"Are you my boogie babies?" she asked us.

We all followed her to the piano. Izzie and Felicia sat on each side of Nana on the bench. Timo and I stood behind. The babysitter was on the phone.

"All right, kids," Nana said with a wink. "Let's swing it!"

I've never thought a piano bench could be a porch swing, but it flew as Nana hit those pedals with her feet, her hands flying so fast over the keys they were a blur. Felicia and Izzie clapped wildly and bounced on the bench. Timo took my hand and twirled me around like boys and girls do on the dance floor. Nana swung into a fast, fast song: "Downtown Strutter's Ball."

The grown-ups found us doodlebugging, as Nana calls it, when they came back from their private rendezvous. Uncle Davy and Mom weren't speaking French anymore, so the secrets must have been passed between them. That's what Nana said.

She's raised a passel of spies for children, that's what Nana told us that night. And they're all plotting against her. Fortunately her job at the CIA keeps her children on their toes, too.

Then Nanpa MacKenzie came home. He looked really tired. "I'm beat," he said and flung his hat so it landed perfectly on the vestibule rack.

"Everything in this house flies," Timo whispered to me, and we started giggling.

"What's the joke?" Uncle Davy demanded. He seemed kind of cross, but I didn't think it was with Timo.

"I was just explaining to Cousin Danny how you got to be a pilot," Timo said.

"Davy is a navy pilot to protect us...and you, too, children." Nana jumped up, knocking Felicia off the piano bench as she ran to take out more cupcakes.

"Yes...protect," Mom said, looking straight at Uncle Davy as she picked up Felicia. She wasn't hurt; the carpet was too soft. Felicia was too stunned to cry.

Uncle Davy sat down beside his little Izzie, who was playing "Silent Night" with one finger. It was the only song she knew, and Timo and I were already sick of it.

"Those Germans *would* pick Christmas to tear apart their whole society," Nanpa grumbled as he sat down with the newspaper.

"I can't believe you'd *complain* about the Berlin Wall coming down," Mom said. "It's the perfect Christmas present...to us all."

"Yes," Nanpa laughed. "But it's like one of those newfangled gifts you don't exactly know what to do with."

"How to use it, you mean?" Mom asked. "Dad, how about just being happy it's happened—the wall is down. Our world will never be the same. We'll have to change."

"If you kids ever read your Bible," Nana called in from the kitchen, "you'd realize what Gorbachev's really up to." Then she added, "Who wants to lick the frosting bowl?"

We all ran in and there was a bowl for each of us. "Go ahead," Nana insisted. "Don't use your fingers like sissies. Get in there with your tongues." She showed us how to really lick the frosting like little dogs, and when our faces came away with all different kinds of frosting, Nana's was the wildest. And then I decided that even though she was kind of dangerous, she was more fun than most grown-ups, and I was glad she was my Nana and not someone else's.

Lickety-split Nana reached out a finger full of Timo's green frosting and drew squiggles on my forehead. "There," she said real happy. "Go show your mom."

In the living room they were still talking about that old wall. It's so important to them, but nobody my age pays much attention to it.

"This is history," Nanpa was telling Timo in his lecture voice. Timo shrugged. "This may be the most important thing that ever happens to you." Timo looked like he doubted it.

Then everybody turned to stare straight at me. Nanpa and

Uncle Davy started laughing, but my mom got furious.

"*Very* funny, Mother." My mom tried to smear Nana's frosting squiggles off my forehead, but I ducked and ran to the vestibule mirror. There I saw the numbers 666 in green swirls. Nana stood behind me with her wooden spoon, pointing.

"The sign of the beast! That's what Gorbachev is up to. And it's your own children who'll pay the price if you fall for this Berlin Wall trick."

"It'll never come down for you, Mother," my mom said softly and slipped the wooden spoon from Nana's hand. "You and Dad wouldn't know how to live without a wall, would you?"

"And you do?" Nana said too loud. She grabbed Mom's chin, shaking it back and forth. "No, you don't know, Missy. So don't lecture me on how to live. You kids have had more peace in your time than your father and I or my parents ever had in our whole lives. Your own children here have never known a day of war the way we did growing up. And *that,* kiddo, is because of our walls and weapons."

"We've known war," my mom said, and her voice was steady. "We live on the home front. The real trouble is not out there, it's here, it's us."

"I give up!" Nana said suddenly and threw her frosting-covered hands in the air. "Just wait until your own children stand here and accuse you of ruining their world when all you did was try to protect them!" Nana swatted my mom on the bottom so fast it startled everyone. Then she spun Mom around and sent her flying into the La-Z-Boy where Nanpa sat. "You handle her, Sam," Nana yelled. "She's always been your favorite."

Uncle Davy jumped up and pulled Nana into the kitchen. My mom sat sobbing on her daddy's lap. Nanpa kind of wrapped his newspaper around her like a blanket and rocked her, even though her legs reached the ground.

Timo and I sneaked into the kitchen and watched Uncle Davy try to calm Nana down. But Nana's hands fly around sometimes without her telling them to. She's like an octopus caught in an invisible net of angel hair. Nana thrashes around but can't get free. Nana's not clumsy, she's just fast. Once, a long time ago, she told me the whole world just seems to her like it's in slow motion.

At the piano Izzie banged out, "Sleep in heavenly peeeeeace!"

"Stop that," Uncle Davy called. But Izzie's banging snapped Nana right out of her sad net.

"Oh, let her play!" Nana came and sat down at the bench with Izzie, playing a jazzy left hand. "She's just getting the swing of it."

"All we need is another boogie queen in the family," Nanpa said. He used his newspaper as a screen when he talked to my mother. "I've got that crazy cantata coming out my ears. Don't know if I can hear it one more time without screaming."

"Communism would have come tumbling down a lot faster if the CIA had sent Mom on a mission to play piano at Checkpoint Charlie," Uncle Davy said.

"Joshua fit de battle of Jericho and de walls come tumblin..." my mom sang. I was glad to see she wasn't crying anymore.

"Now, Davy...Therese...show some respect for your mother," Nanpa said.

"You don't, Dad," Uncle Davy said.

"Oh," Nanpa sighed straightened his newspaper, patting my mom on the bottom as she jumped up. He turned to Uncle Davy. "Still angry about *that,* are you? I'm sure the U.S. Navy has a lot more on its mind than one little report." Nanpa stood up and added, "The navy has lots bigger accidents these days."

"But they wrote *me* up for what happened to Izzie," Uncle Davy said, "not Mother."

"Well," Nanpa said in his reasonable voice. "Izzie is your daughter, not ours."

"Thank God for that," Mom said.

I couldn't understand why Mom was suddenly angry with Nanpa when she'd just sat in his lap. Mom's family always blows up just when you think they've settled down.

"With what's going on in the world right now…" Nanpa shook his head like he was very disappointed in Mom and Uncle Davy. "And all you can talk about is yourselves. Or things that happened ages ago."

"It's still happening," Mom said so low her voice shivered.

"It's starting all over again, Dad," Uncle Davy agreed. "Second generation."

"I'm keeping a scrapbook on all the accidents in the past months," Timo said suddenly. He wasn't bragging, but it got everybody's attention.

"What accidents?" Uncle Davy demanded.

"Your navy, of course," Timo said and held his face very still like at military attention. But I could see Timo's mouth trembling. He hates his dad sometimes just like my mom hates Nana. It seems to me that the way nuclear families are put together with so many people hating each other, and yet stuck circling around the same center over and over—it just makes sense they would explode. That's what they're made to do.

"If you're talking second generation," Nanpa told Uncle Davy, "why not talk about some of the good things for a change? Like the fact that your children here will grow up not even caring there was a Berlin Wall. Maybe they won't even remember what Communism is. Wouldn't that be a wonder?"

"I'll remember!" Timo suddenly shouted. "I'll remember everything…especially that wall. You made us go there, Nanpa."

Nanpa was startled. He looked down at Timo over his world news and gave him a look like he was searching for something he lost. Timo does look a lot like Uncle Davy.

"He means the memorial wall, Dad," Uncle Davy explained. It was like he took pity on Nanpa.

Even I knew what Timo meant. Nanpa had taken us sightseeing to the Smithsonian National Air and Space Museum, climbing up the Washington Monument, and then the Vietnam Veterans' memorial. It's just a black wall in the ground running straight across the mall with millions of names on it of everyone who died in that war. It wasn't a world war and there were no nuclear bombs; but plenty of people blew up anyway. It was kind of like a practice war, I think.

At the wall, lots of people left flowers stuck in the cracks by their own family names or husbands or sons. Timo and I saw a teddy bear, a tiny U.S. flag, a red toy truck, and a pair of mirror sunglasses people had left at the wall like the way we used to leave treats for Santa when we still believed in him. For some reason Timo cried, but he got mad when I asked him why.

"Honey," my mom now got down on her knees, eye-level with Timo, and took him gently by the shoulders. You could tell he hadn't been around a mother in awhile, except Nana, because he flinched. "We're talking about a wall that went up before you were born, a Cold War wall that went up when your father and I were just children like you. We've never known what it's like to live without a Cold War. But you children will...we're going to work very hard to make sure of that."

"Is that why you're leaving Uncle Hawkins?" Timo asked Mom. He wasn't trying to be mean, I knew that. But it wasn't exactly the right thing to say. Even Timo admitted that later, when we were getting ready for Nana's cantata. But that moment when Timo said it, all he could do was look miserable as soon as those words left his mouth.

It was like he'd slapped my mom. But she tried to smile and stood up. "I know you're angry, Timothy," my mom said, looking at him straight in the eye. "I get angry, too. Very angry."

Timo hung his head. Next to his mother, I know he loves my mom best.

"You're all still here lollygagging around?" Nana ran in, her arms piled high with boxes of cupcakes. "Let's get this troop on the road," she ordered Nanpa, who sighed and folded his newspaper.

"Snap to, kiddos. Let's not miss your mom's cantata."

I got dressed quickly in my new winter, pink party dress, so I still had time for some finishing touches to my *Key West Christmas* present. I added Timo and Izzie to the underwater nativity scene. They were little white fur-seals; Uncle Davy was a flying fish, of course. And then I added Greatnana Felicia who was see-through with little purple dots of Timo's special glitter glue. Christian fishes nibbled her in communion.

At the church cantata, called "Night of Miracles," we kids sat with our legs dangling off the pew listening to our Nana play boogie-woogie with those fast hands we couldn't see but loved. We couldn't see Nana at all because the choir director, Mr. Shumaker, put her and the organ behind a wall of potted plants so people wouldn't be distracted by her grinning face and feet flying across the pedals as she swung the choir higher and higher. The whole service was songs, no sermon. It was beautiful, all the singing, like mermaids and mermen.

Timo and I watched Mr. Shumaker very closely because we heard that the man had a steel plate inside his forehead from the war in Vietnam. Watching Mr. Shumaker trying to slow down Nana for Mrs. Zimmer's solo was the best yet. Mrs. Zimmer had to sing so fast she slurred her words so it sounded like this: "Glorriuss night of miracless...wondrousss night-f-miraclllles. They all...combine 'n' shine to make...thsss...night...dviiiiiine!"

The choir sang their cantata in half the time because Nana carried them along on her speeded-up tempo. But when we all got home Nana was not so fast and grinning anymore. She was shaky and snapped at my mom when they were in the kitchen fixing us sausage cookies, cupcakes, and Russian tea—it's a combination of Tang, which the astronauts drink, and black pekoe tea.

Nanpa tried to break things up between my mom and Nana by saying, "So who wants to open a Christmas present early?"

Before Timo and I could jump up to volunteer, Nana said, "I do, Sam! Let me go first."

"No," my mom turned to Nanpa as if he were a judge. "This tradition is for the kids."

"What have *they* done tonight?" Nana demanded and fixed Timo with what we call her evil eye—one eye popped open and angry, the other clamped shut. "I played my heart out, dragging that slowpoke Shumaker through every song. I swear that man came home retarded and no one's telling him."

"It's the steel plate in his skull," Timo suggested.

"Whatever..." Nana waved her hand and spilled some Russian tea. "He's living in 4/4 time. One day Cornelius Shumaker will just drop dead of boredom."

"It's not boredom, Mother," my mom told Nana. "It's shell shock. Just think, Shumaker survived the Viet Cong to come home to *you*."

"No more ancient history," Nanpa held up his hands like a referee. I thought maybe Timo and I should put our allowances together and buy our Nanpa a loud whistle for Christmas. Maybe he'd like something practical instead of my drawing.

Just as I was feeling that I should take back my nativity from under the tree, Nanpa must have read my mind because he disappeared into the living room and returned with an armload of presents. I caught my breath when he handed my carefully wrapped drawing to Nana.

"For you, dear, from Daniella."

Happily, Nana acknowledged Nanpa's offering of the first gift, but as she tore at the pretty wrapping paper—it was a Snoopy's Christmas—her face fell. Nana took one look at my undersea nativity. Then her hands suddenly flew out of control.

"Sacrilege, pure and simple!" she said and tore my nativity into a trillion tiny pieces. "Do you think God sent us a...a slimy old fish for a savior?" Nana demanded.

"But you said fish were first holy, Nana." I looked down at my nativity drawing scattered over the floor like New Year's confetti and felt a blackness inside I'd never felt before. I could never paste my picture back together, not in a million years. Maybe it meant there would be no more Christmas miracles. Maybe Mrs.

Manatee would die and her baby would never be born. Maybe at this very moment a boat propeller was ripping up her back just like Nana tore my painting. Maybe there would not be a Christmas next year for anybody.

Then I realized something they don't teach us in school. The nuclear family is just as dangerous a thing as the nuclear bomb. Even a child can trigger it, like I made my Nana explode. And then the war, the end of the world and my family will be all my fault.

"Fish aren't holy," Nana screamed at me. "We *eat* fish!"

"We eat God's body, too. In communion…"

"Don't smart-talk me, Missy! God hates liars!" Nana grabbed my arm and twisted it. I cried, not because it hurt—but because I didn't feel anything right then. It was like I didn't have a body, just the blackness.

"You hate me, Nana…," I heard my own voice say, but far off and funny sounding because my teeth knocked the words together.

Then everything stopped, or at least I was still, flying up from the floor into my mother's arms. I was so dizzy, it took me a minute to see that Uncle Davy had Nana's arms pinned back like those wrestling holds Timo taught me.

"We're leaving, Mom," Uncle Davy announced, his face real white.

"You can't," Nana cried in shock. "What about the children? They haven't had their cupcakes yet!"

My mom started laughing, but not a real laugh. She told Nana the boycott was now complete—she and Davy had joined it.

I felt the hardness in my mother's arms, like all her muscles clenched in a big fist. She doesn't hit anybody when her body gets like that. She just cries real hard. But now Mom didn't cry at all. She just moved. Faster even than Nana. She bundled us kids upstairs and packed our suitcases. In a flash we left—me, Felicia, Mom, Timo, Izzie, and Uncle Davy.

As we drove toward Washington, D.C., I saw all the Christmas lights twinkling like cold stars. There was some snow still left on the ground so everything looked like those Christmases in storybooks. But I wanted to be back home with my daddy and Mrs. Manatee. I'd rather things be hot in Key West than freezing in Nana and Nanpa's city—I don't care if it is where history happens. Besides, I don't like history; it's not very scientific.

"Where are we going?" Timo asked. He was happy, I realized. Happy to be leaving our grandparents' house, happy his dad was with us and not in the sky. Timo's happiness helped me, especially because he didn't tease me for being a girl and crying.

"To a motel," my mom answered. She was crying, too.

Maybe it was a Christmas miracle, because at the exact same moment Uncle Davy reached out to put his arm around my mother, Timo took my hand. His fingers were sticky; he must have sneaked a cupcake from Nana's cupboard. Timo squeezed my hand and our fingers stuck fast.

As we drove past all the white stone monuments lit up like someone really lived there, instead of just ancient history, I made up my mind: when I grow up to be a scientist, even if Mrs. Moray flunks me, I will discover a way to make what's outside people and what's inside people come together. Like that small Vietnam War memorial wall inside Mr. Shumaker's skull that keeps him slow but still alive; or the slow-motion world outside Nana that might someday come together with the secret ocean that floats Nana's brain like pink coral while all around holy fishes flash, making their own brightness—a light that Nana can see, too. That would be some science project, wouldn't it? That would be some miracle.

7

ROCKET MAN

Davy, 1989

I

I was prepared for anything but this: me, my sister Tia, and all our kids crammed into Motel 6 off the Capital Beltway two weeks before Christmas Eve. Of course, the kids love it. Timo and Daniella are kissing cousins; Izzie and Felicia are little dolls like the ones they fuss over when they play sweet miniature mammies. And I like kicking back and sipping bad motel machine coffee with my sis. The problem is, we aren't just hanging out; we're staging a tactical maneuver—a family boycott.

Now, the navy has used strategies such as boycotts and blockades for good purpose: Remember when the Soviets were steaming their way toward Cuba with missiles reportedly aboard and Kennedy called a navy blockade? I was only six when it happened. My naval history instructor in flight school told us the official story. Seems our intent was to signal the Soviets to back off. Somebody asked the admiral leading the blockade, "What if the Soviets don't understand our signals?" The admiral replied, "We'll just fire a few warning shots." The other guy asked, "And what if they misinterpret and think we're starting World War III?" Well, the admiral had no answer. He'd reached the limits of his military logic. Fortunately, the Soviets recognized the carrier's threat, read the blockade correctly, and turned tail because Khrushchev called them home.

But war games are serious business, signals are hard to read in our family, where everybody seems to speak a different language, and I've reached the end of my military logic. Sydney started the whole thing. Even though she's always meditating, my oldest sister is a firecracker. You put her together with Tia and warning rounds will be fired—sometimes a wild shot, sometimes a broadside hit. But it always strikes home. So now, because of Sydney's boycott against my parents until Mom sees a shrink, Tia and I sit here in this budget motel like we're carrying out orders we don't understand. Who's calling the shots? Who's in command here? Where are Tia and I with our little troop going to march off to tomorrow? And now that I've taken the kids from my parents' house, what am I going to do with them when I report for special duty at Guantánamo Bay, Cuba—the base where I've been angling to get temporary detachment ever since I got my wings? What am I going to do, call my wife and say, "Hello, Mathilde, I know I kidnapped the kids but you can have them back now"? She'll know she's won custody and she'll sue me anyway.

"I've got it!" Tia says just then. She's fresh off the phone with Sydney, and I expect the worst.

"Is this Sydney's idea?" I ask my sister. "Or Mathilde's?" It's hard having two older sisters and an ex-wife. Most jet pilots are the oldest kids in their families. Their command skills come naturally; I've had to work for mine—and what's worse, I've had to do it in a woman's world where nothing really makes sense. It's all leaps and bounds, no logic. But maybe these acrobatics some-times give me an edge in the cockpit; I certainly understand that every one of my instruments has moods and fits of temper. After living with sisters, flying through fog is second nature.

"We'll all do a cross-country," Tia announces.

For a minute I think she means by plane and I get really excited.

"Great!" I say, and all the kids start happily jumping on the motel beds. All except my son Timo, of course. He kind of freezes and goes tight and gives me his "I hate you" look. Then I remem-ber, Tia is afraid of flying, too, just like my son. It's all in their minds, so there's no hope of reasoning with them. "Oh…" I shake my head, trying to stall her. "You mean overland? That'll take *for-ever*, Tia."

"When do you have to be back to Boca Chica?" Tia asks.

"December 18. When do you have to go back to the Keys?"

"Oh, we can miss a little more school," Tia says and glances over at Daniella, who acts as if she's just been given her one Christ-mas wish. Daniella takes my son's hand, and for a moment I think Timo might even fly for her. But then he gives me that look again.

"Cross-country where?" he demands.

"How about Seattle?" Tia says lightly as if she hasn't just dropped a bomb. "We could have an early Christmas with Aunt Sydney. And Davy, your children could see their mother. So we can keep our holiday *and* our boycott."

"You forget," I tell Tia, so hot I don't use my French. "I'm boy-cotting my wife."

"Your children aren't," Tia says, but her voice is so soft it's like she's singing me those old lullabies, rather than opening my gut and just reaching in to grab my heart. I tell you, there is no prepa-ration in a man's life for women. Not even war.

"Yes! Yes! Yes!" All the children screech, and those Motel-6 beds might as well be trampolines. "Cross-country to Aunt ShiShi!"

"The continent drops off there into another ocean," Daniella tells my little Izzie as if she's explaining the facts of life. "But it's too cold to snorkel. Do you know the water temperature in Puget Sound only varies three degrees, from 45 to 48 degrees, between winter and summer?"

"We know," Izzie shoots back. "It's our home."

"You don't live in Puget Sound," Daniella reminds Izzie and laughs. Then she turns to Timo and says as if this, too, is a proven fact, "Not everyone can live underwater."

They all giggle and bounce, making so much commotion I can draw Tia aside. "Who dreamed up this?" I demand. "Don't tell me Sydney and Mathilde didn't have a hand in it."

"Actually, Davy," Tia says and her eyes well up. Now I know I'm in trouble. "It's my idea and I just okayed it with them. The truth is…well, I think I'm leaving Hawkins. I might be in love with another man. And Daniella almost died."

"I don't know why I'd take my orders from the most confused person in this family," I say. But Tia puts her hand on my shoulder and gives me that deep look. It doesn't say "I hate you." It says just the opposite, but it has a much more devastating effect. I've often felt sorry for Hawkins. Here's a guy who has to try and handle Tia every day—and he never had a sister or mother to give him the slightest hint of the chaos that he would have to control.

"Not orders, Davy," Tia says softly and smiles. "A request."

"An official request?" I try to ask her, but instead I return her smile, just like I was programmed. Maybe all those years ago when she held me on her lap as her living doll-baby, Tia programmed me with some secret code so she can subliminally call on me whenever she wants something.

"No, sweetheart," Tia says. "It's personal."

"Maybe I'm the one who should see the shrink," I tell her, and she hugs me fast before I change my mind.

"We'll go by train, of course," she tells the kids, who hoot and holler and make locomotive sounds.

"No," I say. At least I can countermand that order. "We'll go by car. We'll drive your van, Tia. It's big enough for all of us. And we'll take a full week for this road trip." I wink at Timo who, for the first time I can remember since my divorce, returns my wink. I don't know which he's happier about—not flying, taking a trip with Cousin Daniella, or seeing his mother. I don't really think it has anything to do with traveling with me. "Maybe we'll take some detours," I promise them.

"Where?" they squeal.

"Top secret," I say, and they're so thrilled I have to admit the idea might be all right. After all, I can ditch out once we're in Seattle, beg duty calls, and catch a military hop from Whidbey Island back to Key West. I don't really know what else to do. Until the court decides custody, the kids might as well spend some time with Mathilde. Besides, I've got Cuba.

And there's something else. If Mathilde gets wind of that navy doctor's report writing me up for child abuse, I'd lose any chance at custody. I should never have taken Izzie to a navy doctor. But how was I to know her arm was dislocated after just one of Mother's hugs? I'll admit Mother's hugs have often left me with bruised ribs, but it was an accident, that thing with Izzie. And completely unfair that the navy put me on warning, instead of my mother. That's what really started this family boycott. When I told Sydney about that doctor's report, she said, "Well, little brother, the navy has taken over where I left off. Bless them."

That's the kind of moral support a man gets from sisters. Just when you're down, they decide to explore the wound. Any man would just tell you to get up and walk. But the facts are that my taking the kids away from Mom and Dad's house might be what I'll need to have any kind of custody case at all.

Actually, it's a long shot I'll ever get custody, being a navy pilot and gone so much. But I have to try. My dad was never home, and I swore that I'd do better by my own kids. So I thought I'd ask the judge to let me have Izzie and Timo the six months of the year that I'm not at sea. And Mathilde could have them the other half-year. Mathilde won't consider this. Like most women she is nonnegotiable. Everyone says if women ran the world things would be different—no wars, no starving Third World children, no weapons. I know different having been raised by them. If women were in command we'd have just exactly what we have now: screwed-up families and civil wars. The women's weapons would also be the same: divorce and children. And since women have no respect for the chain of command, there would be anarchy. Oh, I know Sydney would say women have rhythms and their own logic just like the earth. She says you can chart a woman just like the tides. But I tell her she's obviously never been at sea in a hurricane or applied her little charts to tidal waves.

"OK, by car," Tia agrees. "But Davy, we don't have to spend the whole week on the road."

Now take Tia. How would you chart her? She's a speed demon, and I'll bet if she'd been born a man, she'd be the fighter jock in our family. For example, even though I'm used to hopping cross-country in five hours, I like to take my time in a car. Really know where I am, the country I keep, you might say. But not Therese. The last time she and Hawkins traveled cross-country to see Sydney, they flew on the ground. They were on their honeymoon, so no children, of course. But do you think they savored the road trip like newlyweds should, stopping to smooch during those blazing Nebraska sunsets or rolling in the hay before it was harvested on a horizontal Kansas farmland? No, those two hooked themselves up to catheters, got extra tanks of gas, and made the trip in eighty-nine hours. They stopped twice.

"For someone who's afraid of flying," I tell Tia as she starts packing for an early departure the next morning, "I'm afraid one day you'll break the sound barrier—and you'll still be on the ground."

"'Slow down,'" she sings as clothes fly into the suitcases.

"'You're moving too fast...' Oops, Davy, I forgot. Before your time."

"One of them hippie songs," I tease her.

"Uncle Davy," Daniella asks, "what are hippies?"

"Hippies are one of those stoned-age tribes. They've vanished now."

"Where did they go?" Daniella asks.

"Oh, they just kind of disappeared in a puff of smoke, honey," I tell her and make my face like I'm telling a sad story.

Daniella turns to the other children as if giving one of her science lectures and says, "They've gone extinct. Thank goodness we still have manatees and elephants."

"Shame on you, Davy." Tia laughs and throws a sweater at me. Then she turns to Daniella. "That's not science, sweetie, that's the world according to Uncle Davy."

Then Timo pipes up. "My Dad's seen a lot of the world," he says, and I'm so shocked I just stare at him. I've gotten used to his hating me; I forgot there was a time when he thought I was anything more than a fighter jerk—that's what he usually calls me, when he thinks I'm out of earshot. I turn to my son and give him the thumbs-up, cockeyed grin that only guys can really exchange. "Thanks for watching my tail, Big Guy." I don't think I've called Timo that in two years. I don't think I've called him that since he quit flying with me.

Sometimes my own son reminds me of someone—it's certainly not me. No, it's my old flying buddy, Faster. We called him that because he graduated top of our squadron in training, but he talked so slow you could be halfway across his home state Tennessee before Faster finished his sentence. He didn't think slowly; Faster just went so deep that by the time the words came out, the subject was closed. I guess Faster knew me better than anybody except, of course, Tia. He told me that a man like me was just doomed to choose a wife like Mathilde—fine-strung, as tense and risky as a high-wire act, which is what I do in the sky. But I'm inside a jet; Mathilde is just up there midair all by herself.

Maybe that's what hooked me on Mathilde—her acrobatics. The first time I ever laid eyes on her she was flying, even though she was on the ground. Before we married, she was a gymnastics and dance teacher. I was stationed at Whidbey Island. Faster and I went into town for a little R & R (which to Tia and Sydney means rock 'n roll, but to me means rest and recreation from military life). Faster and I were practically blind from staring at instrument panels. But I told Mathilde when I asked her out for a date that I was blinded by the dazzling sight of a woman in skintight red-white-and-blue somersaulting through the air.

Faster tried to warn me off Mathilde. "She's like a dead stick over water for a rocket man like you," Faster said. "Blub, blub, baby. And you're drowned like any stillborn bastard."

Faster suspected that Mathilde would soon drag on me; I should have listened. After all, Faster was my Naval Flight Officer—we call them ECMOs, short for electronic countermeasure officers. It was his job to tell me how to navigate. Faster was the best ECMO, bar none. Every pilot in the squadron wanted him. For a pilot, who you have in the cockpit is just as important as who you marry. A pilot can't shack up with too many different ECMOs. That's why I wanted Faster beside me. In the air he was my guardian angel—cool and calm like he belonged in the sky, like Mathilde. But unlike my wife, Faster never fought with me, never raised his voice, just told me where we were, what our options were, and held us steady so we could really go for it. Without Faster, I'd never have gotten my call name: Rocket. They called me Rocket, not because I was the fastest, which I often was, but because I could hang ass and then explode out of nowhere in a dogfight. Never let Rocket and Faster see your tail—that's what they said in our training squadron at flight school on Whidbey Island. Faster and I belonged together; and we belonged to the thin, blue spaces of heaven.

II

"We're off again!" Timo tells everybody as we hit the road for the fourth straight day of our Christmas cross-country. Tia and I are in those plush seats of Hawkins's van; the kids all lie sprawled on the backseats, glued to the VCR. They're watching *Help!* for the second time, even though they were born after the Beatles broke up.

"Tune it down, buddies," I order the kids. But Tia is humming along. This van is really too much. Full bar, VCR, double bed, shag carpet on the ceiling with a few Tootsie Roll Pops stuck in it from other road trips. There's even a small wind surfer in case we are tempted to try these frozen South Dakota irrigation ditches. "Hawkins sure does spend a lot of money on his boy toys," I tell Tia. "I let the navy buy them for me."

"If Hawkins could figure out how to buy a fighter plane," Tia says with a laugh, "he'd have his own."

"The kids tell me he cut off your credit cards," I say low so the munchkins can't hear. Tia leans over and turns up the radio, which drowns out "A Hard Day's Night" from the backseat. "You managing?"

"Savings," she says and sighs. "This road trip is Daniella's college education."

"What an asshole. I'll talk to Hawkins," I promise.

"Tell him you'll swap him child support for an F-14. That'll get his attention," Tia snaps, and I recognize that voice. It's right before tears. But even now she rarely cries. Tia is more likely to scream or slap back.

"Have you really lost him?" I ask as quietly as I can.

"He lost me, little brother. He lost me."

I nod. In the backseat, the children are all screeching loudly, "'Heeelllp!'"

I glance over at Tia, who's taking her turn at the wheel. Her eyes are the fierce blue of a turbulent sky; though tired, those eyes constantly sweep the South Dakota flatlands as if any moment she'll find what she's searching out. "Oh, sis…" I have to laugh. "You and I, we're miles away from what we want, aren't we?"

"You hungry again?" Tia demands. But I know she hears me. "You're always hungry, Davy."

"I don't run on empty," I tell her, "like you. A man needs fuel to fly a jet plane."

"What do marriages run on, Davy boy?" Tia asks me with a quick, rueful grin.

"You're asking *me!*" I laugh. "They don't teach Marriage Maneuvers 101 in Flight School."

"There are schools for everything else in the world," Tia comments drily. "But when it comes to marriage, we fall back on our parents—the very people we *know* have blown it!"

"Oh Tia, Mom and Dad are just people—what works for them isn't right for us."

"I'm not blaming them for the mess you and I have made of our marriages." Tia frowns and glares at a passing Stuckey's as if by sheer force of her will none of the kids will notice it and clamor for more pecan logs to stick in the van's shag rugs. Like magic, the kids remain in their televised trance. Tia sighs, but not with relief. "I just mean, it's so hard to stop the parental programming. It's like we're little pinball machines put together in a certain screwed-up way to simply respond to familiar stimuli. I don't know how to undo or rewire or reroute what's so deep inside me."

"Well," I suggest simply, "if you were a machine we'd just tear you down, see what makes you tick, and then rebuild you from scratch. Like we upgrade planes or make new model cars."

Tia laughs and slaps the steering wheel. "Now I know what you and I are doing in the middle of nowhere, with our poor kids in tow. We're in the tearing-down stage, right?"

"You got it, sis."

"Maybe you and I should have a big race to come up with the best new-model marriage of the year."

"I'll sit that one out," I tell Tia. "I don't have the heart for any more research and development."

I turn to Tia. Here's her opening to tell me about the new guy, the one who might win the compare-and-contrast test Tia's running on her marriage. But she says nothing and I don't push her. That's the difference between men and women. We don't demand to know every little nook and cranny of someone we love. I like to stand back and give women a chance to come out to meet me. Mathilde called this coldness, distance. I call it respect.

"Who knows what we'd be like, little brother," Tia has a faraway look. "If our parents had told us the world would never blow up, that we'd never move again, that Satan or the Communists weren't lurking, ready to steal our very souls..."

"Well...maybe you wouldn't be such a good OR nurse saving lives and maybe I wouldn't be fighting for our country," I point out. Tia shrugs and I get kind of miffed. We've made a pact not to talk politics among the siblings in our family. She was breaking our treaty. "We wouldn't have any survival skills...ever think of that? We'd be like all those other ordinary bozos who think making jam is big news."

"Or making love?" Tia asks softly.

"You're not convinced, Tia," I snap. "Otherwise, you wouldn't be asking *me*. It's not fun without a good dogfight, even in a marriage. Someone has to stand up to you."

"Mathilde's certainly done that!"

"Yeah, but she waited until she had a judge and lawyer between us. Otherwise, she just cries. How can you fight with a goddamn waterfall?"

"You slide down it," Tia laughs, "into the hot springs."

I snort and shake my head. "At least I didn't marry a nuclear reactor."

"Hawkins does up the ante considerably, doesn't he?" Tia nods.

"I mean *you*, sis!" I say. It's a joke, but Tia is so surprised she swerves on the road.

"Lunatic at the wheel!" comes a gleeful munchkin chorus.

"Pipe down!" I tell the kids. "Another prairie dog lives to see the sunset."

"Prairie dogs are underground in winter," Daniella reminds me just like my third-grade teacher—I forget her name. I forget which state or country we were living in then.

Dad's diplomatic career moved us every other year or so, and it's mostly a blur to me. Sydney, Tia, and I used to joke that we'd be better off in the military with all our travels—at least we'd live on a base and speak only one language.

"Nuclear reactor?" Tia frowns. "That's a rotten thing to call your own sister!"

"I just said you're a goddamn power plant, Tia," I defend myself. "That's a compliment."

"Oh, right, try to weasel out of it, Davy," Tia says, and I can see her ire is up. If she were a guy, I'd take her on easy. But she's my sister, and it makes me nervous when she or Sydney gets angry with me. For a moment I feel real panic, as if I've lost my ECMO and don't know where I am or how to navigate my way home. For so much of my life Tia and Sydney were my home. I can live without a wife or even my kids or even my parents. But if my sisters ever boycotted me, I don't think I could stand it.

Faster told me this was my problem—I'd never really made my own family with Mathilde, Timo, and Izzie. But how do you hold onto something that self-destructs after less than a decade, especially when you've had a lifetime with your first women?

"Listen, sis…" I soothe Tia in a way I never would Mathilde. The difference is simple: I trust Tia with my life. "You know we're all spitfires in this family. Not just Mom and Dad. If our parents had been pacifist Quakers who ran a little collective called Friends Fresh Down-Home Preserves, we kids might have ended up even worse. We might have been terrorists!"

"Who says we aren't?" Tia demands. Then she laughs in spite of herself and I know she's with me again. She's also way over the speed limit. But I don't say a word.

Tia and I settle into our truce. The kids snap off the VCR and play house in the van. "Have kitchen, will travel," Tia laughs, and we change driver's tasks so she can rustle up some microwave pizza, orange juice, even a salad—though this midwestern produce is slim pickin's in the dead of winter.

"At least marriage to Hawkins improved your standard of living, sis," I call back as she tosses the limp-looking greens. "If not your faith in the American Way." Tia zings a cherry tomato my way, and it splats against the dashboard with a little red, pulpy burst.

"Bombs away!" Timo shouts and waves his plastic cutlery. He and his cousin engage in some serious fork fencing until the prongs break off.

"You know, kids," I call back, "once someone forgot to strap down a ballpoint pen in the cockpit, and when we hit the boat, that pen flew through the air like a dart and stuck right in the back of my neck."

"Wow!" Timo hangs on my seat. "Neat!"

I show him the scar, and he raises a finger to trace its little crescent moon in my skin, but suddenly he draws back. "I'm not a girl, you know, Timo," I laugh. "I don't have cooties."

In the rearview mirror I see Daniella gearing up to give us a lecture on invisible mites; but she thinks better of it and disappears into the van's tiny head. This van has everything; we never need to stop, except for gas. We can go on forever across these dark flats. The land is so repetitive it begins to seem familiar—about as familiar as any home Tia and I have ever had.

We chow down like contented cows and all the kids kindly conk out. As Tia and I sip our coffee, perked perfectly in the van's little galley, Tia plops her feet up on the dashboard and smiles.

"This is perfect," she says. "We're between everything, like when we used to move, remember Davy boy?"

I nod and start an old revival song, "We'll Leave It All Behind." We miss Sydney for three-part harmony, but our voices blend as well as always. "You know," Tia laughs and slings her arm around my shoulders as I drive, "It's supposed to be heaven we're going to in that hymn."

"A little bit of heaven right here on Interstate 90," I say. It feels funny for a second, to have a woman's arm around me. I'm trying to think, but I can't remember Mathilde ever just draping her arm around me in the movies or when we sat together on the couch. That's a guy's move, I guess. But it feels good, and this is one of the times I feel sorry for the guys who didn't grow up with sisters.

Tia and I sing "Over the Sunset Mountain," as the South Dakota fireball finally flows into so wide a horizon you can see the curve of the earth, just as if we're flying.

"Do you..." Tia takes a deep breath. "Davy, do you ever miss Mathilde?"

"You sure know how to ruin a sunset," I say, startled. "Do you miss Hawkins?"

"I miss Hawkins...," Tia begins slowly, "but like you miss someone you've moved away from. Remember how that was, Davy? We'd leave everyone we loved, swear to keep writing, and about six months later...well, the longing changed to something you could live with."

"So who's the someone else you're really missing now?" I ask her. Still she says nothing about the new guy.

Tia is quiet, then very slowly shakes her head. "Not even him really." She sighs and shrugs, turning to me with those pretty eyes full of tears. "I'm just lonely...I don't know who for."

I take her arm from around my shoulder and hold her hand. It's warm and about the same size and almost as strong as mine. "I know, sis...," I say. We drive like that as the sky turns darker. We're alone on the highway.

After awhile, when I think Tia might be sleeping, I say softly, "You'll get over Hawkins long before he gets over you, Tia."

"Is this an expert's opinion?" she laughs, and her voice in the dark is throaty like she's just waking up.

"Hell, no!" I laugh. "I'm an expert in only one thing..." But before I can say it, Timo pipes up between us in front.

"Aviate, navigate, communicate...," he recites. "That's what you do, Dad." He jumps back before I can give him a little swat.

Ever since we started this trip, Timo is a different boy. It's like we're flying buddies again, but on the ground. "All right, all right, son," I say and tousle his hair, not like a mother, like a man. "You know I'm trained as a pilot, not a parent."

"You ain't been shot down yet," Timo comments from the backseat.

"*Haven't been,* Timo," my sister corrects him. "No he-man, hee-haw, redneck talk allowed in this van."

"Then the two of you can't talk French, either," Timo bargains.

"All right," Tia cinches it. "We'll all speak the same language on this trip."

We settle in for the night drive—this flat prairie's low, black sky and yawning horizon our one dream. No one on the road for miles, except the red, zigzag lights of a trucker or two. You know why they have those ham radios and their own language. This is lonely land for a man. I've never been lonely for anybody in the sky, except sometimes for Faster. When I'm midair I never miss my family—not the way I would if I were a trucker boring straight down a flat interstate. Something about the earth makes a man feel less lost, alone. I look over at Tia and know she doesn't sense this earthbound loneliness as much as a man. She's more at home here; that's why she never gets off the ground.

"Can't you speed?" Tia asks with a yawn.

"I'm already indicating 80!" I laugh. "Hey, sis, remember that family cross-country when we got caught in the Sahara Desert?"

Tia slaps her thigh and tells the kids. "Your Nana was barreling down the road in the middle of the night and suddenly this rubber-tip arrow thwacks against the windshield. We almost drove off the road."

The kids clap as if that would have been wonderful. Someone in the back makes a *bmeeep-bmeep* like the Roadrunner cartoon. It's Timo who asks, "Was it Indians?"

"No, honey," Tia says. "It was a state trooper shooting speeding tickets smack dab down on cars."

"That's what the sign 'Patrolled by Radar' means?" Timo asks. He inches up and perches between Tia and me in the front seat. I allow it, though it's a safety hazard. I also notice he kind of nudges his elbow onto the armrest alongside mine. "Right, Dad?" he demands.

"Yessir," I tell Timo. "Those cops are in planes spotting on poor suckers like us."

"Radar in the air is the same as sonar in the sea," Daniella informs the general populace.

"Let Dad tell it," Timo snaps.

I'm so startled by Timo's mutiny of his favorite cousin, I glance over at Tia. She nods and says, "Tell us, Rocket Man."

"How'd you get that name?" Daniella asks in her sweetest tones, quick to find her way back into Timo's favor.

"My buddy Faster gave me my call sign," I tell them. I don't mean to get stuck doing bedtime-story duty, but all the munchkins settle back as if I'm the chosen. They'll fall asleep, I figure, soon enough. So I say, glancing over at Timo, who's hanging on my word and my arm now, "Faster was a lot like you, buddy."

Timo ducks his head. "Except he's not afraid to fly."

I gave my son a little pretend sock in the arm. "That boy ain't afraid of anything now, Timo."

"Why not?" everyone clamors. I look to Tia and she shrugs. I'm really trapped now. So I try to distract Timo, who sticks to my story like a little heat-seeking Sidewinder missile. I change the subject. "Next time we're in Whidbey, Timo, I'll take you into the cockpit of an F-14 Tomcat."

"Those F-14 jets are crashing all over the place at Whidbey,"

Timo says. "I've got the newspaper clippings in my scrapbook."

"You know, old Faster always wanted a son…" I give Timo a hard look and he backs down. "Don't know why."

"Why is Faster like me?" Timo asks, though I can tell it costs him some pride.

"Why?" I hem and haw. "Well, because Faster was a lot smarter than he looked."

Tia reaches over her thick sweatsock foot and thumps me a good one upside the head. "What your father means," Tia tells Timo, "is that Faster was smart enough to keep Davy from falling out of the sky."

Timo nods, decides to be pleased, and then bugs me for more. "So why *did* Faster want a son?"

I sigh. "Because he only had daughters, that's why, Mr. Nosy. But if I tell you about Faster, you can't put it in your goddamn crash scrapbook." I look him right in the eyes. They're the same gunmetal gray as his mother's. "Deal?"

"Deal."

Tia hands me a thermos cup of coffee. "Well," I begin, none too pleased to find myself telling a story I never told anyone, not even Tia. "First time I met Faster, he was bunking down the hall. Most guys have girlie pictures, military insignia, other macho stuff on their walls, you know. But Faster had his daughters' drawings and baby pictures. It looked like a playschool there beside Faster's bunk." I sip my coffee and Timo squirms, my signal to go on. "One night I come in and hear Faster humming to himself in his bunk. Then I see he's got a Walkman tape recorder, singing lullabies to his girls. It was so they'd recognize him when he got off the boat."

"Like you sang to us, Dad, on those tapes…," Timo says. "So what happened to Faster?" Timo insists on asking. "How come we never met him?"

I look at Tia and she nods encouragement. Both she and Timo are leaning near me, and I feel so crowded I turn down the heat.

"Well, it was a night landing, you see," I tell it to them straight. "The most crazy-ass difficult thing a pilot ever does, even in combat. I mean, think of it: those air force jocks can land on any wide strip of desert with their sweet little parachutes to stop the drag. But for us navy boys, every carrier landing is like a car accident going 35 mph. What if I slammed on the brakes right now?" I tap the power brakes a time or two for emphasis, and everyone jerks forward. "Well, imagine yourself strapped in just so...because if you aren't, bam! You'll break a backbone or skull, just landing." They all make appropriate ooohs and ahhs. "You see, we have to sight on a postage-stamp–sized carrier pitching around in an ocean wild as a bronco bull. We sight on that teeny 700-foot landing strip, shoot the deck at 150 miles per hour and..." Here, I really slam on the brakes. Everyone's buckled but Timo and I stop him with a wide, outflung arm. "Yeah, like that! We stop in two seconds flat." I start driving again. "That is, *if* we manage to hook the wire with our tails.

"So Faster and I, we're doing all this—and on a moonless night. You tell me about fear. You can't see the horizon. The sea and sky are one." I notice Timo is clutching my arm; and I don't mind. "I was sweating buckets when Faster's voice comes over the ICS so smooth and sure, like silk. He's *singing* lullabies to me. Can you believe it? Then he says, 'You got it, Rocket Man, let's take her home.'

"I take her in, but at the last minute the landing signal officer waves me off to take another turn. I do. We come back. The deck looks like a little football field studded in Christmas tree lights. 'Eeeeesy,' says Faster. 'We're in...we're in. Beautiful, baby boy.'

"But the ship pitches wildly and I pull up, just missing the ramp. My heart is doing double time, and inside my mask I suddenly can't breathe, like inside a coffin. Faster stays calm. 'You're OK, Buddy,' he says. 'This time, you'll ace it.' But I don't, 'cause there's this fog out of nowhere and control tells me to fly around until it lifts. It's better to keep flying. Keeps my mind off having to hit the boat again.

"That's when it happens. We're flying with only instruments and Faster says real soft, 'Something's wrong, Buddy...we're losing altitude. Ten thousand feet....' 'No, no, Faster, we're fine,' I tell him. Faster shakes his head. 'Engine warning lights on and I've got secondaries,' Faster says. 'We're dropping....'

"And we are. Fog clears for an instant, and we're goddamn upside down right over the water like some seagull swooping pretty as you please. 'Holy Jesus!' I yell. "Faster, what d'ya got? Where's the boat?' He's real quiet, then says, 'Both engines down. Punch us out, Buddy! Command eject.'

"'No!' I yell, and I'm pulling on that dead stick for all she's worth. I know Faster's right to eject; but I still think I can save us. 'We'll stay with our plane,' I order Faster. Then he says, real quiet, 'Not me, Buddy. This plane ain't no kin to us. Let it go, Rocket.'

"'I can't, Faster!' I tell him. 'We can make it!' Faster says so soft it's like he's singing, 'Won't die with you, Davy boy...I'm outta here. I got people waiting on me.'

"His seat explodes out. I see him shoot sideways like a goddamned star and sizzle. Then my plane suddenly shudders like it's going to blow. But it's only the engines. How in the hell did they start up again? Suddenly the fog clears. I can see my boat straight ahead and the ICS comes back on. 'Stay with us, Rocket,' the carrier tower talks me down.

"I hit the boat. Perfect. When they're lifting me out of the cockpit, they cheer and say I'm a big hero—saved my plane. But after helicopters search the black sea for Faster, I know I didn't save my buddy. I feel that goddamn fog is inside me now and I know that no one will ever sweet-talk me in the air again like Faster."

On a flat highway somewhere midcontinent, I downshift. For a long while no one says a thing.

"They never found Faster?" Timo asks, leaning against me very carefully.

"Never," I say. "Never did. Never will."

I didn't tell them the rest of the story. How I took down all the pictures from Faster's bunk and sent his unfinished tapes to his wife and girls. Except I kept one tape for myself. Sometimes I still listen to it. But never on days that I fly.

"Faster died before I was born?" Timo asks.

"Right before." I give him my best military nod. "But aviators never die, son. They just *auger in.* Anyway, you were born a little before your time, kiddo. When your mother got word of Faster's and my mishap, she went into labor and bam...there you were, Buddy."

"Maybe they never found Faster because he came back to you," Daniella suggests, her voice soft behind me like another little ECMO.

"What?" I demand, yanking my head around to stare at her. If it weren't for science, this kid would be a complete space cadet.

She hesitates. "I mean, as a baby...like Timo. Maybe that's what happens when someone you love dies and then someone else you love is born—all at the same time!"

"Jesus H. Christ!" I explode. I don't like to swear, but it slips out. I turn to Tia because Daniella is cowering in the backseat like I've hit her. "Did you teach her that?" I demand of my sister, who is grinning as if she thinks this is amusing. "Or did Sydney?"

Tia throws up her hands. "Not me, brother. Since I've never been dead, I keep mum on the afterworld."

It's times like this that I long to be midair, jamming enemy radar in my EA-6B Prowler. I long to be soaring above, the gold in the glass dome of my cockpit glinting in the sunlight. It's not just all that gold poured into the very glass of our windshields that makes the Prowler so valuable. Prowlers are the first planes the enemy takes out. That's because we're up there jamming radar to protect all our pretty planes. Protecting everybody else won't bring Faster back, but it does keep him near me.

"Faster was a good ECMO," Timo says. He's talking to me but also to his cousin who has the sense to keep her mouth shut. "And now," Timo concludes with a short nod, "he's never afraid."

I look at my son, and his face is illuminated in the headlights of a passing truck. Timo doesn't look like me or Mathilde. Maybe he does have something about Faster in his face—although I would never say this aloud. "All right, that's enough for one night. Hit the sack, kiddos."

I pretend to lunge at Timo, but he's way ahead of me. He grins and makes a swan dive into the shag rug. Tia beds down the kids, then rejoins me up front. We travel for awhile in silence, then Tia says softly, "I'm sorry about Faster. You never told me how you lost him."

"Oh, sis," I say. "I don't think we lose people so much as we just kind of misplace them. We put them aside for something else. When we look behind us, they're gone."

"You're not talking about Faster," Tia says, her voice as flat and smooth as the highway. "You're talking about your wife." We're both quiet, then she adds, "Want me to take my turn at the wheel?"

"Thought you'd never ask."

Wearily I pull over and we switch sides. We're another half an hour down the road before I fall into a weird half-sleep. It's always the same dream—the way I dream my death:

I'm flying above everybody, watching over my Tomcat buddies, my E-2C Hawkeye electronic whiz-bang kids below, my bomb-babies in their bravo A-6E Intruders. They know how to deliver the ordinance right on target; because this isn't any drill. This is real, what we've all waited for, we ace students of war. I'm protecting them all from high above, jamming the enemy's radar so fast it makes their heads and planes spin, with no hope of recovery. I'm thinking about my Timo and little Izzie still safe behind our front lines—saved from this fight because of us guys up here in the sky. And just when I know that we've won, when I see that last enemy plane sizzle black smoke through the sky, I say, "That's for Faster, motherfucker!"

Then all is still, just me, the vast blue, and my ECMO buddy beside. He tells me in a voice as soft as Faster's that the enemy has launched a heat-seeking missile. I twirl and dip my wings. Yes, she's meant for us. But I'm not worried; I've practiced eluding these babies a million times. They've never scored a hit off me. But this old girl is different.

I hang midair; so does she. She's on my tail. I turn, so does she. Jesus! There's no logic to her. I tell my ECMO, "It's OK, buddy. I was raised by women. I'll get us out of this." I close my eyes. Forget the instruments. I just have to feel where she's aiming. And I do.

Then I know she was always meant for me, but the others got in the way, protected me from her hands. My mother's hands were wild but right on target. They never hit me. Others got in the way and let me spin, twirl into safety as my sisters stood between me and my mother. My arms were too short, you see. And afterward, after the strike, my mother collapsed. Then I'd reach out real slow, real sad, and I'd touch my sisters' shoulders. Sometimes they cried; often they were hurt. But they never told on Mother. They never told on me—that my arms were too short and I was no good in a fight.

Just then the missile hits me, right on target, right where she should have struck long ago. I should have saved everybody then; and now I finally do—I save a country, a whole world, my family.

This is my last thought as my Prowler explodes in a brilliant streaking light. I open, too, an ecstasy that bursts my body into thin air, nothing but spirit rushing up through the sky—80,000 feet, I see a few Blackbirds cruising in Mach 3—but I'm Mach gone! And then it's black space while I whiz through stars, an astronaut without a shuttle, with no need for the slow drag of a body. It always was a tight fit, my body. It always came between me and God, between me and my wife, between me and everybody I loved. How it held me back, my body.

But here there's no gravity, just a soaring and spinning in this orbit around God, who shines so bright that if I had eyes to see

Him I'd be struck blind. But my soul sees. Only now can I look down at the earth. She is blue and round and so beautiful that I can love her at last—after I'm gone.

III

"Shhhhh," somebody whispers, and I wake up so disoriented I don't at first recognize my own sister, her face hidden in the darkness. "Turn that down…Davy's sleeping," she tells the kids.

I stretch my legs and yawn. In the backseat Timo and Izzie are watching another video. I don't know what it is, but it sounds like a horror flick or a UFO movie—lots of screaming and unidentifiable animal noises.

"What time is it, sis?" I feel so heavy, straitjacketed by sleep.

"Zero-three-hundred-hours, Lieutenant."

"You awake?" I ask.

"No," Tia laughs. "I'm on automatic pilot. Go back to sleep, Baby."

"I'll take my turn." I stretch and Tia gratefully pulls over. She's asleep the minute her head hits the seat.

I pour another cup of thermos coffee and settle in. In the rearview mirror I see that Timo and Izzie have at last passed out against the little litter of Izzie and Felicia. Daniella has plopped down on a big pillow she's strategically placed on Timo's head. It's a kid sandwich there in the backseat. I love watching my kids sleep. When they were little and I was lying next to Mathilde, who does gymnastics even in her sleep, my kids cured me of insomnia.

I'd slip out of bed, avoiding Mathilde's flailing, and go into my kids' room. Sitting cross-legged between Timo and Izzie's beds, I'd close my eyes. First their breathing—so untroubled, that old reptilian brain just sucking sweet air in and out for them— then their smells, sour and musty and sweet all at once. Sitting there on the floor listening to my kids breathing in their sleep, that's what I'd remember most the many months I was away at sea.

Tia shifts around in her seat and sticks her long legs up on the dashboard. Behind me the kids are bathed in that eerie, flickering flow from the VCR. I'd like to turn that thing off, but stopping would wake the kids. So I just kind of tune into the soundtrack as if it were a radio. And because it's so low and I can't see it, soon the screams and growls of otherworldly creatures are like music from outer space.

Somewhere in the rolling Badland hills, I recognize that damn movie. It's *Creature from the Black Lagoon*. I haven't seen it since I was Timo's age. And maybe it's the midnight driving, or the ghostly black-and-white Dakota landscape, but I get spooked. An image hits me like double vision: I'm sleeping in the same room with Sydney and Tia. They're sharing a double bed; I'm in the crib. I must be pretty small. I didn't know you could remember back that far. There's a TV going in the room, lowlike, and suddenly the door flies open and a big woman I guess must be my mother, because I know her voice, strides in and jerks the covers off my sisters. "Get up!" the woman says. "We're late for Sunday school!" The blinds roll up with a bang, and this thin, watery light falls into the room. Then Mother turns, "You girls left the TV on all night when I expressly forbade you to watch it." She's mad, too mad. Tia is slower than Sydney in rousing. Her hair is wild and tousled as she pulls on her Sunday dress.

"Come over here, Tia, and let me brush that hair." Tia stands in front of Mother, who starts singing a fast revival song in rhythm to her strokes. She's laughing and brushing real fast, and the girls start singing, too. But there's something wrong. There's a smell in the room that I recognize. It must be fear because it makes me start howling.

"See to the baby," Mother orders Sydney, who comes and pats my back. Sydney keeps singing, but real soft. A lullaby, not a march like Mother sings.

"Hurry up, hurry up, Sydney!" Mother says loudly and stops singing. "And will you please stay still?" She grabs Tia by her small shoulders and scissors her between her knees. Then Mother starts brushing Tia's hair so fast and furious it's like rubbing down a racehorse.

"Ouch!" Tia starts wiggling around and trying to grab Mother's hand. And because Tia is quick, too, she succeeds in disarming Mother. With a howl, Tia throws the brush across the room. "You're supposed to hold the tangles when you pull!" she screams at Mother. "That's what a real mommy does!"

Like lightning Mother lunges for my piggy bank on the vanity table. Before Sydney can interfere, Mother is on Tia and hitting her again and again. Hard clay strikes bone with a soft knocking sound like my popgun makes. Tia slumps to the floor like she has no more bones left in her body.

"She'll be OK," Mother says and tosses the cracked piggy bank to Sydney. Mother steps over Tia's body and looks down impatiently. "She'll be fine."

"You'd better hurry, Mother," Sydney says as she kneels by Tia's body, touching her wrist, her head. She's done this before; she knows what she's listening for. But I've never seen it; I've just heard the sound of screams. Until this morning. "Hurry," Sydney wards off Mother, "or you'll miss choir practice."

And just like that Mother turns on a dime and flies out the door. Only when Sydney hears the sound of the car door slamming does she start to shake. And she cries a little as she gets a cold washcloth and puts it on Tia's face. I'm standing up in my crib, looking down, real quiet.

"It's OK," Sydney says to me and to Tia, who starts to wake up. "Shhhhhh…" Then Sydney starts singing one of those lullabies and rocking Tia. In the background there's still the television, and now I can see the picture. It's a man covered in black slime trying to pull himself up out of a lagoon. I get the hiccoughs and Sydney gives me a bottle.

Years later Tia still had that soft spot in the back of her skull. I remember paying her five cents of my allowance to stick my finger into that secret spot—hematoma, doctors called it, but only after we were all grown-up and Tia was a nurse. For all the years as kids we just called it the black hole. And Tia's skull made her a lot of money—so much so that we always owed her most of our allowances. I beat up Billy Perkins in fifth grade when he called my sister a miser and said he'd never pay another nickel for her freak show.

Two years ago, when Tia finally had neurosurgery on her skull, they found there was indeed a hole in her head through which some of her brain was pouching out—sinus paracranii, the surgeons called it. From early trauma. Mother says she remembers that the garage door fell on Tia's head when she was in third grade. I never knew what hit her. Not until tonight.

But you can't always trust memories. Especially at night on a winter road through the Badlands. Once, driving in the desert going back to Fallon Naval Air Station—Strike University we call it—I actually followed a green truck for two hours. When my buddy said, "You're going too slow, Rocket, boy," I said, "I don't want to pass that old green truck. It's easier to follow someone when you don't know the desert." Well, my buddy says, "Pull over, son. There ain't no green truck anywheres. You been following a green phantom."

I almost wake up Tia to take her turn at the wheel, but she's so sacked out, it's not fair. And we're miles from the next town. I turn on the radio to drown out the soundtrack of that stupid *Creature from the Black Lagoon*. Then I start humming along, singing a tenor harmony to a country-western tune. I drive with my family behind me. This is what a father does, I tell myself. This is what Faster would do—as I sing to all my children while they sleep.

IV

"We're sick of Christmas carols!" the kids complain. We're in the Cascades, only an hour out of Seattle. But it's snowing like a son of a bitch.

"I can't believe we made it all the way across the winter-whopping wonderlands of Wyoming, Montana, and Idaho to get snowed in here!" Tia shakes her head and leans forward to peer through the whitewash that is our windshield.

I know this old Snoqualmie Pass. Me and my buddies used to go skiing here when I was stationed at Whidbey Island. That's before Mathilde and I moved into Seattle—and all our trouble started. On the base, all the other navy wives kept Mathilde in line; but in the city, Mathilde got the notion that the navy was a four-letter word for Never Again Volunteer Yourself.

We're all bone-weary; even the kids aren't bouncing around anymore. Seven days on the road will do that to you. You run out of songs to sing, license plates to spot, stories to tell. During that final day, you notice everyone's got glazed eyes, even the kids, who don't drive.

I have to smile thinking that when we drive up to Sydney's house, all six of us looking like we've had close encounters of the cross-country kind, I can tell my big sister we're not dazed, we've just been meditating.

"We could stop the night here as long as nobody's moving," I suggest. Ahead of us on the blizzard-whipped winding road is a line of cars, all with their heaters running full blast. We're waiting to see if the troopers will close the pass before or after us for their confounded avalanche patrol. The truth is I'm glad for the snow. Nearing Seattle, it's really hitting me that I'm closer and closer to my ex-wife. It's kind of like pilot's vertigo this dizzy, sinking feeling in my head and chest. I'd rather be hitting the deck at night than sitting like a damn snow goose in this blizzard, just waiting to return to my so-called mate. Unlike geese, humans don't have to mate for life, I remind myself. "What d'ya say, kiddos. Wanna stop here at a nice little ski lodge and play?"

"Noooo!" They all shout me down like we're in a game show and I'm the big loser.

"How're ya doing, sis?" I ask. She's looking pretty ragged. Didn't even bother to put makeup on this morning. I'm probably the only man in the world who has ever seen my sister without makeup. But I like this backstage privilege. Tia without her make-up looks really young, more like a girl than a mother of two. And she's kept her graceful figure. Like Mathilde. But unlike Tia, I've never seen Mathilde without her makeup. She never let me behind her mask. I could be as deep inside her body as any man could go and I'd look at Mathilde's face: Her eyes were closed to me as if I were an intruder. I never wanted to invade her. I just wanted her to let me in. Like she would a brother; like she did our children. Hell, Mathilde even let my sisters really see more of her than she allowed me. And that's virginity for you. A man is only a virgin until he has his first woman, whatever age. A woman can be a virgin all her life, even though her body's practically been a motel.

Sometimes toward the end of our marriage, Mathilde would look at me when we were making love as if our bed were a war zone and her body were occupied territory. She'd smile at the enemy and do his bidding; but behind his back, she spit on him. And those nights when I'd enter her gently to signal her I was no enemy, I'd find myself ashamed to be so aroused by those lean thighs and high buttocks as she let me thrust deeper, even raised her feet to push against my own ass. And the light, urgent pressure of those feet, pretty pink toenails and all, pressing against my buttocks as I exploded into her so high I heard myself crying out, is what I remember most about my wife.

Even now. Even after I've had a continent and several other

women between us. But there's never really been anything between Mathilde and me, except ourselves. I realize this now, too late to turn back.

"I'm hanging in there, honeychile," Tia's answer startles me. "Still a bit of that stupid headache. How you doing?"

She turns and gives me a real deep look like she sees through the sunglasses, the dark circles under my eyes, straight to the darkness in the center of my chest. Creature from the Black Lagoon, I want to tell her. But instead I say, "Oh, I'm right where I want to be: grounded, in the middle of a blizzard, sixty miles from a she-devil."

Tia laughs. "And who's your ECMO?"

"A worser she-devil!" I say.

Behind us the peanut gallery laughs and claps. They've run out of videos, so they're watching us in the front seat like some situation comedy. "Mind your own business," I tell them. "Play a game or something."

And surprisingly, they do. A low humming comes from the backseat, and I know the kids are playing "Elephant Talk" again. I take advantage of this noise to turn up the heater and ask Tia, "Say, conchhead, do you remember charging us our allowance, plus interest, to stick our fingers into your goddamn skull?"

"Sure, little brother," she says. "Some of those savings we're probably burning up in gas bills even as we speak."

"Yeah, I'll bet you've still got half of every dime you ever made."

"Ah, but do I have half of every dime Hawkins ever made? That's the real question!" Tia says and sighs. "He's never saved a penny in his life."

"So...what happened?" I ask. "I mean, really?"

"It just flew out of Hawk's hands," Tia says.

"No, not the money. I mean...what really happened to your head?"

Tia turns to me, and even though she's staring me straight in the eye, she doesn't see me. For a minute it's like she disappears inside herself, not as if I were the enemy, the way Mathilde shuts down, but like she's trying to remember something she lost a long time ago. At last Tia shrugs. "Don't know, do you? Mom says it was the garage door fell on me. Dad says it was a sledding accident. Sydney says it was Mother. I don't know…"

"But didn't they take you to the hospital and file some report?" I ask.

She is quiet a moment, then speaks so low the kids can't hear. I hardly can. "Too bad we didn't have the U.S. Navy to protect us back then."

"Hmmmmmm," that's all I can say. And it sounds a lot like the humming going on in the backseat.

Then before I know it, Tia is leaning over the gearshift and stretching, a stretch that includes an arm around my neck. She embraces me quickly, like it was just a casual hug. But her eyes are wide open to me—blue and clear as the sky. "I'm so proud of you, little brother," she says.

"Why?"

"Because you're brave," Tia says and smiles, though I can see she's sad. "Because you're here…with me…with your children."

"Right." I laugh. "It takes a real man to stick around with this ground crew."

"Right, Rocket Man," she says and gives me a kiss on the cheek.

Maybe the cops somehow get her signal, because just then they wave us on through the pass. Timo looks behind and sees they closed Snoqualmie just five cars behind us.

And no sooner do we get through the blizzard and barrel down I-90 straight for Seattle, no sooner do we pull up at long last to Sydney's door than I see what I should have suspected all along: we've walked right into a trap. If I were in my plane, I'd pull up on my stick and climb so fast it'd make your head spin. But what can you do with a van full of screaming kids and a five-speed stick shift? You park the car and unload the kids, who run happily up into Sydney's arms. You give both of your older sisters a look that could kill, and then you suck in the air through gritted teeth and try to smile.

"Hello, Mathilde," I say. She's standing right behind Sydney as if for cover. "Fancy meeting you here."

"Welcome home, Davy," my ex says. She tries to smile, but it fades into tears.

"Thanks," I tell her. It's hard for me to see Timo and Izzie hugging their mother so hard. But what knocks the wind from me is seeing Hawkins step out from behind Mathilde. He's a mess. Looks like he hasn't slept for days, and it's obvious he's been crying. He doesn't even try to hide it.

Everyone freezes, and then Hawkins says, "Happy holidays."

All his kids and all my kids crawl over him, shouting. Tia hangs back, right beside me. I know what she's thinking. *Get back in the car and drive. Anywhere.*

"I'm right with you, buddy," I whisper to her. "Let's fly outta here!"

But I said the wrong word. "I don't *do* flying, baby," she says. Just like a guy, she squares her shoulders and walks toward her husband like she's still at attention.

Me—I walk, too. The other way. No van, no plane, no partner. I just start walking down the street. They'll be a phone booth somewhere. I've always made it a practice to travel light. I can work on a beard until Tia brings my suitcase back to Key West.

"Davy!" Sydney calls after me. "At least come in and get warm." She starts walking with me, even though she's without a jacket.

"Et tu, brute," I tell her. But it's hard to be really angry with my older sister. Mathilde's always tried to stick her in the middle. Syd usually slides out, but not before some damage is done.

"Come back in a couple hours," she says. "After…well, after they've all gone."

"Listen," I tell her, "I just left one hell of a D.C. family reunion to walk right into another night of the living dead. And I'm outta here!"

"But..." We both almost collided with a scraggly gaggle of carolers.

"But nothing, big sis. I've just had it! Tell Timo and Izzie I'll come back for them...soon," I say. When Sydney hesitates, I ask, "Please, sis?"

She sighs. "We'll miss you, little brother."

She's shivering and I put my arm around her. My flight jacket keeps us both warm. We've almost reached the phone booth.

"Let me drive you to a motel," Sydney offers, but I know she's stalling for time so she can talk me into staying.

"No, thanks, sis. I'll just call a navy buddy and be gone."

"Whidbey Base, then a little hop back East?" she asks.

"*Sí, señora.*" I laugh. "But don't forget Cuba."

"How could I ever forget Cuba?" Sydney says and embraces me. She starts walking back home, then turns and looks at me fiercely for a moment, as if she's not going to let me go. Then she says, "Call us when you get..."

"Home?" I ask. "Where's that?" I shrug and grin, but I know I don't look right with this cockeyed grin when I feel like I've been gutted.

We stand gazing at one another. "Fly safe, Rocket Man," Sydney won't fake a smile. She stares at me steadily, her eyes holding mine.

"Of course," I say. Then for some reason I add, "Hey, Syd?"

In the streetlight her face is so familiar—it's my face, too, only pretty. But we have the same eyes—blue-gray and deep like fog. "You believe in reincarnation, don't you?"

"Yes..." she says slowly. "But you don't."

"Well," I tell her and laugh. "Well, if I could come back, how do you think I'd come?"

"A bird, baby brother?" she says. "A beautiful bird?"

"No," I tell her. "I'd come back just the same. I'd do it all over and I'd do it right. But just before I shot through that old birth canal, I bet I'd say to myself, 'Oh, no! Not *this* family again!'"

Sydney starts laughing, too. "Just keep coming back to us, baby brother," she calls. "You got people waiting on you."

8

DO NO HARM

Hawkins, 1989

I

If I weren't a surgeon, I'd be a murderer. I've never killed anyone on purpose. Everyone who has died under my scalpel did so as I struggled to save them. But I know what I'm capable of; I know that if things really went wrong inside me, I could kill.

Most people don't know this about themselves. They're too busy defending against a first strike. But think about it. Even a murderer twirling his thumbs on death row will tell you it was self-defense and he's a victim—his mama didn't love him, his wife left him for another man, his boss axed him. When do you ever hear a guy say, "I woke up this morning and felt so bad I wanted to kill. So I did."

You see, I know the harm I can do. I took a Hippocratic oath and rerouted my natural instincts. The first law of medicine is: Do no harm. For a heart surgeon this is only half-true. We don't work by osmosis, but by breaking and entering the body. Yet we wound with the whole in mind. I make my violence a choice, not an impulse I repent of afterward when the damage is done. Here's how I've worked it out: If I'm going to wound, it must be to save another's life, not my own. Even so, I keep the murderer in me nearby, so he doesn't take me unawares. We even have polite sit-down chats like at a summit meeting.

For example, just before Christmas, when Tia took the girls and disappeared from her folks' house without a word, my mur-derer—I call him Joe Blow, because a blow is his solution to everything—well, Joe says, "Hire that sleaze-bag Cuban cousin of yours to track down Tia and take your kids. Then shanghai them to Grandmother Felicia's abandoned nunnery near Camagüey. Let Aunt Marelis hide your daughters better than any nuns bricked up babies. Your wife will be barren then—that's as good as dead for her. Your girls will love only you. They'll forget their mother—and so will you."

That's the kind of advice Joe gives—go-for-the-jugular-and-never-look-back. Or forward. After considering his plan, I say, "If I steal the children, Tia will hate me forever."

"So what's new?" he counters. He thinks he has me.

"Well, she hates me now, but that woman changes her mind a lot."

"Awwwwwh." Joe Blow shakes his close-cropped head. I imagine he looks like a veteran drill instructor. Sometimes I even think I can faintly hear the rattle of his dog tags when he throws up his well-muscled arms and wishes he could nuke me without killing himself, too. "Ahh, you're such a sap. If you really want her back, you're a jerk."

I admit I am; I do.

"Well, for *that,* chump, you'll have to call in the damned diplomatic corps." Joe Blow shrugs contemptuously. "That's a job for...civilians."

He can never say the word without spitting. Then he marches off to his quarters to brood and play war games. I don't barrack my murderer in the back of my mind; I keep him front and center. I always want to know exactly where he is and what he's plotting, because if he ever goes AWOL on me or undercover, that's when I'd really be dangerous.

My wife Tia, like most people, especially women, doesn't ever dream she might be harboring a dangerous criminal, much less a murderer inside herself. That's why she married me. I'm the asshole she'll never allow herself to be. But if you're living with an angel, there's nowhere to go but down—that's what Satan must have thought. Someone had to balance out all that heavenly bliss. The real truth is, God gives *and* takes away. It's the taking-away job Tia assigned to me, the dirty work. A man's job. And then she turns the tables: she takes off and takes away my children.

Funny thing is, I kind of liked her for it, for being so low-down mean as to desert me with Christmas just around the corner. Don't think I didn't get sympathy. Operating-room nurses who usually act like I'm Attila the Hun brought me Christmas cookies and invited me to supper. Nubile candy stripers came caroling to my apartment. As a finale of Christmas compassion, the anesthesiologist who once said that operating with me was like playing high priest to Khomeini—this guy asks me to go fishing with him. I brought my spears.

I was so surrounded by sympathizers that when I called Sydney to find out where my wife had absconded, I expected solicitude even from Tia's big sister. "Well, Syd, I guess ya know my wife and girls have run off and left me."

"What am I supposed to do about it?" Sydney asked matter-of-factly.

I snapped at her no-nonsense tone. "You don't have to do a thing, Syd," I said, reorienting myself. "Just tell me where Tia and the girls are, and I'll leave you alone."

"No," she said. I thought she would hang up on me, but then I remembered: her southern family is excruciatingly polite. They simply say the most terrible things in their angelic voices.

"Then I'll fly to Seattle and camp on your goddamn doorstep until Tia gets there. Where else would she and Davy go but to you?"

There was a silence as if Sydney were tuning in to her own summit meeting. And I'm sure at that moment her murderer had the floor. Oh, she has one, all right. It's one reason Sydney and I have always had a standoff affection for one another.

"Maybe they've hit up the Hilton for the Homeless," Sydney suggested. "I hear that hotel takes canceled credit cards."

Sydney was fighting mean. Joe Blow exulted in his element. He had all sorts of ideas for Tia's sister. *Threaten her,* he suggested gleefully. *Tell her that when you operated on her five years ago, you left in a sponge.* Bad idea, I told Joe. My minor surgery on Sydney's ulcer was a complete success. Besides, surgeons never leave sponges in their patients. Scrub nurses do.

"That was wrong," I heard the diplomat in me tell Sydney. "I was wrong to cancel Tia's credit."

"And unfair to the children," Sydney added.

"All right, all right," I said. "Don't make me bleed, Syd."

She was quiet a moment. "Tia didn't tell you where she was headed?"

"No," I said and suddenly felt a moment of panic. What if Tia wasn't with her brother, but another man? Maybe they were all in some cozy Christmas cottage singing and making plans for next Christmas? In my mind I saw my daughter Daniella swimming with the old manatee in my backyard canal. Next Christmas I'd have a newborn manatee, but I wouldn't have my family. I'd be alone again as I was now, a bachelor, an ex. My heart rate went up, as it always does when I allow myself such thoughts. I hate the future. I've always hated the future when bodies grow old, falter, and finally fail; when families fall apart and there are only photographs on dusty bureaus of beloveds whose eyes follow you, without seeing you at all.

I grew up like that, in a big house full of photographs instead of people. My mother's eyes, my father grinning in his marine uniform. He was a surgeon, too; but a lot of good that did him when we dropped the bomb on his POW camp.

As a kid I used to imagine that Cuba was a lost continent that sank into the sea after we left. I'd rather believe that than remember I had a big family living on without me—while I stayed in a dilapidated big house with a crazy grandfather and a grandmother who gave me her healing hands but never would tell me why my mother left. Still can't fathom it.

"I'm sorry Tia didn't let you know," Sydney said softly.

"Do you know why she...why Tia left?" I had to ask. Women tell their sisters such things, not their husbands.

"I think it has more to do with our parents than you, Hawkins. Although of course, you're part of it. We're boycotting our parents, you know."

"Again?" My heart steadied and I could even laugh. Sydney laughed, in spite of herself. "You know those boycotts never work."

"Well," Sydney said, and I heard the slyness in her voice that I've always admired in her, "it's either that or nuke 'em."

"And that's so messy, isn't it, sis?" I called Sydney sis when she'd let me or when we didn't mean anything we said.

She let me get away with it, but then she asked. "So what dastardly plan do you have in mind when you greet Tia on my doorstep?"

"I want to tell her to come home."

"Where's home, Hawkins?" Sydney asked.

"With me."

"No," Sydney said slowly. There was some sadness in her voice. "Not anymore..."

"Maybe Tia is just boycotting me the way you do your folks?"

Sydney hesitated. "Maybe...," she said. But you could tell she doubted it. And she doubted me.

"Sydney...," I began and then kind of gasped as I heard myself say it. "I have never been so alone."

There was dead silence. Joe Blow was holding his breath on this one. Even the entire diplomatic corps advised against such total surrender.

"I know," Sydney answered.

And then I remembered—Sydney was alone, too. Years ago her husband upped and killed himself. Sydney knew all about solitude and surviving the loss of someone you love who just checks out like life is some unacceptable motel. No thank you, room's not right. Think I'll pass.

"Well, Syd...," I suggested, "maybe you and I could have an orphans' Christmas in Seattle. If Tia shows, we won't say she's not invited."

"If you stay in my house...," Sydney started to say, again in her no-nonsense voice. "If Tia lets you stay...it'll cost you."

"How much?" I asked. Joe Blow hit the ceiling at this.

"One year's child support for every night you sleep on my couch," Sydney said.

"Holy moly, Mother of God! You think you got the Taj Mahal there?"

"No," Sydney said, and this time there was an edge to her laugh. "I've got your family."

"That's called blackmail, Sydney."

"No, honeychile," she said, and her voice was just as sweet, southern, and deadly as can be. "That's called paying the rent."

"Do you need my credit card number to hold my room?" I demanded. I heard Joe Blow lobbying, screaming his bloody head off. But I assured him it was the only way I could get where I wanted to go.

"No," Sydney said with that extreme politeness women use

when they're about to disembowel you—it's kind of like those Oriental guys who bow to one another before a dropkick to the kidneys. "I've got your number, Hawkins."

Well, at that I just had to laugh. Sydney laughed then, too. "You taught Tia everything you know, didn't you, big sis?" I asked. "Too bad you didn't teach her she's no angel."

"Tia attacks your basement boiler, slashes the waterbed, and you call her an angel?" Sydney laughed as if I'd given her no end of amusement.

"Before that, I mean. All these years she played Mrs. Sweetness and Light to my Mr. Godzilla."

"Well, now that Tia is misbehaving, I guess there's nothing left for you but to play the gentleman caller."

"I'll be a model tenant," I promised, even though Joe Blow had other ideas.

"Right," Sydney said. "And I'll be an imperfect hostess."

II

She was. Sydney was never there, those first days in Seattle. Every morning she'd disappear to her houseboat office on Lake Union where she sees mentals all day and gets paid to listen. I'd never be a psychologist. What little shrink-stuff they forced on us in med school, I endured. Who can really work with the mind? Even neurosurgeons with God's quick hands can't fix someone's thoughts. Who can cut Joe Blow out of me? Someday scientists will discover that it's all a matter of neurotransmitters and chemicals. No more listening to patients drone on with no cure. There will be sophisticated pharmaceutical treatment. Just like one day all of us hotshot surgeons will be replaced by bioengineering machines that bypass my bypass surgery. Instead of scalpels, they'll have 3-D motion pictures of organs at work, and rays or lasers that enter the body without breaking the skin. Until then, they'll need my hands, because no machine has ever duplicated the complexity of the human hand. Hell, it takes half our brain just to operate our hands. Maybe that's why we have so little else on our mind besides grasping, seizing, holding, and making.

Those first couple days at Sydney's, Tia wouldn't let me touch her at all. Then I knew we were really separated. If she wouldn't let my hands near her body, she wouldn't have much use for the rest of me. Except, of course, my money. But Daniella practically lived in my lap, and Felicia curled next to my sleeping bag on the couch like a kitten.

"Puget Sound is too cold for manatees," Daniella was reading one of her aunt's books and making notes in her schoolgirl hand. Of all the things I've ever done, making my daughters was the best. Tia's and my genes got together and said, "OK, for once let's pass on the best and brightest of both these parents."

I want to tell my daughters this: that whether your mother and I make it, we made you. And that is miracle enough for one life. But I can see it's really not. I can see my little girls' sadness, and there's nothing I can do to save them, especially since I had a hand in it. This is something I don't discuss with Joe Blow. He blames. That's his job, just like it's my job to cut open a chest. Without Joe Blow I could never be up to my armpits in blood and gore all day. But there's more to me. Like my Grandmother Felicia said, *the same hand that harms can heal.* And that's why I still keep my bloody hand in this marriage. Even if the prognosis looks grim.

"It's like I told that old gal when her husband bought it on my table," I said to Sydney who was making early morning coffee for us all in her small kitchen. "There's good news and bad news. Bad news, he's dead. Good news, he won't be paying taxes."

"Are you talking about your marriage?" Sydney asked casually. It was always hard to get a rise from her. After all, she listened to Joe Blows all day. "It's dead. But you'll have more money?"

"There's no community property in the state of Florida," Tia remarked. I hadn't noticed her coming into the kitchen. Her hair was matted and she wore a blue silk nightgown I bought her years ago.

"I sure do like lying here on my celibate's couch while you two sleep like virgins in Sydney's little bed."

"At least that futon doesn't slosh and make me seasick," Tia yawned, reaching for her coffee cup as if she'd always lived there.

"You two sisters have slept together as long as Tia and I have," I found myself saying. I didn't know quite who was talking. It wasn't Joe Blow's style, and I couldn't see how the diplomatic corps could use this for any type of negotiation. Surprisingly, it made them both laugh, and for just a minute I felt what it must have been like to be their brother. It wasn't that bad a feeling. And it meant I would always be part of their family.

"Who do you think Tia fought with first?" Sydney said. "We used to pretend there was barbed wire down the middle of our bed. Sure enough, if I crossed that imaginary line, I'd wake up the next morning with bloody scratches up my legs." She nudged Tia. "Then one night I caught Tia cutting her toenails in little zigzag patterns—human barbed wire."

"Yes," Tia shot back, but she was smiling. "And who picked me up like a sack of potatoes and threw me against the radiator because I wouldn't get you a Coca-Cola?"

"Violence runs in our family." Sydney shrugged. "Who knows what we kids might have done to one another without a common enemy to unite us?"

"Sibling rivalry always took second place to our war against the Evil Empire." Tia nodded.

"She means Nana and Nanpa," Daniella piped up as if I needed a translator.

"Are your mother and I the Evil Empire to you kids?" I asked.

There was a moment's hesitation as Daniella glanced around for Timo. He was with his mother, of course, after Davy turned tail and left for Cuba. Daniella missed her cousin. But I didn't think Timo was such a good influence on Daniella; he obviously hated his father. And Davy's recent desertion seemed to have sealed his fate in his son's estimation.

"Darth Vader and Princess Leia are cartoons of real people," Daniella pronounced as if she were a tiny professor. She turned up her nose and went back to her book on marine mammals. "They're OK for outer space, but they'd never make it under the sea."

Would we? I wanted to ask my daughter. But I guess I didn't want to hear her answer. Instead I turned to Sydney. "How about I take us all out for dinner tonight?"

"Not me, thanks," Sydney said. Already she was reaching for her raincoat. "I've got a gathering to go to."

"Christmas party?" Tia asked and poured herself a second cup of coffee.

"No, Gregory and I are leading a winter solstice celebration," Sydney said.

"What's a solstice, Aunt ShiShi?" Daniella put down her book.

"Spare me the details, Syd," I said and made for the john. "I'll just go to the library and read my *Whole Earth Catalog.*"

This was the part of Sydney I stay away from—all that mystical juju left over from the sixties. I'm older than Sydney, but I didn't spend my college days on railroad tracks or grooving with the earth. I should have been in Vietnam, but medical school meant deferment. Still, I did my part. The moment I finished school, I spent my military service as a doctor in Panama. In fact, I don't look back on those war years the same way most men of my generation do. No ambivalence. I was a doctor in the bush and glad of it. If I had it to do all over again, I would. For me, it was like going back to Cuba without Castro. And the people—the Cuna Indians took me in like I was their *mestizo* son. Only problem was, the minute I went into military service my grandfather, the Captain, cut off my inheritance. I was the poorest doctor I knew—and I was happy. I had my native language and people who could pass for my family. I had my skills, and I was saving lives when other guys my age were doped up in Asian jungles

killing and confused and coming home to sneers. I was lucky—
wherever I went in that country, I was wanted. And that's the best
definition I know of a hero.

When I came back to the kitchen they were still yakking
about the solstice. If I hadn't wanted another cup of coffee, I
wouldn't have braved the cross fire.

"Tomorrow is the darkest day of the year," Sydney was telling
Daniella. "Still today in some tribes they believe that by prayers
and rituals we literally turn the sun back from its dark journey
away from the earth. We can call back the light and spring."

"The sun comes back OK without us," I assured Daniella, and
I noted that the little scientist in her was satisfied.

"I know, Daddy," Daniella said, but she was still riveted on
Sydney. I could just see what growing up without me around
would do to my daughter. She might even forget her science and
study some nonsense like ecological astrology. She might not end
up a marine biologist at all. One day I might find her practicing
medicine by plopping huge slabs of crystal on a patient's body
and ommmmmming to that poor guy's organs. Problem with my
wife's family is they've got religion like so much voodoo in their
genes. Why couldn't they just be good Catholics? You don't see
simple Catholics worshiping snakes or high on Armageddon.
Most of the Catholic mystical shenanigans are in their past, all
their saints and such. Nowadays it's just business as usual and a
nice little hierarchy that keeps order—nuns take vows of silence,
and most priests are stunned into submission by their celibacy.
Martyrs are the only troublemakers, and they usually die before
they can do too much damage.

I knew that with all that voodoo blood in my daughter, I'd
have to satisfy it with some sort of religion, so I chose Catholicism
as the safest bet. It wouldn't interfere with science. But when I
saw Daniella's rapt face as she listened to her aunt's ancient-
history lesson, I realized that her Cuban blood just might some-

day conspire with her southern backwoods god-struck gene pool, and I could have a fanatic on my hands.

"Stop with the wu-wu, will ya?" I had to say. Everyone looked at me, and I realized for the first time just what it felt like to be surrounded by females. Not a pleasant feeling. Kind of like the mixture of pity and terror those conquistadors must have felt when they first encountered a tribe of Toltecs or Mayans.

Joe Blow ordered me to stay and fight, but I'm not at my best in the kitchen, so I walked out to the front porch for the newspaper. Somebody had to remind this little nunnery of reality.

Truth was, I was glad for the air, even though it was raining. It was hard on a guy to willfully be part of a pecking order not his own. If this had been an OR with its perfect hierarchy for which I'd paid plenty of dues to reach the top, I would have known exactly what to do. Women were nurses; they took orders. And most men, too. Everything from the smallest stitch to the most rebellious resident knows its proper place. There are rules of conduct. I don't make them; I've just mastered them.

Face it. How many women surgeons—not counting ob-gyn—do you ever see in one hospital? That's why my time in the trenches surrounded by women has been limited. If my plan to bring Tia back with me—even if we had to drive—didn't succeed soon, I'd have to go back to work at the hospital.

I flapped open the newspaper like an accordion and sat down on the front porch to read, even though I was still wearing my scrubs as pajamas.

But I didn't stay put long. "It's about time!" I had to crow a little, even though I knew it would irritate my hostess. "We finally did it!"

"Did what?" Tia asked lazily. World news has never been her forte.

"Panama! We took that bastard out!"

"Which bastard?" Sydney said coolly.

"Noriega, of course," I said and showed her the front page: "U.S. Troops in a Massive Strike against Panamanian Army Bases."

"He's no bastard," Sydney said very calmly, but I saw her grip her coffee cup a little tighter. "He comes from a long family line of CIA-backed tyrants."

"Now, now, Syd," I said. "Let's not bring your mother into this."

Sydney frowned and snatched the newspaper from my hands. It pleased me to see her so downright inhospitable. "It says here 'Noriega Eludes U.S. Assault,'" Sydney pointed out, but she knew her argument was weak.

Tia dropped her coffee cup. It shattered on the floor, but no one made a move for it. We just all stood looking at one another. It must have dawned on us all at the same moment.

"Davy…" Tia said it for all of us. "Davy's there!"

"He would have told us…," Sydney began but stopped.

"I don't think he knew," Tia said.

"It's the darkest day of the year…," Sydney whispered softly. Then there was silence. And in that stillness there was so much feeling it struck me dumb. Sometimes when I hold a heart in my hand and feel it pumping, its pulse beats in my blood, too. I feel a kind of awe at this brave little workhorse that just keeps on going even when it doesn't have a body. The heart must be where God lives. No one ever dies of a broken brain—but people die all the time of a broken heart.

That morning I felt a single pulse between these two sisters; they held a brother in their hearts. Who knows whether, a world away, this same brother felt their hearts beating for him, willing him to stay in the world with them?

I envied Davy, even though he might be dead. Because, except for making love, when I listen to Tia's heart pound in perfect sync with my own, I have never known what it is like to feel someone's heart beating also for me. Women don't love their husbands that way, even though all the songs say it: they save that heart-song for their sisters, and their brothers, and their children.

We waited, all of us, the four days it took to have word of Davy. We waited while the world went crazy: bombings of civil rights judges in Georgia, unarmed Romanian protestors murdered by the thousands in the streets, and hourly reports of fighting and looting in Panama. When the phone call from Mathilde came, she was so hysterical I could hear her halfway across the kitchen.

"I will never again marry a soldier," she said, her voice shell-shocked. "Why did I marry a soldier?"

Sydney listened intently, then said, "We'll be right over, Mathilde. Stay still."

I drove us halfway to Mathilde's house before anybody bothered to tell me anything. Tia and Sydney were talking telepathically. It wasn't until I said "They'll fly his body here and give him a hero's funeral…" that they both turned to me as if I'd said the most monstrous thing.

"Just like you to assume Davy is dead," Tia snapped. She was fighting back tears and not succeeding, but I dared not touch her. Her anger was like another body between us.

"Daddy…!" Daniella cautioned me. She was in on it, too.

"Well, will somebody mind telling me what the hell is going on? I'm not tuned into the family frequency."

And just like that Daniella got this dazed look on her face and said softly, "He's under the sea. Uncle Davy is remembering how to breathe water."

"Where, honey?" Tia asked Daniella as if she were some sort of psychic instead of a little girl scared to death.

"Stop it!" I said. "She doesn't know what's going on." It was dangerous to put it on a kid. My daughter would think she had some hand in Davy's death, simply because her magical powers didn't save him.

Tia opened her mouth, then thought better of it. "It's all right, darling," she soothed Daniella. "We'll find him."

That was it. I just blew up. "You going to astral travel to the goddamned Far Side? Will somebody please tell me what's going on?"

"Nothing you can help with," Tia said simply. "It's not your OR."

It was Sydney who took mercy on me. "Davy's plane is down," she explained, each word so clear it was as if she were teaching me a foreign language. "In Cuban waters. He was coming back to Guantánamo Bay from an aircraft carrier off the coast of Panama. He was doing air support for the invasion. But on the way back to the base, he had some sort of mechanical trouble and...and his jet...well, they don't know."

"Do they know where he went down?" I demanded.

"Yes, but there's been no radio signal from him since...," Sydney stopped. In the rearview mirror I could see she was crying, holding Daniella.

"Where did they last hear from him?"

"Off the coast of Cabo Cruz," Sydney said.

"I know those waters!" I picked up the car phone and called the airlines. There was a nonstop midnight red-eye to Miami. I booked two seats without thinking. One for me and one for Tia. Sydney could stay with the girls and maybe drive the van back with Mathilde and her kids—the women and children's caravan—while Tia and I went on ahead.

"What are you doing, Hawkins?" Tia asked. "We've got to get to Mathilde."

"We've waited around long enough!" I told her, and I noticed she snapped to attention at my tone. It was like in the old days when I was the surgeon and she my most brilliant scrub nurse. Before we married, before she ever talked back to me or dreamed of leaving me—when she was still my right hand.

"Hawkins!" Tia cried as I turned the van around and headed back to Sydney's.

"I know those waters, Tia," I told her. "I can find your brother. I know the reefs; I know places the navy would never look. I remember them as a kid. And if Davy's there I can find him."

"You'll find him when the radar can't?" Sydney asked.

"Your family has its own radio station, WU-WU—my family has celestial navigation in our blood."

"This is another one of your crazy survivalist plans," Tia snapped, but I saw she was halfway tuned in to my thoughts. That hadn't happened between us in months.

"You don't want your brother to survive?" I demanded. Tia's eyes filled, and I said, "That settles it. You and I will fly back and find Davy."

I expected Sydney to intervene on her sister's behalf, but Sydney surprised me with her silence. From the back of the van I could see her watching me in the rearview mirror. She was also watching her sister the way a mother bird must gaze at her offspring in those terrible moments before she pushes it, spindly and terror-stricken, from the nest.

It was Daniella who spoke the family fear. "But Mommy doesn't fly. And what if your plane falls from the sky, too?" Daniella began to cry and Sydney held her. I noticed that Sydney kind of muffled Daniella's tears in her raincoat.

No one said a word. I just kept on driving fast toward Sydney's, but in my mind I was heading home *and* with my wife in tow. I knew she would follow me—not as my wife, but as Davy's sister.

At last Tia gave a short, I'd almost say military nod, and reached forward. "Hand me the phone, Hawkins," she said as if our roles were reversed and she were the surgeon asking the nurse for instruments. I almost refused, but my hand automatically answered her request. It was unsettling to suspect that my wife had more control over my hands at that moment than I did. But sometimes my hands are smarter than I am.

She dialed, and we all waited to see who in the world she was calling. "Timo," she said firmly, even though her voice was shaking. "Hawkins and I are flying back to Miami tonight. We're going to try to find your father. Will...will you come with us?" She paused. "Good, honey. Good for you."

Joe Blow hit the roof and I slammed on the brakes. "All we

need is a kid along!" I shouted. It was the first time I'd raised my voice since this tentative reunion. But this was insane! The blind leading the blind, the scared leading the terrified. "Forget it, Tia! We'll leave the girls here with Sydney. She and Mathilde and the kids can drive the van back to Florida over Christmas vacation after we've…"

"Davy is Timo's father and he's my brother!" Tia yelled right back as if she were across the street instead of right there in the passenger side of my van. "We'll fly back and find him, even without you, Hawkins!"

The thought had never occurred to me that Tia would fly for the first time in seven years with someone other than me. Even a little kid could rescue her from her phobia.

"It's my boat!" I yelled even louder.

"I'll rent another one," Tia snapped and turned her face to glare out the window.

"You don't know how to navigate as far down as Cuba," I reminded her.

"I'll rent a skipper."

"No one will take you there. No one else knows those restricted waters."

She was silent, her jaw set. Silence, too, from the backseat. I sighed and started driving fast again. At least now I could hear a static sound whenever Tia, Sydney, and my own daughter were tuning into one another's thoughts. If only I knew what conspiracy was brewing in their minds.

It wasn't until we were midsky, midcontinent, in the middle of the night—me, Tia, and Timo—that I realized the truth. Of course they were all in on it, that's why no one had to say anything out loud. Even Daniella, even my own baby girl knew: there was another man. Must be! Who else were these women and children relying on, if I was out of the picture?

I sat bolt upright in my seat and glared at Tia. She'd strategically placed Timo between us, and he was slumped against her shoulder, with a thin, red woolen airplane blanket over his head. I suppose he slept. Or else he was paralyzed by fear. Tia had lodged a pillow between her head and the porthole. Her eyes were closed but I knew she did not sleep. Her breathing was ragged, and her hands were clenched so tightly, the skin showed splotches of red and white where no blood flowed.

If I hadn't hated her at that moment, I would have held her hand in mine. But if I held my wife's hands now, I'd break every bone, every memory of every night when she lay beside me dreaming of someone else. *How long has she been unfaithful to you?* Joe Blow asked softly. He didn't have to shout; he had my full attention. *When did it begin? Before the separation? Did she leave you in her heart before her body abandoned your bed? When you made love to her, did she think of another man's hands stroking her thighs? When she threw back her head and screamed in pleasure, was she calling out for someone else? Does she think of that man even now when she's so afraid, when you're sitting right here next to her?*

My hands were so hot, I was surprised not to see third-degree burns raised on the skin. And the roar inside was so loud, I couldn't hear the noise of the plane engines. My eyes blurred as I looked over at Tia. Her hair was wild, that dark curl that first drew me to her. *Morena bonita,* I had whispered to her the first time we made love. It was in a linen closet off the OR. It was the darkness—hers, mine, and the room's—that drew me to her that midnight.

Tia and I had never dated; our romance was the OR. No surgical nurse had ever read my mind so easily or anticipated my every want. I didn't have to ask Tia out on dates—I always demanded that she scrub every important heart with me.

That night they brought up a gunshot aorta. There was no time to open the guy up properly; we had seconds before his heart pumped out all its blood. I glanced across at the resident, then Tia. Over their masks, their eyes watched me expectantly. What else could I do? This guy was a goner anyway. I grabbed the scalpel, made a perfect stab, ripped that poor bastard wide open, and stuck the transfusion needle straight into his heart. We gave him so many pints of blood as I worked to sew up the wound that by the time we closed him up the guy had a different blood type. It wasn't sterile, but he was alive. And he wasn't the only one pumped up.

After they wheeled that gunshot back to the ICU, I turned to Tia and said very calmly, although my own heart was beating so hard I thought she might overhear it, "Nurse, I want you in post-op."

She was waiting, but she had exchanged her bloody green scrubs for blue ones. I hadn't bothered. "Yes, Doctor?" she'd asked, a smile edging her mouth—that mouth I so rarely saw because it was usually hidden by a scrub mask as tantalizing as any harem veil.

I said nothing, simply reached across and took off her little operating cap. Her hair tumbled down in a mass of matted curls. Sweat still stood on her temples, although I was sure she'd washed her face along with her hands. "Where's your scrub cap?" I teased her. Then I gallantly opened the linen-closet door and invited her in as if it were the most seductive boudoir.

She was the one who locked the door. I liked that. It showed spunk. I could feel Tia's smile in the blackness as she turned the lock. "Can you operate in the dark, Doctor?"

"Yes," I said. "I carry my own generator."

In the same way that the nurse in her always anticipated the healer in my hands, Tia's body intuited my touch. Somehow she knew I'd be aroused most by arousing her. When I reached out for her breast, she caught her breath a split second before my fingers felt her nipple stiffen, stand at attention. Her skin was so warm even though goosebumps raised up to meet my fingertips. If I ran my tongue along the inside of her thighs, her whole body tensed, then yielded. One touch and her skin hummed, a high, electrified sound like a human tuning fork.

In doing so little, I was never so powerful. Simply the suggestion of my tongue in her mouth sent subtle waves of pleasure along her limbs. Her back arched, her belly pulled taut, and her hips moved slow and sure as though she was dancing a samba. Her whole body invited mine to dance there in the dark with the sharp smell of starch and astringent everywhere. I moved in and out of her as easily as waves on a body of warm, surrendering sand—and we slow-danced like that to the same rhythm although there was no music, to the same beat though there was no drum.

It wasn't wild, it was slow and deep—and I don't suppose I have ever left that woman's body since that bloody, black linen closet. But she has left mine.

I looked at Tia one seat away on that midnight flight to our separate homes, and I thought she might as well be across an ocean from me. And right there in the darkness of the airplane with the roaring all around and inside me, I watched the small, strong pulse in my wife's throat and let tears ease out my eyes without even hiding them. There was no one to see, there was no one to explain why every woman must leave me.

III

The other man, if you can call him that, was waiting for us at the airport gate in Miami.

"He's a goddamned nurse, Tia!" That was all I could say as this small Cuban guy walked toward us. I recognized Gabriel Alvarez from my own hometown hospital. He struck me now as he had then, which is not at all. Quiet, unremarkable, the kind of guy you lose in a crowd.

Joe Blow just shook his crew-cut head and spat. *Some competition,* he said. *Probably got bounced from boot camp because he's too small to fight—like those pathetic Third World countries.*

"Any guy who's a nurse has got to be very gay or very confused," I muttered to Tia. At least she had enough grace not to embrace him right there in front of me.

"Timo...Hawkins..." Tia took her nephew's arm as if that ten-year-old boy were the only male around. "This is Gabriel Alvarez. He'll drive us to the naval base at Key West."

"Hello, Doctor Costarella." Alvarez nodded.

I turned to face what little there was of him. "How's the hospital treating you, Nurse?" I said.

This was a worse nightmare than Joe Blow and I had ever prepared ourselves for in our end-of-the-world scenarios. I know how to survive the big bomb, but it never occurred to us we'd have to train to survive a firecracker. *Maybe he's more like those terrorists,* Joe Blow theorized, but I knew he was scratching his gray, stubbled head, as confused as I was. *They don't look dangerous, but it's what they carry hidden inside that does the damage.*

As we all passed back through the airport security gates, I half-wished they'd run Gabriel Alvarez through the metal detectors. But the diplomatic corps gave me some unexpected help by reminding me that a man like Alvarez was the most treacherous when he talked. Heart in the right place, and all that. God knows, Tia wasn't alone among women in wanting a man to talk to her. Trouble was, when I told Tia what was on my mind, she never allowed Joe Blow into the conversation. So how could I really level with her? Then there is the other problem: sometimes I just don't know what I feel. It's not something they teach you in med school.

Like that morning in the Miami airport. We'd flown all night and I was so tired I didn't even remember it was Christmas Day. There was my wife walking alongside her nursing buddy as if I weren't around—do you think she wanted to hear me express my real feelings? "I'm so glad you've found a girlfriend in your hour of need, Tia." That's all I could say. Joe Blow had much worse in mind. The civilian corps asked me to consider if this Alvarez really might be just a friend. I've heard that divorcing women sometimes take up with pansies because it's safe, but they're still in male company.

It was a good thing we all had our winter gear from Seattle because Miami was as cold as a witch's tit. A freak nineteen degrees on Christmas Day. Not exactly the best weather for a boat ride.

But a plan is a plan and what alternative did I have?

So, waiting outside for Gabriel to bring the car round, I made my last pitch. "Listen, Tia," I said, "my boat is ten minutes from here. We'll bring a heater. Christmas is a good cover-up. We can make it down in...oh, I'd say..."

"I'm not going," Tia said. "Don't you. It's too dangerous."

"Well, why did we fly all the way here for?" I demanded. "We could have waited for word back in Seattle—and been there when they shipped your brother home."

"It was time for me to take my turn in the sky," Tia said softly. "I'll fly down and wait for word of Davy at Guantánamo Bay."

You could tell this was against her better instincts. Like Sydney always says, the emergency personality dies hard in her family. I could see Tia was debating whether or not to go with me on my search and rescue mission.

"Look, Tia," I pressed her, "I don't know who this Alvarez is to you. But I know he can't replace me. I mean, *look* at the guy. He turns sideways and you can't see him. What kinda protection you gonna get from a man like him?"

I realized too late I'd said the exact wrong thing. Tia flared at me. "I don't need protection, Hawkins!"

Trying to salvage something, I softened my tone. I even took her reluctant hand. "What do you need, honey?" I asked.

Tia was quiet a moment, considering. Her expression changed so quickly I couldn't follow it. At last she looked me right in the eye as if we were sparring off, and she practically shouted, "I don't know! I don't know what I need!"

She was exasperated with herself and taking it out on me. But

I'd let her. I'd let her rant and rave, as long as she didn't leave. "Listen, darlin'," I began, "how are you going to live on a nurse's salary? What about our children? You going to take them from riches to rags?"

"His nurse's salary *and* mine," Tia said and craned her neck to see if Alvarez was returning with the car.

"Tia," I said and grabbed her gently. I took her face between my hands and held it. "If you wanted someone like him...why did you ever marry me?"

She frowned, but I knew I'd made her think. For a long while she was quiet. Then she laughed, but there was despair in her. "I'll always be married to you now, Hawkins," she said. "I've got you...under my skin."

We stood there eyeing each other, and I couldn't believe it was really happening—that another man was driving up to the curb, with Timo in tow, to take my wife away from me. Everything was in slow motion, the way an oncoming accident changes time, warps it down to this: Something's coming. It's going to hurt. You'll never be the same.

"Tia," I hardly knew I was speaking, my voice was so low. "Don't do this. I'll fight you...I'll fight for my daughters..."

"And I'll fight you right back, Hawkins." Her voice matched mine. In that moment I knew she would—it would be the bloodiest mess between us—and my Daniella would bleed the most.

"It's not fair," I told her. I felt like I was choking, then pains in my chest. Not angina, something deeper. "You're only losing me. I'm losing my whole family."

Tia shook her head. "I'm sorry, Hawk, it just doesn't work anymore." She waved wearily to Alvarez, signaling him to the curb. "I don't know what does work. I just know that *we* don't anymore."

Alvarez drove up like a taxi-to-hell. Tia threw her own bags into the trunk. Alvarez didn't even help her. Then she turned back to me. "Why don't you wait with us at the navy base for word of Davy, Hawk?" she asked.

It startled me, her request. I'd assumed Tia didn't want me along. "Why?" I demanded.

"Because if you go off on a one-way trip to find my brother, who may already be dead, I'll lose two people I love."

"But you don't love me anymore," I said softly.

"I'll love you even less if you leave your daughters without a father," she countered.

Right then I had a mutinous thought. I camouflaged it from Joe Blow. He was already way ahead of me arranging, strategizing: How much gas to get to Cuba? Was the Lowrance still on the blink? How much food and water to survive the ocean trip?

I actually thought about agreeing with Tia's request to stay with them and wait like a bunch of old women. But what would Joe Blow do if I waited out the war? He was already retired and he was nowhere near off duty. Maybe if I sent him for a little R & R? I tried to imagine how Joe might take it. Say, if I sent him off to Hawaii, a favorite stomping ground for sailors on leave?

I pictured Joe in a high-rise Hawaiian hotel, luxury even. I had the money and he'd served me well. We wouldn't call it a pension; we'd call it an expense account. I could add him to my child-support checks each month. Imagining Joe Blow in a double-occupancy ritzy room, I saw his distress. What would he do without me to drill all day—flirt with pretty Polynesians, hula like hell in his skivvies? Would Joe take up scuba diving instead of spear fishing? Could he ever exchange his jungle fatigues for Hawaiian shirts?

Closing my eyes to concentrate, it all came clear to me: There was my drill instructor on vacation in his navy-issue jock shorts, crisp T-shirt, dog tags dangling. He was bored, bouncing Susan B. Anthony dollars off his perfectly taut and tucked bedsheets. He was slack-faced from brooding.

"Don't you want to rest, Joe?" I whispered to him, as intimate and insistent as any of his worst suggestions to me. "Aren't you sick and tired of playing the tough guy?"

His grin was menacing. "I'll get you for jailing me in this mandatory peacetime paradise!" He flexed his arms and spat. "I'll get you back *bad*!"

Maybe Tia glimpsed fear in my face, because her voice was soft so as not to startle me. "What are you going to do, Hawkins?" she asked.

"Do?" I exploded. "I'll do what you'd expect of a doctor. I'll do no goddamned harm!" I was yelling, but I didn't care anymore. I'd lost her anyway. "Maybe I'll scratch this suicide sail to Cuba and go back to Panama instead. They need bush doctors there. And there are plenty of women there without husbands. They didn't throw their men away, they just lost them!"

"Go be a hero, Hawk," Tia got in the car and slammed the door. Then she rolled down the window and said, "Find yourself a good, grieving widow!"

As the car drove off, I yelled after her. "At least those women know what they're missing!"

I watched the car curve around the cement parking garage until it was just a speck on the tropical horizon. With a shiver, I realized I was freezing my ass off in nothing but a sports shirt and raincoat. At least my Miami apartment had heat in it. It gave me slight pleasure to think of Tia and Alvarez in our Key West home without a boiler. Unless Tia had reconstructed it by now.

As I signaled a taxi to take me to my Miami bachelor's apartment, I tried not to imagine my wife and that weasel Alvarez bundling up in our bed for warmth. Maybe they'd go straight to the Boca Chica base and catch a hop over to Guantánamo Bay, without stopping, without making love. But what about all the nights, all the years to come, when they'd lie together as if I'd never been a part of Tia's body, as if my children had never come from her? What about Daniella and Felicia? Who would be their father now? Who would stitch Daniella's knee when she fell; who would tuck her in with stories?

Not that nurse. He didn't have any children of his own. He couldn't know my daughters. They didn't belong to him. But they might learn; they might learn to love him, too. Like their mother.

I couldn't stand it. I couldn't stand the thought of them all together. So I made my plan: The minute I got home, I'd pack my boat and just head out. I'd probably camp out on our SONS secret island—after all, it was already fortified. I wouldn't tell anyone I was there. Tia would begin to worry. Maybe her money would run out and she'd try to find me. Yes, that's what I'd do. Disappear. Call it R & R.

"Freezing, mon, yes?" The Jamaican taxi driver pulled up to my apartment. "How con it be so sunny, and so cold?"

I gave him a tip instead of an answer. Once you talk to taxi drivers, you end up saddled with their life's story—or telling them yours. I didn't want to talk with anybody, not even the hospital. But by habit, I called in. None of my hearts had died; that was the good news. The bad news was that they'd scheduled me for surgery the very next morning. Seems the hearts were stockpiled, waiting for me to come back from Christmas vacation.

There went my disappearing act idea. Stuck on the home front. Just like Joe Blow, I didn't know what to do with myself. Even though we'd flown all night, I couldn't nap with the sun so bright. And it was too cold to go spear fishing. I thought about giving Daniella a call to tell her we'd arrived safely, but it was only five o'clock in the morning Seattle time.

I fixed myself an espresso and toast and ate my breakfast while I paced the kitchen, watching the clock and waiting until I could call my daughter. If I could just hear her voice, I knew I'd be OK. Daniella will never leave me, even if I'm far away from her.

Mid pacing, I heard a familiar noise—but the sighing was shallow, not the deep expulsion of air like a great wind shaking the palm trees in my backyard. I ran outside, cursing the blast of icy cold.

"C'mon, girl!" I called to the feminine floating island always adrift in my canal. Then I froze.

Everything about her was so wrong: those tiny eyes squinting, almost shut, her respiration light and labored as an asthmatic. Even from the bank, I saw her shivering, that blue-gray sagging skin trembling in rippling waves across her scarred back. She was freezing to death in this freak cold spell which had turned the warm waters fatal as arctic wastes. Why hadn't I thought of her before? Mrs. Manatee might have died of hypothermia while I was sipping my espresso and munching my toast, oblivious to her struggle in my own backyard.

"Hang on! Hang on, old girl!" I shouted and ran for the boat shed and my wet suit. "Don't fall asleep!"

That's how it would take her. This great, gentle creature who spent so much of her days drifting and dreaming in a kind of half-sleep as she held her breath, sank to the bottom, then slowly bobbed back up to breathe. This siren to my bachelor days, this companion to my daughter—she'd just fall asleep with the cold and never come up again. Certainly there'd be no Christmas manatee miracle baby.

Hurriedly I pulled on my wet suit and dove into the canal. The chill set my teeth on edge, but my thin layer of rubber protected me, whereas Mrs. Manatee's blubber did her no good at all. Her naturally low metabolism left her defenseless against such cold. The old girl has no natural enemies, except man and cold weather. Well, the boat propeller hadn't killed her off, and I'd do my best to stop her from freezing.

But what good was my best? It was only me and this big mammal floating in the frigid waters. My body wasn't long or large enough to keep her warm. My hands weren't strong enough to jump-start that sluggish heart. Everything in her was slowing down, drifting into a deadly dream. If she fell unconscious, she'd never wake up.

There was only one thing I could think of—the warm waters around the nuclear power plant. If I could tow Mrs. Manatee that mile or so down the canal without her losing consciousness and drowning, the churning, warm waste waters would revive her.

"Easy now, darlin'," I told her. Her small eye fixed on mine with recognition, but her pupils were dilated and her lack of coordination showed her deep disorientation. Several times as I was wrapping the rope around her thousand-pound body, she helplessly bumped into me, her flippers as useless as frostbitten hands.

With my fishing winch, I hoisted her half out of the water and rested her head up on the rubber dinghy behind my boat. It was a strange procession, me on the outboard motor, towing my dinghy like an inflatable yellow pillow to haul Mrs. Manatee through the water. I had to go slowly to keep from harming her. Several times waves washed over her round, barnacled snout with its natural smile as she gasped for air.

My heart went out to the old gal as we at last reached the warm confluence of canal and effluent waters from the nuclear power plant. She stirred slightly. I don't know whether it was the warmth or the nearby herd of other manatees—all floating here to fend off freezing.

It was so strange. They were everywhere in the bubbling waters; and every manatee I saw had white scars and gouges crisscrossing its back. Even the babies. That's how you recognize a manatee, by the scars. I was the only human here. Maybe the manatees thought that I was just another man who'd run over one of them. Maybe they wondered when I jumped into the water—Jesus, it tasted foul—and wrapped my arms around this swollen old girl, pressing my ear to her heart.

Slow. Much too slow. I reached around her great girth as far as my arms would stretch and floated with her—belly to belly, her snout resting on my shoulder, her breathing faint as a whisper. All around me, they gathered, the other manatees, gently bumping against my back as I floated with Mrs. Manatee, careful to keep her head above the water.

If I had any voice at all, I'd have sung her to sleep because that's where she wanted to go—into a dream, down into the deep. I don't know if I was crying, there was so much salt water stinging my eyes.

We floated like that in those warm, toxic waters—it seemed forever—with her head thrown back, her small eyes closed. I held the whole world of her in my arms. Then with a sigh, Mrs. Manatee slipped backward into the dark water. I dove after her and we spiraled down slowly, my arms around her, my head against her silent heart.

9

THE SECRET CITY

Samuel, 1989

I

It is difficult to practice the art of diplomacy with children—especially one's own. I've had an easier time negotiating with terrorists and Third World factions than handling my daughters and son. Take this Christmas boycott. It was Sydney's idea from the start and the others followed suit, even my son Davy, who has the distinction of seldom siding with his sisters.

"What is your purpose in this boycott?" I asked Sydney when she announced it at Thanksgiving during one of our usual family conference calls. Our family is accustomed to living so far-flung from one another that linking up by satellite is one of our holiday traditions.

"What do we want...?" Sydney mused. I knew only too well the face that belied her soft tone. It was Sydney's stalemate face:

jaw jutted out, gray eyes alert, almost audibly electric. I've seen jaguars stalking South American jungles with those same eyes. Like those elusive cats, Sydney hasn't a spot of night blindness.

Long ago I taught my eldest daughter to play chess with me after dinner. Sydney took to the game with a devotion one rarely sees in children. But she never played fairly within the limits of logic. Sydney practiced a kind of psychic chess. I'd never see her ponder a countermove for more than a moment. That was because she was not strategizing. She simply glanced at the chessboard, sensed where my real attack was aimed—no matter my elaborate feints or camouflages—and she'd protect her threatened players. It was maddening to play my daughter at chess; it was also, I admit, mesmerizing—a glimpse into the irrational mind like the one I tried to fathom for those twenty years of diplomatic service in Central America. Career-wise, it was good practice to spend my evenings playing chess with a child.

From the time Sydney was twelve to the year she left home— let's see, in 1968 we were in Honduras blissfully bypassing the Stateside sixties' hippiedom—I never once beat Sydney at chess. Nor did I lose. We always ended in a stalemate. Even though Sydney's defense was impenetrable because of her own intuitive early-warning detection system, Sydney hadn't the first notion of how to carry through an attack. She could never win, only check me.

I must say, I made two crucial errors in raising my eldest daughter: I never should have sent her back to the States for college. (The first letter she wrote us was about passing by that People's Park demonstration on her way to the university library. When Governor Reagan dropped tear gas on the campus, a canister rolled into Sydney's psychology carrel, sending her and all the other students, weeping, to the infirmary.) My other mistake was teaching Sydney chess. Maybe if we hadn't had all those years of stalemates, Sydney wouldn't be so inspired to lead her siblings in these unsuccessful coups against her parents.

"You know," I had to say to my telephonically gathered off-spring. "You children are acting like your mother and I are the government you want to overthrow. Be careful how you use your power. After all, you're adults now."

"As adults we're exercising our simple right to say no, Dad. No to another screwed-up family Christmas." Sydney paused. Her weary voice told me she'd dropped that stalemate face. "I give up," she sighed. "I surrender."

"No one's asking you to surrender, Sydney," I said. "This is not a war."

"I just can't pretend everything's OK for one more holiday," Sydney added, her voice breaking.

I considered my next move. Sydney's defenses were down, Tia and Davy seemed to waver, looking for leadership. But just as I opened my mouth, Sydney spoke again.

"Let me put it another way, Dad. I retire as the family shrink. Get help from the outside."

"Do you all think you're helping your mother by refusing to come home for Christmas?" I was asking them to look into their hearts and find some compassion for their mother. But Sydney interpreted my request as a demand.

Without missing a beat, she said, "Yes, we think so, Dad." Not satisfied with that countermove, she launched a surprise attack. "Don't *you* ever think about retirement yourself, Dad?"

Sydney knew full well it's the last thing in the world I want to do. One of my hunting buddies sums it up: "Man is not evolutionarily prepared for retirement or celibacy." Retirement doesn't make sense for a career man like me. Even so, at sixty-four I've had to give it some thought. And Sydney knew this because I'd made the mistake of confiding in her my modified retirement plan: At sixty-five, I'll buy myself a Cessna and kill two birds with one stone. I'll still be available as a diplomatic courier, and I'll conquer my family's fear of flying. My idea is simple; I won't have to travel the world alone if I can teach my daughters and wife how to fly. It's giving up control that frightens the women so much. If Sydney, Tia, or Madeleine had the throttle in their own two hands, they'd believe air travel was safe.

"Do you also mean to retire as a member of this family?" I had to take a stern tack with Sydney. Once she gets on her psychological high horse, it's the same as if you've given the girl her head.

"I'm just following in your footsteps, Dad," Sydney said, and her tone put me on red alert. "I'm taking a leave of absence from family life."

"Now, I take offense to that, Sydney. I travel for my career, not to drop out, as your generation is so fond of doing."

"I'm not dropping out, Dad," Sydney said in a low voice. "I'm staying put. Putting down roots…deep. Down deep."

"*We* are your roots," I argued sensibly. "Your family."

"Most of my family lives midair," Sydney said.

Again her tone warned me off, but I accepted the challenge. I called on the strategy that always undermines even Sydney's most brilliant offense. Besides, Sydney can never sustain an attack— she overidentifies with the queen or bishop or knight who is about to fall. "You're not making sense now, Syd. You're beginning to sound like your mother…"

"Hot air!" Tia chimed in giddily, the way she does when her beloved sister and I fight. Tia has made such an enemy of her mother that she can't bear it when Sydney and I—the "good guys"—quarrel.

"You know, Dad…," Sydney said in her quiet voice that feels spring-loaded. "Mother may be the hurricane, and you the so-called calm center. But I think you're *both* part of the same system. And I'm staying far away from that rough weather. What would you do, Dad, without Mother's violence?"

If Sydney were still small, if she'd been next to me instead of across a continent, I would have spanked her, as I rarely did. But I did take my belt to her on certain occasions when she was so out of hand with that mouth of hers that it would drive any father to fury. "This conversation—and I'm being polite to call it that—is over!" I said.

I didn't expect Tia's voice. It was muffled, as if she were crying. "Why did you...why did you let Mother hurt us?"

My jaw dropped. Defection, from my favorite daughter. "You're overwrought," I soothed. "You're all overwrought."

There was a long silence on the line, interrupted by static that I realized was much too close. Then I realized my wife was listening in on the bedroom extension. I prayed the kids wouldn't hear their mother, but the noise was so loud it sounded like Madeleine was eating potato chips in my ear.

"What do you expect of me?" I heard myself shouting, hoping to drown out Madeleine's phone tap. But I'll admit I was also good and mad. It's just like Sydney to lead this children's campaign against me right before a national holiday. I've always insisted my children behave like civilized people even though underneath I suspect they are savages. "I'm not superhuman! I don't have a satellite preview of your mother's moods. They come out of nowhere. *She* comes out of nowhere!" I dearly hoped that my wife would stay off the line, and in my own way I was warning her. "I'm not a weatherman; I'm a negotiator. You can't sit down at a summit table with a high-pressure system."

"Weather Men go underground," Sydney said, and her cryptic reference cost her. It sailed right past her siblings. I could feel their confusion as they waited for Sydney to explain.

I took the upper hand. "The real issue here is that each of your own families is in such turmoil right now—everything is up in the air."

"That's why we never fly," Tia managed a hoarse laugh. I knew she was in pain. Madeleine told me she wheedled it out of Davy that Tia is seeing another man. Even if we believed in divorce in this family, Tia's running around is hard to watch. It's bad enough that Davy's marriage failed. Being divorced is like being a man without a country.

"So, Tia…" I tried to keep any emotion from my voice. No sense in betraying myself; and I certainly wouldn't beg. "You're not coming home for Christmas?"

I knew Tia wavered by the long time she took to answer. Tia is my hotheaded child. Where Sydney is cool and contemplative, Tia's feelings are right there on the surface. I once watched Tia knock two boys' heads together because they laughed at Davy singing falsetto in the joint embassy school's play. Unfortunately, the two boys were the sons of the ambassadors from Guatemala and El Salvador. We were posted in Panama at the time, and Tia's temper almost sparked an international incident.

But for all Tia's moods—which Hawkins managed to suppress for a surprisingly long time—Tia is the child closest to my heart. If Sydney has my temperament, Tia inherited the high spirits that first attracted me to my wife. The difference is that Tia also got the MacKenzie gene for pragmatism. Even midtantrum, Tia can hear any sensible appeal. This is not true of my wife.

At first I thought Madeleine was simply prey to coquettish pouts. To a Tennessee country boy like me this seemed a wealthy town-girl's luxury. Madeleine used to meet me at the doorstep for our date, casting a glance at my unpressed trousers or inevitable cowlick. "I don't feel like seeing you," she'd flounce away in a perfumed cloud of curls and chiffon to leave me dazzled on the stoop. I thought I would gently break her like a favorite filly; I thought motherhood would make some sense of her town-bred high-handed manners, what we in the hills called "uppityness." I even believed that my rise as a diplomat and the worldly education of an embassy wife would mature Madeleine's ebullient flair as a hostess into the solid skills of a backstage negotiator.

Like most men in love, I was wrong. I've come to see my wife as a small fanatical country, say like Iraq, who steadfastly insists on seeing reason as an insult to its sovereignty. Sometimes I even think my children are my wife's hostages; she threatens my children in order to get her way with me. I've never told a single soul this: when the children were little there were times I considered leaving Madeleine. But in those days and with my country-hopping career, I knew Madeleine would get the children. The irony, of course, is that because of my loyalty to my wife, I might now lose my children.

"Just say you haven't taken a position yet on the boycott issue," I urged Tia.

"Well, *I* haven't, Dad."

It was Davy. I keep forgetting that boy. I know it's an over-sight, especially since he's my only son. I even know that Davy's made a military career more to please me than himself. Davy wanted to be a singer, of all things. Some lounge lizard with noth-ing more to do than lurk and croon to lonely women in dark bars. I put the kibosh on that idea long ago when I sent him off to a military academy. We were in El Salvador and the situation was not stable. When I found Davy in the basement making a Molo-tov cocktail with his little Salvadoran friend, I dispatched my son post haste to a fine boy's academy with a reputation as a stepping-stone to West Point.

"Haven't what, Davy?" I asked.

He sighed. I could just see him shrugging those square shoul-ders. "Taken a position yet."

"I doesn't matter, son," I said. "I assume you'll be home with us and your own children for Christmas." I pressed my advan-tage. "Listen, let's all be together as a family for Christmas. Come home, kids...and we'll all sit down at the table to work this thing out."

There was a long silence interrupted only by Madeleine's crackling again. Then Sydney said at last, "I'm sorry, Dad. I just can't."

"Sometimes I think I'll forget what my oldest daughter looks like," I told Sydney. "If it weren't for the photo your mother keeps on my study wall, I might not even recognize you, honey."

"Oh, Dad...," Tia said sadly. I knew then that my second

daughter wouldn't boycott me. Of course, she wouldn't capitulate on the phone, but come Christmas, I knew Tia would come home.

It seemed a good way to finish the conference, but before I could call an end to it, Madeleine made her unfortunate presence known.

"Now just a darn minute!" Madeleine's voice was so loud, not only because she was upstairs, but because she always shouts on long-distance calls to compensate for the fact that we're talking cross-continent. I never let her use the phone when we were posted abroad. "You going to let Sydney get away with going AWOL, Sam?"

"I *knew* Mother was eavesdropping!" Tia snapped. "And you said this was a private call, Dad."

"Was that you munching on the line, Mom?" Sydney laughed. Even though she boycotts her mother, Sydney has always been my wife's favorite. As a child, Sydney was absolutely attentive to her mother, straightening Madeleine out when I was away. Madeleine used to call Sydney her "feeling-eye dog," because Sydney gave her mother all the right cues for getting along with people. It wasn't until we ended up in Central America that Madeleine finally fit in without much coaching. The Latinos loved Madeleine's ups and downs. When we were in Cuba during the Batista regime, if Madeleine had led a people's revolution instead of Castro, she might well have become a beloved, national tyrant. Then my children would have left me for good—braving shark-infested waters on one little raft rather than endure their mother's unchecked rule. Fortunately, in 1959 we got called back to the State Department in D.C., right before the revolution. My children were safe with me in their own country for awhile. And then there was our Honduras stint, which was like a siesta compared to what was happening in the States overrun by hippies and Cuba under the Commies.

"Having yourself a little CIA snack attack, Mom?" Tia said,

but her tone had none of Sydney's affection or amusement.

"Those of us relegated to the peanut gallery make do," my wife said in her most injured tone. But we all knew that wouldn't last long. A moment later she was on the offensive. "You all *make* me crazy! If I don't listen in and then tell Sam I know the whole family is talking behind my back, he'll say I am paranoid. If I do listen in, you all say I'm spying. Well, I think it's pretty gol-darn sneaky to talk about putting me away with some shrink in a funny farm!"

"No one's talking about putting you anywhere, Madeleine," I soothed her. Although at that minute I admit I wanted to put her off. Once she got going she'd make sure the kids' boycott went into full swing. We wouldn't see any of the kids come Christmas.

"Mother," Sydney said. "I know you're scared of seeing someone, but…"

"How do *you* know?" Madeleine shot back.

"Because I was scared, too, at first."

"Yeah, but you beat those shrinks at their own game by joining them. Now all you have to do is sit there and listen and get paid lots of money. But me…I'll have to tell all my secrets."

"Go ahead, Mother," Tia said. "I think the nation will survive."

"And you think the CIA is cold-blooded!" Madeleine shrieked so loudly it blasted my eardrums, and I had to hold the phone away until the high-frequency ringing in my ears faded.

No matter. These conversations always ended the same way: Madeleine slamming down the phone, usually when Tia was talking. There was a crash upstairs and then a droning dial tone on the phone.

No one rang back. It's a point of honor in this family when one is hung-up on, to answer with the loudest, longest silence. But that was the official story; behind the scenes I knew all my kids were back on another conference call, plotting and strategizing their Christmas boycott. And even though, as it turned out, the boycott was lifted enough for Tia and Davy to make their pre-holiday visit, then disappear without a word—I knew at Thanksgiving when I sat downstairs in my study with a dead phone in my hand, staring at photos of my children, that in spite of my best negotiating, my wife and I would be alone at our Christmas table.

II

There is no isolation like that of the Secret City. Yet one is never alone; TV cameras and screens are everywhere broadcasting fake news of the outside nuclear holocaust. These phony newsreels might seem like horror movies aboveground; but buried under a mountain of stone, the images take on an urgent realism. Perhaps because everything underground seems so unreal: the fluorescent sunlight, the filtered air, the steady whir of the little battery-powered cars that shuttle us around on rubber wheels like go-carts for grown-ups; the eerie gleam of the spring-fed artificial lake; the blotched, pale faces of bureaucrats whisked from the Situation Room to sleepless private quarters where we wonder if we did the right thing and saved a world already savaged by radiation.

At any one time there can be several thousand of us underground in Mount Weather staging war games. Most of the personnel are high-level representatives of the various departments of the federal government—men like my colleague Ray Sawbury, who's an assistant undersecretary in the Agriculture Department. His job is to act as the cabinet-level head of Agriculture, memorizing and reporting on how to handle a mass postnuclear evacuation from San Francisco into the Sierras. Or Ray might have to remember, under pressure, the exact location of California's wheat, corn, and grain storage silos, buried in case of catastrophe for a time when every other food source is contaminated.

Then there's my long-time pal Buster Brannigan, who is called to act as the emergency secretary of Health and Human Services.

During a thermonuclear war, it will be his job to round up the construction workers needed to do excavation work for the necessary mass graves. It was Buster who told me that his department's biggest worry is not radiation sickness, which is slow, but all the countless victims killed by the most common of all nuclear deaths: the blast throws people to the ground with such force they die on impact.

My area of specialty from years with the State Department traveling South America is to cite possible remote areas where chances of surviving World War III are the highest. I suppose that's because our military tacticians have deemed most of the Southern Hemisphere not worth targeting. So I have to recall specific villages high in the Andes or hidden in the Brazilian rainforests where isolated tribespeople won't recognize a nuclear blast. Ironically, these primitives might have the calmest heads during a nuclear holocaust simply because they believe it's possible to negotiate with even the angriest fire gods.

After several days in the Secret City, with its double-blast doors and retractable antennae, we can grow as remote and superstitious as any of those inbred, stone-age tribes I studied in the jungles. During the latest drill, there were times when I stared at huge color videos portraying American cities leveled, overrun with looters whose faces were burned past recognition by radiation—and I just marveled that there was no mention that in 1989, the whole world above us had changed. In my diplomatic work I've often noted the military mind is the last to perceive the present reality. That's because the military begins with an assumption—say, nuclear attack—and then spins off into future scenarios. A diplomat's imagination is always curbed by reality. We live in the present tense. The difference between a military man and a diplomat is the difference between a man with a recurring nightmare and a man who must negotiate his polite and careful way across a small but politically sensitive mine field.

That's why it is always like entering a dream world for me to do my twice-yearly drill in the Secret City. Even in this most recent stint underground, there was no mention of the Berlin Wall falling down, of Castro's imminent fall, of a U.S. administration admitting there was no longer the possibility of a Soviet first strike. Perhaps that dreary repetition of the Cold War military mind—combined with the fact that I'd been called up along with other lower-level personnel right before Christmas—gave me what my kids call "a bad attitude."

That December morning when I sat bleary-eyed and pale-faced over my cafeteria coffee and the first images of the Panama invasion flashed on our video screens, I didn't take it seriously. The entire Situation Room erupted in a hoopla of hoorays and huzzahs as we watched footage of American soldiers, men and a few women in camouflage fatigues attacking the Panamanian Defense Forces headquarters. Of course, we didn't think it was real, this U.S. Christmas invasion.

It was the typical war-movie plot: the United States launches a localized military incident to which the Soviet Union responds with a full-scale nuclear strike. We waited for the reports of the atomic blast, but instead the "news" broadcast shifted to other reports: racist mail bombs in Georgia and the like. Then we were back to Panama with a shot of an air force honor guard carrying the casket of a U.S. soldier.

Not for a second did I take this John Wayne invasion seriously. Perhaps I have spent too many years out of my country. All I could think of was that this Panama business was an unrealistic scenario because of the hostile reaction it would elicit from Latin American countries.

Finding myself underground watching these scenes of fighting in Panama made me strangely homesick. I still don't know whether I was longing simply to be above ground again or to be back in Central America. As if sensing my despair and seizing upon it, an aide delivered to me a telegram: EMERGENCY STOP LT. DAVID MACKENZIE DOWNED IN EA-6B PROWLER STOP HOSTILE WATERS

STOP CONTACT COMDR. BOLTON BOCA CHICA AIR STATION KEY WEST
STOP.

While the young aide loitered around waiting for a reaction
from me, I called over to Buster. "I wish they'd leave my family
out of it," I grumbled. "Last time it was my wife held hostage by
terrorists demanding sanctuary in Mount Weather from radiation."

"Right," Buster nodded, still glued to the television screens,
where U.S. tanks were rolling down a main street in Panama City.
Looking closer, I thought I recognized that street. "They really got
me a couple years back…told me my entire family had been mas-
sacred in their fallout shelter by marauders looking for supplies.
You'd think that having to enact World War III over and over
would be enough to test any man's mettle under fire."

"Well," I snapped at the young aide. More often than not
these innocuous-looking kids are in training for CIA jobs. "What
am I supposed to do with this?"

"I'm sorry about your son, sir," the fellow said.

I turned back to the television screens. "Of course, I have no
response," I flattened my voice. "We are sealed off here from any
personal matters not affecting national security. You may go."
When the fellow hesitated, I barked at him. "Dismissed!"

"Well done, Sam," Buster said. The news had switched to
scenes of mass destruction not unlike those shots they're always
showing on late-night movies of Hiroshima—blackened wastes,
no sign of life.

I did not contact this Commander Bolton or anybody else for
that matter. I spent Christmas Eve in the Situation Room at a
round-table discussion of the scenario of Iraq attacking Iran with
unexpected nuclear capability. The heat was on me especially
because I was supposedly an expert on family feuds, even though
the Arab world is not my usual negotiating neighborhood.

If it hadn't been for my wife's high-security clearance, I might
have served out my entire week-long stay in the Secret City with-

out ever knowing that Davy's plane really had crashed in Cuban waters. I'd no idea he had participated in the Panama invasion. I thought he was in some motel who-knows-where spitefully spending Christmas together with Tia and all my grandchildren.

Madeleine still can't divulge how she managed it, but on Christmas Day she got a call through to me.

"What are you *doing* down there, Sam?" Madeleine's voice was so loud, as if by sheer force she'd penetrate the solid stone between us. "Davy's plane crashed off Cuba. He's in the navy hospital in Guantánamo Bay."

"It's...it's true, then?" I managed to say. I noticed with a certain detached calm that my breathing was labored. Suddenly I had to fight off the feeling that I was buried alive. "His plane...shot down?"

"No...some sort of malfunction flying back to the carrier after the Panama attack...say, wasn't that wonderful? Our guys did great! And now that low-down Noriega's hiding out in the Vatican Embassy. But he'll get his! Just like the Ceauşescus. Did you hear, they were executed by a firing squad?"

"What about Davy?" I demanded.

"Broken leg, but otherwise OK I think. I've been praying night and day...no help from you. Didn't they telegram you?"

"I thought..." I stumbled and again felt breathless. "I thought it was just..."

"Oh, a drill. I thought you might take it that way. You would make a great military man, darling."

Madeleine's comfort is so rare that when it was offered I didn't recognize it. Just as I didn't recognize my son's very real danger.

"I feel terrible," I said.

"Well, you couldn't have done anything anyway. The boycott's still on."

"What!" Now I was yelling.

"Tia's down there with Davy and, as usual, she won't talk to me. I can't get a thing out of her. But Davy's squadron commander is a wonderful guy. He told me Noriega was practicing black magic."

"The kids are *still* calling for a boycott?" I asked. "Is Sydney down there with Davy?"

"She's in Seattle with all the grandchildren. Just think, if Sydney is in a car accident, we'd lose our entire next generation..."

"I've had enough of that kind of thinking," I firmly told Madeleine. "Listen, I'm getting out of here. Can you meet me at Dulles about five o'clock?"

"I'll pack our suitcases," Madeleine shouted. Her voice was full of that overwrought gleefulness that is always a warning signal. But I didn't care. "You know we aren't supposed to bust through the kids' boycott..." Madeleine laughed.

"This is a family emergency," I said and at last mastered myself. My breathing steadied, and I felt my competence and control return as it always does in any real diplomatic crisis. Leave the war games to the military; I am in my element, I am most alive, not in the shadow of death, but when handling people who hate each other but have to survive together. "*Our* suitcases...?" I suddenly remembered. "But dear, you don't fly."

"Oh, I'll load up on Librium, Sam. I wouldn't miss this for the world. I've always wanted to see Guantánamo Bay again and right under Castro's nose!"

I had to ask, "You're not...you're not on some CIA business now are you, darling?"

"Of course not! I just want to spend Christmas together as a family."

III

As it turned out the navy transferred Davy from Cuba to the Boca Chica naval hospital, which put Madeleine in a foul mood, as if her presence might have hastened Castro's fall. When Madeleine and I entered Davy's hospital room, Tia did not block us from

Davy's bedside, though she did give her mother a warning look as Madeleine made for Davy, her arms outflung. "Shhhhh, Mom! He's still sleeping," Tia said.

Madeleine turned on a dime and passed us on her way out. "Well, then," she said, "I'll get us all some snacks. I'm starved."

Tia sighed and embraced me tightly. I knew she was glad to see me, boycott or not. Except for one white-clad leg raised high in traction and a nasty gash running from elbow to hand, Davy seemed all right. His head was thrown back on the pillow as if he had abandoned himself to some dream.

"How is he?" I asked Tia.

"Well, Dad…," she hesitated. "Davy's not really all the way back yet."

"Not brain damage?" I asked in alarm.

"No."

"Then what?"

Tia shrugged. "Maybe he was hypoxic and he hallucinated. Who knows?" She turned to someone nearby, and only then did I notice another man in the room. "We flew all night."

I don't know which surprised me most: Tia's flying or her companion. The we was not what I had expected. Instead of Hawkins by her side, a stranger stood near Tia. He was slight of build with dark Latin eyes that met mine without challenge. The man was almost unsettlingly calm. He reminded me of a small stag I'd shot once—magnificent animal who gave me a good chase and then at the last moment turned toward me to meet my startled gaze. That animal's eyes were so intelligent, so—well, I'd have to say candid—that I lowered my rifle a moment. It was only years of hunting instinct that at last quickened me to take the shot. That stag's antlers were undersize but I had them mounted, head and all, with the other trophies in my study. I keep him nearby not for his horns, but to preserve those expressive eyes.

Tia's companion—Gabriel Alvarez is his name—looked Cuban to me. Tia has always liked Latino men. Maybe it's her adolescent years in Central America. None of my children has married one of their own countrymen. Sydney's late husband was half-Polynesian, of all things. A man she met in a Taoist yoga class. I fully expect my oldest daughter to one day end up with her version of the Dalai Lama. Then Tia with her Hawkins, and even Davy followed suit by marrying Mathilde, a Canadian who seems permanently startled by what she calls this country's "aroused consumerism."

"Is Mathilde here, too?" I asked, nodding politely to Alvarez. He returned my gesture with a slight smile that said he expected nothing more. The man kept his place at the edge of things. I liked that. Maybe he wasn't Tia's boyfriend; maybe he was simply a friend.

"No, but Timo is here," Tia answered. She had noted my silent exchange with Alvarez and visibly relaxed. "Timo and I both braved the friendly skies…" She glanced over at her brother. "Although not so friendly for some."

"What exactly happened to Davy?"

"Well, that's what everyone, including the navy psychiatrist, is trying to find out."

"Psychiatrist?"

Tia's face clouded. "I want to hear the story from Davy himself," she said. "Besides, a navy psychiatrist is a contradiction in terms."

"Just like you to be so prejudiced," Madeleine swept back into the hospital room with an entire tray of Cheez-Its and bear claws from the cafeteria. "They have psychiatrists at the CIA, too. And thanks to you kids, I've even looked into it."

Tia rolled her eyes and was about to speak when my wife spotted Alvarez. Tia took the man's arm and said softly, "Mother, Dad…this is Gabriel Alvarez."

"And who's he? Are you with the embassy or the navy?" Madeleine asked. She eyed Alvarez up and down as if looking for his rank.

"Neither, Mrs. MacKenzie. I'm with Tia."

He said it so simply and with such dignity that even Madeleine couldn't take it much amiss. She shrugged and offered him a bear claw. "So you're the new beau. Well, I hope you marry my girl...*after* her divorce is final. She's high-strung and needs a man to settle her down." Then Madeleine threw her head back and laughed easily and a tad flirtatiously—as is always her way with Latin men.

It was hard to believe that my wife would accept our daughter's divorce with such nonchalance. It was easier for Madeleine than for me. It also surprised me Madeleine didn't take this chance to blast Tia for her blasphemy against our belief in marriage. But Madeleine never ceases to surprise me.

She even left me once. It was way back when we were first in D.C. I was just out of the navy and studying Spanish in the State Department's language school. Perhaps I neglected my filial duties as any young diplomat-in-training might, but I returned to our apartment one evening to find my wife and child gone. Sydney was about two and Madeleine was pregnant with Tia. No note, no word for a week, and then Madeleine returned, red-eyed with weeping. As it turned out, she'd met an evangelist who had a passion for Ping-Pong. After the service—during which she was saved, as she routinely is every summer revival—they both lit out for a Ping-Pong championship in Macon, Georgia. As she tells it, my wife beat her evangelist paramour in the mixed singles competition and he snubbed her. After that escapade Madeleine never left me again—or at least not that I know of. Sometimes I wonder about that undersecretary to the Brazilian ambassador back when the children were teenagers.

"I assure you, Señora MacKenzie," Alvarez said with a playful flourish, "I'll do my best by your daughter."

"For me," Tia told her mother, "that might *not* mean marriage."

"Well, you can't just live in sin!" Madeleine exploded. "I thought you'd gotten over that, Tia." Madeleine took the only chair in the room. "Besides, if you two don't get married, Hawkins will probably murder you both. You know how he feels about adultery."

Timo ran in just then and almost tripped over his grandmother. "Oh," the boy said flatly. "It's you two."

"Look what your granny brought you, Timothy," Madeleine offered him two packages of Cheez-Its.

In spite of himself, Timo hungrily took the snacks. Only after he'd torn into the package and his mouth was full of those unnaturally orange crackers did he say, "I thought we were boycotting you both."

"Don't be silly, dear," Madeleine laughed. "In times like these, families stick together."

Timo made a face. "Well, I'm staying with my dad. I'm not going back with you again."

"What makes you think we'd want you back?" Madeleine snapped.

"What your grandmother means," I explained, "is that we're not here to force any issues. We just want to make sure your father is all right."

As if on cue, Davy groaned. He stirred violently, sat straight up in bed, seeming to notice his leg dangling for the first time. With a confused grimace, he lay back in bed. He was very pale, his lips drawn tight as if even torture would not make him speak.

Madeleine reached him first, even though I was standing right by his bedside. She ran a quick hand across Davy's forehead and kissed him on the cheek. We all had to laugh at the lipstick marks left on my son's bewildered face.

"You don't have amnesia, do you Davy?" Madeleine demanded. "Like in those war movies? Don't you remember your own family?"

"Yes...," Davy said slowly, but there was something warbly about his voice, as if he spoke from a great distance. "I do...I do remember you. I just didn't...didn't expect..." His voice faded, and he stared at each of us as if there was something in our faces he'd never really recognized or didn't want to forget. "Timo...," he said at last.

I have never seen such elation as when my grandson heard his name called first by his father. It was almost pathetic, the boy's gratitude. Timo ran to his father's side. "Here!" he called as if being counted.

"Timo...," Davy said again in that slow-motion voice. "Maybe you'll be the only one to believe me." He shifted painfully, muttering, "No one else does. Not the doctors, not my squadron commander, not even the other pilots." He glanced over at Tia plaintively, the way he used to as a child, seeking support from his older sisters. "And you'd think after all the trouble...after having to come back here...you'd think someone would want to hear what really happened..."

"We do," Tia said simply and came to sit on the other side of Davy's bed. Flanked by his son and his sister, Davy calmed down. "We've been waiting to hear it from you, Davy." Tia took his hand.

"Tell me, Dad!" Timo practically bounced on the bed, then seeing his father wince, he quieted down. "I've got a *big* imagination. I believe in everything!"

At that Davy smiled and looked almost like his old self. He reached up a hand to cup Timo's head, speaking so softly that Madeleine and I could hardly hear. I noticed Alvarez kept his place, neither moving closer nor farther away.

"Well...," Davy began slowly, taking deep breaths as if he were running a race; I noticed that on those electronic machines monitoring his vital signs, my son's heart rate rose considerably. "I was flying alone indicating about 450 mph and half-listening to the ICS chatter. I was on my way back to the boat and all the radio guys were carrying on about the strike...you know, Operation Just Cause..."

"Oh, yes, we know!" Madeleine piped up. "In my office, we knew the night before!"

Davy looked over at Madeleine as if noticing his mother for the first time. Slowly his eyes traveled to me. But they rested on Gabriel Alvarez. The two men exchanged a look that was oddly intimate, as if they'd met many times before. "So that's him...," Davy murmured to Tia. "Your dolphin man?"

Tia nodded gently. "I hear you've had your time under the sea, too," she said.

"Yes..." Davy closed his eyes. "I knew you'd believe me, Tia."

"Me, too!" Timo practically shouted and Davy opened his eyes.

"Yes, son. You, too." He eyed Timo. "Listen, if they ever tell you that your father was grounded because he cracked under pressure, it's not true! The only thing that cracked under pressure was the canopy."

"On your jet?" Timo asked.

"Yes...even the lie detector says it's the truth." Davy closed his eyes again and began, "One minute I was cutting my engines to hit the boat, the next moment there was this incredible fog. It was...it was just like with...with Faster. Like an instant rerun of that night, except it was daylight, but dark because of that awful fog. Suddenly I heard Faster's voice." Davy sat up, grimaced, and gazed at Tia, his face ashen. "I couldn't believe it! After all these years, my buddy back behind me. And he...he was singing to me!

"'Stay with me, buddy!' That's all I remember yelling to Faster. My instruments indicated I was losing altitude, but I couldn't tell with all the fog. There was nothing I could do except pull up on the stick with all my might.

"Who knows when the fog changed to ocean? It all looked

the same to me diving straight down. I don't remember feeling any impact, so maybe I blacked out before my plane hit the water..." Davy paused and drew a long breath. Again I noticed that wavering, far-off tone in his voice. It was disturbing—his voice was changing again as if he were between two worlds.

"All I remember is that when I came to, Faster was still with me, singing, for God's sake! I tried to turn around to see him, but I was wedged into my seat from the crash. I couldn't even reach out a hand to pop the canopy top. Worse yet, the glass was cracked and water was rushing in. I started laughing. I'd survived the crash, only to drown, trapped inside my own cockpit. I was still on oxygen, but that wouldn't last long. And then what? My plane was my coffin."

Davy stopped, staring for awhile at his own leg raised up in traction. He was smiling, but I didn't like the look of it. There was something skewed about that smile.

"Daddy, go on!" Timo tried to contain himself, but he was practically exploding there beside his father.

When he looked at his son, Davy's smile changed. He was his old self again. "Aren't you scared, Timo?" he asked playfully.

"I'm not scared," Timo protested. "You didn't die."

Abruptly Davy dropped his grin and looked away. After a long time, he said softly, "Maybe I did, kiddo...maybe I did. That might explain it."

"You saw something terrible?" Timo pushed him.

"No," Davy answered slowly. "I saw something I can't believe. So I must be crazy..."

"We're *all* crazy in this family!" Madeleine blurted. "So spit it out, son!"

Davy looked at his mother and burst out laughing. Everybody joined in. Anybody passing by might have thought we were a laugh track, we made so much noise.

"All right, all right!" Davy finally said. "So I was going to drown. Water filled up my canopy and I just lay there trapped, breathing the last of my oxygen. And all the while Faster was with me singing. He wouldn't talk to me, just sang lullabies. And maybe I went to sleep as the plane sank deeper and deeper. In a way it was beautiful, like being in a diving bell as we descended past layer after layer of coral reef. There were schools of butterfly fish, you know, those bright yellow babies with four black eyes, two real and two false to confuse predators. I saw meadows of sea grass wave good-bye to me as my plane scraped against the reef and kept sinking. Down...down...I don't know...1,000 feet... past coral-reef caves and caverns and pink terraces...3,000 feet...

"And then I was so deep, where coral cities don't grow. It was just darkness and silt as the nose of my jet struck bottom and lurched, then lodged in the sand. Everything was swirling and my oxygen was almost gone. I gasped and gazed out thinking, *This is the last thing I'll ever see.* If I'd had more air I would have screamed at Faster to stop singing those damn lullabies. Maybe he heard my thoughts, because suddenly there was silence. And heaviness. All that pressure caving in on me. I looked out and saw something I'll never forget: It was a sunken plane right there on the sand beside me...maybe World War II vintage, maybe one of those missing Cuban aircraft...or some training MiGs who had crashed. It was incredible. The sea life had covered over the cockpit with orange and purple sponges, with algae and a beautiful rainbow-colored coral like intricate beadwork all over the instrument panel. It was a goddamn eerie work of art right there. I was breathless with the beauty of it.

"Well, I was breathless anyway. Because that's what all those little polyps and algae and sea anemones were going to do to me—embroider and engrave my plane, my skeleton. Soon, sea cucumbers would be swimming in and out of my eye sockets. I shuddered and started gulping my air. It must have been a full minute before I realized that the air was sea water now. I was surprised that I felt so little panic. Air to water...oh, back to this again. It was easy. It even felt familiar, comforting. I just let go and breathed it all in, but instead of passing out, my vision became even clearer: an octopus oozed by and schools of fish so brilliantly colored it was like staring straight at the sun. There was light everywhere because of that bioluminescence, and I just basked in it like I had all the time in the world..."

Davy broke off and gazed at Tia. His voice was almost a whisper as he said, "It wasn't like dying, sis...it was like dreaming. And I didn't feel trapped anymore, even though I was still inside my body."

"Yes, baby," Tia soothed, "like dreaming."

"Then what?" Timo demanded.

"Then they came for me," Davy said. He closed his eyes and lay back. "They were all around me. At first I thought they were fish, those great blue-green tails shining with scales like mica. They had black hair that streamed out from their faces, and the women were beautiful, their breasts bright as abalone. The men were so graceful but supple and strong like dolphins. They were all singing—I guess that's their way of talking. Then...and then I saw him. Faster. My buddy. He was back, but changed. He was one of them!"

"Who...of who?" Timo cried.

"The mer-people...Faster belonged to them now..."

"You, too! They wanted you!" Timo said excitedly.

"I thought so..." Davy opened his eyes and looked straight at his son. There was regret on his face; even Timo saw it. "But then why am I back here?"

"Because we need you more than they do, Dad," Timo said and burst into tears.

It startled Davy to see his son cry. With one finger he reached up to touch Timo's face. "What does it taste like, Timo?" Davy said tenderly. "All those tears."

Timo was crying so hard he started hiccuping. "You know...," he managed to get out.

"I won't leave you anymore," Davy said quietly.

"It's true, then?" Madeleine demanded. Hysteria rose in her voice. "You're grounded?"

"Yes, Mother," Davy said, and again that unnatural smile. "Think they're going to trust me with all that expensive navy property? Think they're going to let me back in the air when I keep telling them about a secret city under the sea where mer-people are trying to help us save ourselves? Oh, sure..."

"Did they save you?" Timo asked.

Davy nodded. "Faster himself popped the canopy. He and another merman floated me up very slowly to the surface. Don't ask me how I breathed underwater all that time. I did, that's all. The navy doctors can't figure it, either. By all medical opinions, I should be dead."

"So..." Tia smiled. "*We're* you're afterlife, honey."

"*This* family again..." Davy laughed.

"What?" Timo said.

"Oh, just a joke I have with Sydney."

"Sydney should be here," Madeleine said. "This is right up Sydney's alley. Remember, Davy, she helped straighten out Mathilde when she thought she had a close encounter with Saint Teresa; I'm sure she could cure you of mermaids."

"Shut up, Mother!" Tia snapped. "Can't you see Davy is upset?"

"I've got a great idea. Why don't we *all* go to see a CIA psychi-atrist? I mean, I'll look normal compared to this crew!"

"Be still, Madeleine!" I had to cut in. I could feel the kids' boycott descending upon us again.

"Oh, heck, Sam!" Madeleine snapped. "Can't you see now I'm not the crazy one? I believe in things that are real. Like God, and my country, and angels." She shrugged, as if wearily resting her case. "*Somebody* in this family has got to live in the real world."

We all stared at Madeleine. For a moment I saw my wife through Tia's and Davy's eyes—a small-boned woman, but wiry and strong as a wildcat. Her eyes were an electric gray like low summer clouds shot with heat lightning. Everything about her seemed to hum or vibrate with a kind of static, from her red-tinted bouffant hair to her hands fidgeting with the crinkly plastic wrappers on another bear claw.

In that hospital room, we all fixed on Madeleine, but what we were really looking at was ourselves. What had we come to? A family that needed to call in a psychiatrist, an outside negotiator, to solve what should be our own business. A son who would soon be dishonorably discharged or like so many of those Vietnam vets, given a "psycho" label and drummed out of the military. I could just see Davy making the rounds of VA hospitals with his little mermaid story. They'd just laugh at him; they'd say it was all his parents' fault, that it ran in my family.

Just like they said my mother was crazy. I can remember her sitting and smoking those hand-rolled cigarettes, reading Victorian novels while her seven children ran the farm. I was the oldest, her favorite, the one she always threatened with the butcher knife when my father took off across the county line with his other women. I remember hanging out my brothers' and sisters' diapers when I had to stand on tiptoes to reach the clothesline. One day the grass was so overgrown it stained all my hand-washed diapers bright green. I started yelling and dragged out my father's ancient wooden mower. I mowed down all the grass, and the diapers got mangled up in the blades, too. I didn't care. I kept right on mowing until I cut down all my mother's dahlias, the spindly forsythia, and finally, the family garden: corn and pole beans and cabbage and tomatoes splattered against the farmhouse shutters. We had much less to eat after that. It was 1935 and I was six years old. My father sent me to live with cousins, sent my mother to the city for electroshock. She never came back. And I never lost my temper or my control again.

As soon as I was old enough to leave that farm, I did. The navy took me far away from all of it, gave me family and a war that was good to fight, no matter what my kids say now. It was the navy that first recognized my calm in a crisis. They shifted me from a teaching job to the diplomatic corps because, even with people screaming at one another in five different languages, I kept my head. In a strange way, I guess the training I got at home, between a mother always making violent threats and a father who wasn't above physical rebuttals, was good training for my future career in faraway countries.

But standing there in that navy hospital room, I wondered if I'd ever really escaped that old farm? Here was my wife, as high-strung and unpredictable as my mother; here was my son, whom even the navy could not save; here was my favorite daughter, who had married a man much more dangerous than Madeleine; and here was my own grandson, who was so full of fear that even the sky, even the heavens were not safe for him.

Could Timo see, could they all see that for the first time in my life, I felt it, too? The helpless panic. What if I couldn't really protect myself? What if I couldn't protect them?

Maybe it is all make-believe, the stories we tell our children that it is safe for them to sleep, the scenarios we devise in the Secret City to ensure our survival. Maybe we can't stop it. Maybe I can't stop it. It might well come—the dark, crazy calling forth of destruction. And we may call it from inside us. If my mother had the bomb, would she have dropped it on her family? If my wife had nuclear power, would she destroy our family? If I had the bomb, would I have used it as a child that day when I mowed down my family's garden? I had to wonder then—what's to stop a crazy country, like a crazy family, from destroying us all? We're all, every last one of us, human beings, just one big family in a feud.

From my head to my toes, I started shaking right there with everyone watching. I'm sure it startled them, my trembling. After all, I am the father; I can't be afraid. I am the protector.

It was not manly; it was not what the navy taught us; it is not anything that will save us or the world or do any good at all. But I went to him, my only son. I took him in my arms. And we both found ourselves crying.

"It's all right, Dad," Davy said and held me tight. "I'll be OK."

Then Timo crawled on top of us and started patting my back and saying, "It's OK, Nanpa. It's OK, Daddy. It's OK."

And I guess we cried like that for a long time.

10

SAFE IN THE SHADOW

Sydney, 1990

I

"Don't all comedies end in marriage?" I asked Tia when she invited me to hers this spring.

"Think of this wedding as covering a multitude of sins, sis." Tia laughed. "It'll officially end our boycott of Mom and Dad; it'll suffice as the yearly family reunion; last, but not least, Gabriel and I can finally sanction our many months of what Mother calls 'undercover adultery.'"

"The multiple-use approach to modern family gatherings," I said. "Of course, Tia, I'll come." I paused. "But *why* are you two getting married?"

Tia was silent, then said, "Gabriel and I aren't really ready to...not yet. But maybe it might restore family peace."

"Restore?" I had to laugh. "Honey, when have we *ever* had family peace?"

We both fell quiet, and as always the sibling telepathy took over. I could feel my sister's sorrow and confusion, but I also felt the pulse of something else—it was a tentative but heartfelt calm, much like the way we'd all felt that summer day so many years ago when we surrendered to surviving our imagined Armageddon.

"You know what I was thinking of, Tia?" I asked.

"Me, too," she said simply. "That day when we thought the world was going to blow up...now, *that* was family peace, wasn't it?"

"But only in the shadow of death," I said.

"Wonder if we could learn to really live like that—you know, safe in the soothing eye of the hurricane." Tia was very still, and I heard her breathing deepen into a resonant rhythm. It was a kind of communion, this silent link of phone lines when we could both simply breathe together across an entire continent. Then Tia said thoughtfully, "If every hurricane has an eye, then I suppose even Mother has some center somewhere inside, doesn't she, sis?"

I laughed. "Suppose so."

Tia sighed, "Well, after living all my life in the path of the hurricane, under the threat of the bomb, with first Mother, then Hawkins...maybe I'm shedding the family's emergency personality and moving into the calm center where it's safer. And *that's* why I'm marrying Gabriel," she concluded softly.

"Do you think they call it the eye of the hurricane because it sees where it's going..." I asked, "what it will destroy?"

"Oh, Sydney," Tia laughed. "Give me a break! Let's not look at the dark side of this marriage before I've even had time to bliss out and pretend I'm the happy bride."

"Are you?" I asked.

"Happy...or a bride?" I could hear Tia shaking her head at me even long-distance. If we'd been side by side, she would have shaken me, but gently. "Listen, dear heart, I realized that with Gabriel for the first time I'm not marrying my mother or father...I'm choosing someone more like...well, like you or Davy.

I have more hope because I've never ever wanted to boycott or divorce my siblings."

I smiled and knew Tia heard my expression, even mirrored it. For a moment more we simply enjoyed the unbroken companionship of our silence, our bond. Then I said, "Gabriel is one of us. Davy and I always wanted another brother."

"Then you'll dance at my wedding, won't you, darlin'?" Tia laughed.

"Wouldn't miss it for the world."

"You'll have to brave the friendly skies, you know, sis. Just like I did."

"The last time I took a red-eye back home, the world ended. Kinda makes a girl jumpy."

"You could hitch a slow ride cross-country with Davy and his kids," Tia suggested.

"No," I said. "Like you, Tia, it's time now for me to take my turn in the sky. Maybe if you and I do our flying time, the rest of the family can stay on the ground."

"Speaking of ground, you know we're having the wedding in Virginia, not Key West."

"Why, on earth?"

"Because too many members of our family are afraid of the sky!" Tia joked and I joined in. But I was thinking that our parents had persuaded Tia to marry in their church. Then Tia added, "Dad wants us to do the deed with their minister."

It has always amazed me that Tia, the most rebellious of us all, also tries hardest to please my parents. "Will we have to listen to a sermon?"

If you close your eyes to block out the black and white of the outfits, Southern Baptist weddings are indistinguishable from Southern Baptist funerals. Both center on a sermon cajoling the backslid, wayward, or wandering souls to come home. Home is not earth; it is heaven.

"No sermon, sis!" Tia promised. "And I get to pick the songs."

"You going to let Mother at the organ?"

"Sure. That'll be the best part. Gabriel's given Mom some Cuban music...just her style."

"Mambo Mama!"

"And Davy's going to sing, 'Slip Sliding Away'...no, no...'Fifty Ways to Leave Your Lover'...no, no, I mean, 'Under the Sea...,' that calypso tune from *The Little Mermaid*."

"Oh, Tia," I protested, "that's not funny."

"We've got to laugh," Tia told me. "Especially now with Davy. I don't mind that he's obsessed with some underwater family— not that it helps me any with Daniella—but at least in *this* family we've got to remember to laugh at ourselves."

"So you've got a job for me, right?"

"Assassinate Mother..." Tia laughed. "No, I mean, yes, I've got a job...should you decide to accept it."

"Spike the punch again?"

"Yes ma'am...but this time don't give Mother any seconds! I don't want to spend my reception setting another broken ankle."

We both laughed, but then I felt Tia desert me to dive into herself. She was quiet a moment and finally I asked, "What is it, honeychile?"

"Oh...I was just thinking about Davy's wedding and how Hawkins got into that fistfight."

"Do you miss him? Hawkins?"

"The children do." Tia's voice was low. "Panama is a world away. I never thought Hawk would volunteer to go back to that bush hospital." There was silence. "Sydney...," Tia said. "Sometimes I find myself so angry...over nothing. I'm afraid I'll take it out on Gabriel. He's so...so kind to me. What if I turn into a terrible person? What if I lash out at Gabriel the way Hawkins did at me?"

"Well," I said slowly, "I guess then maybe you'll forgive..."

"Forgive Hawkins?" Tia asked plaintively.

"Forgive yourself, honey."

"And what about them? Does ending our boycott mean we forgive them...everything?"

Them always meant our parents. I didn't know what to say; I hadn't figured that out myself. "Well, Tia, I don't know. Forgiveness is not the same thing as agreeing to be together." Then, I was startled when I heard myself say, "I'm...sometimes I'm even lonely for them. I know it's crazy, but I am."

"Vell, Doktor," Tia laughed, "ve'll cure thot! Von day. Von day—und you'll be over it."

"Over what?" I laughed with my little sister, as we have all our long years together.

"Your homesickness."

II

It was a Soviet cosmonaut who said that on looking back at earth, so blue and bright against black space, he felt a piercing loneliness that he at last recognized as homesickness for his own planet. With all its wars and violations, its boundaries and betrayals, earth was where he belonged.

Flying east for Tia's spring wedding, I gazed out the small porthole and watched the blond curve of prairie change to cities clustered tightly, as if for protection; then old, blue mountains worn smooth by wind and long-ago glacial waters. The world below looked so vulnerable. I understood, perhaps for the first time, why my father and brother loved flying. Being above it all isn't only escape; it can also be mercy. Everything below blurs, landscapes flow together like watercolors blending, allowing each other's way. From the air, from this distance, the earth's own gravity reaches out to hold onto us as if it were lonely, too.

It had been a long time since I enjoyed flying, about ten years, really. Since the death of my husband Josh. His suicide grounded me for several years, just as surely as my brother Davy now never leaves the earth. I can see in Davy what I felt a decade ago: The world has cracked wide open. You must stay very still because the earth is so fragile, as fragile as your life. No startling movements, no flying off into space. Just hold on to yourself and maybe you'll keep the world spinning smoothly on its axis; maybe there'll be no more earthquakes.

Davy has chosen to drive cross-country with Timo and Izzie even though he lives part-time with me now in Seattle. That is, when he's not up in the San Juan Islands near Canada studying marine biology. The navy gave Davy a medical discharge with continuing psychological disability for what the military psychiatrists have decided is traumatic flashbacks and delayed stress syndrome. Davy's belief in a tribe of undersea people doesn't seem that strange to me, especially since Northwest Coast Indians have told such stories for thousands of years. The problem is that Davy is out to prove it.

My niece Daniella can hardly grow up fast enough. She plans to someday join her Uncle Davy in a diving bell at the bottom of the ocean. My nephew Timo still cherishes a futile hope that his parents will get back together, even though their divorce is final and Mathilde has custody, Davy full visitation rights.

I had half-hoped to fly to Tia's wedding with Davy and the kids, but as it turned out, it was better to be alone with my own fear of flying than trying to calm my brother's newfound phobia. I have spent half my life telling my sister and brother that everything was all right, when it wasn't. It's good to have developed a survival skill with which I can make a living. Except now I tell people that it's not all right when they are pretending it is.

There is no use pretending. Sometimes the world does stop spinning. Sometimes the world does end and the shadow overtakes us. I know this, not only from living right in the rain shadow of this city which seems so often underwater, but also from my own life.

Ten years ago, on the very day Mount Saint Helens exploded, Josh took his own life. My years with Josh were like living under a volcano. I thought my childhood with a mother like Mount Vesuvius had lent me an advantage with Josh. But, as my father would say, Josh held the "terrorist's trump card"—his negotiations would include suicide.

It's kind of like nuclear war. Suicide is the part of the equation we never talk about—why we want to die. Just as we never speak of fearing ourselves, only the enemy.

I was seven years old before I realized that the Soviet Union had never dropped the bomb on anybody. We had. I was folding fresh-smelling laundry with my mother as she tuned in our brand-new television.

"Oh, look, look!" Mother shouted. She stood so fast to turn up the volume on the television that she overturned the laundry basket. I had to begin folding all over again. "Isn't it something, Syd? Beautiful, even!"

I peered at the squat Magnavox: a tropical island of coral sand and palm trees with smiling dark people dancing for navy men in white shorts. I'd never known my father's naval reserve uniform to include shorts, and my parents didn't believe in dancing. It was a party, I concluded, in a far-off place where adults included children in everything. Not like my parents, who were always leaving us with the embassy aides as reluctant babysitters. We were living in Cuba during the last days of Batista. My mother watched this Stateside broadcast with the rapt attention she usually only gave preachers.

She pointed proudly at the screen. "There're our boys, Sydney." I saw an aircraft carrier full of navy boys with white caps, all covering their eyes. Then another shot of men in black goggles. "They're only ten miles away from it, can you imagine?"

"Away from what?" I asked. I could see navy ships tiny as toys floating on the black ocean, with a few clouds wafting above. Then a shot of a propeller plane, a countdown, a voice intoning, "In ten seconds the Bikini Atoll will be gone forever...five, four, three, two, *one*!"

A roaring noise as a round, white blob rose up from the sea, exploding upward the way my mother's birthday cake once splatted against the ceiling when she threw it sky-high.

"It's like Old Faithful in the middle of the ocean!" I cried out. Then the picture on the television frothed and fell down into a many-tiered wedding cake, frosting in globs hanging over a bright, blooming plume.

"No, silly." My mother jumped up and down clapping her hands. "It's the bomb. The atom bomb!"

"A light as bright as another sun," the television announcer marveled. Then there was the blast sound which almost broke my eardrums because Mother had the volume so loud. I did what I would be carefully trained to do that next year in third grade when we moved back to Washington, D.C. I covered my ears and dove under a pile of hot laundry. I still remember the smell— Fab—my mother used it because she said it reminded her of honeysuckle and soap, like summertime in the States.

It was the summer of 1957, the Cold War was hot, especially in Cuba. It was the ten-year anniversary of that Bikini Island atomic test. The television program concluded with a warning that the Soviet Union was neck and neck with the United States in H-bomb production. "Remember...," the announcer warned. "It's not safe to hope for the best without preparing for the worst."

My mother gaily dragged me out of the tangled laundry. She danced with me around the living room as if she were electrified. I don't know which startled me most—my mother's giddy dance or the memory of that brilliant blast.

"Did they all die?" I asked. To calm myself I folded the clothes once again, careful to turn Tia's and my undershirts right-side out.

"Who?"

"Those people on the island."

"Of course not, Sydney. Didn't you see our navy boys evacuating them?"

"What about all the boats?" I insisted. "Did the bomb sink them?"

"They were official observers, Sydney...I wish your father had been one of them. But all he does is *talk* to Communists all day. Now, if I were a man, I'd be right where the action is! I'd be in the air dropping bombs or at least watching them with the navy boys..." Then she stopped dancing. "Your father was a navy boy when I married him. But then he got distracted by the diplomatic service." Mother grabbed my chin, as if to size me up. "Say, Sydney, don't you want to go into the military when you grow up? You'd make a great WAC."

"Not me," I remember saying firmly, fending off the migraine I could plainly see gathering about her head. After that I used to think that tiny atom bombs exploded in my mother's head—bright lights flashing, misfiring. After that my mother got her wish for a military offspring; she got pregnant with Davy.

"The Soviet Union wants to drop a bomb like that right down on us, Sydney," my mother warned, her voice low and wavering. She put a hand to her head. "They'll make another Nagasaki out of us...oh, my head is killing me! Too much light...pull the shades, will you?"

As I lowered the blinds and the tropical heat took us, Mother told me about those first two bombs we dropped—how all the buildings were leveled and people's bodies were melted down into permanent shadows on the street; how the Japs' hair fell out and their eyes were burned shut and the radioactive black rain pitted their skin. For years those Japs glowed in the dark, Mother said.

Everything around me started spinning; I thought maybe I'd gotten my mother's migraine. She went on and on until she collapsed onto the couch, right on top of my folded laundry.

I didn't dare move her. Let the laundry wrinkle, only so long as Mother could go unconscious. I folded a few of my father's shirts to make my mother a pillow, then I flicked off the television. But I could still see it: that birthday cake exploding right in our faces, blinding everyone with its brilliant light. It was beautiful, but it would blow us out like so many little birthday candles on one big cake.

I thought of my mother's "atomic migraines," as we came to call them, that day many years later when I was called to the morgue to identify my husband's body. Though I only glanced at Josh's face when the orderly pulled back the cold sheet, I will never forget what one bullet can do to one head. A head I'd held in the crook of my arm, a head I'd cupped with one hand, twirling those dark curls as if we had all the time in the world—as if I'd never see this familiar face congealed with a black glob I only later realized was his blood, his brains. Josh's head had exploded from the inside out, a tiny bullet, a gunpowder bomb. Only then did I understand that suicide is murder.

As I drove away from the morgue I thought at first I was hallucinating when I saw a fine, white ash falling from the sky. I knew Mount Saint Helens had exploded that morning, but I didn't expect to see or feel its eerie fallout this far away. On the Seattle streets, people stopped their cars to get out and stare at the strange blizzard from a mountain blowing its top. My hands shook so violently on the steering wheel that I, too, pulled aside. It was unsafe for me to drive. It was unsafe to be in the shadow of so unstable a mountain. It was unsafe to be alive. Most of all, it was unsafe to love anyone—because in a minute, in the twinkling of an eye everything could blow up.

I stood on the street corner with other bewildered people as the white ash fell on us. And I felt blasted wide open, as if in the center of my chest my own heart were exploding. But it was only a sob that shook me head to toe. An old couple standing next to me waited respectfully until I stopped weeping, then they each reached out a tentative hand. They said nothing; the woman patted my back lightly.

"It's not the mountain," I managed to tell them. The white ash fell on their white hair. "It's something else."

"We're so sorry, dear," the woman said.

And I believed them, even though they were complete strangers. I nodded, unable to say anything more.

The man tipped his ash-covered hat, "Might be something in it...might be good for the garden."

They passed on. I got back in my car and drove straight home. I did not call Tia. I did not call anybody to come. I stood in my shade garden and watched brave, white-weighted bumblebees fall down all around me. With my garden spade I dug a deep, deep hole where I would soon bury my beloved's ashes.

That was ten years ago this spring. A decade of gardens have been planted every spring since. I suppose Mount Saint Helens' and Josh's ashes have been good for my garden. I have come to prefer shade gardens to those sunny displays of gaudy gladiolus and marigolds. Give me instead the delicate tulip trees, the subtle, dark trails of mayapples, their flowers and berries growing on the underside. Somehow it is in the shadows that I feel the safest.

A few years ago, one of my clients told me the story of a dinner party at which one of the guests was dying. Conversation was strained because no one would talk about the woman's condition. After the polite and nervous chatter was exhausted, a silence fell on the table. At last, the ailing woman turned to another guest—a woman who spent six months of every year alone in her Alaska cabin while her husband fished. This sturdy yet rather regal woman had endured an attack by wolves, days of darkness when the sun never rose, and the yawning stretch of solitude.

"How do you do it?" the dying woman asked her Alaskan friend. "How do you survive it?"

To which the Alaskan woman reared back and laughed, then replied with a deep-throated voice, "Why, I just shine on it with my dark light."

I thought of that Alaskan woman that midnight as all around me on a plane bound cross-country I saw passengers sleeping in the semidark. Heads thrown back as pinpricks of reading lights shone on their faces, the people in the plane slept soundly. I have always loved watching people sleep. Perhaps it's those early years of taking my turn to watch over Davy and Tia as they slept safely in the shadow of my mother's spent passion.

I once did a study on sleep patterns among my couple clients. Those who slept effortlessly together tended to stay married; those who tossed and turned, suffered bouts of insomnia, and complained of bed-hogging rarely lasted long together. I suspect we begin to divorce our mates in our sleep. It may take us years to wake up and make it a conscious act.

Looking around that plane on the way to Tia's wedding, I saw couples in various stages of separation—the balding man who twitched every time his wife's head fell onto his shoulders; the woman whose mouth gaped open, her eyebrows raised as if in permanent astonishment. Next to her a small child slept upside down, arms and legs sticking out in the aisle. All the sleepers were so utterly open, trusting. I have never been able to sleep on a plane. People sleep on flights perhaps to dream and so defy death, because in our dreams, we never exactly see our own death. In our dreams, too, that moment is a mystery.

My father, who's just bought his retirement Cessna and is giving Tia a series of flying lessons as a wedding present, tells me the sky is really the safest place on earth to sleep. On that plane bound back home, on that flight to finally end my boycott, I saw his point.

Tucking in my legs, I turned to the porthole window and stared down at all the twinkling stars below. Then I surrendered to the darkness, the communal breathing, the dream in which we go on and on.

III

It was no easy task spiking the punch for Tia's wedding reception. We'd all forgotten about the South, that Virginia's blue laws forbid buying liquor on God's Day. It was Sunday morning before we realized we had not a drop of alcohol to sparkle up the wedding punch.

"Wine vinegar won't do," Tia complained as she searched our parents' refrigerator in vain for something vaguely alcoholic.

"I can't believe they still have Alcoholic Beverage Control stores here," Davy muttered. "Is D.C. dry on Sundays, too? I could just jump the county line and…"

"Then you'd miss my wedding," Tia said.

For a moment we all stared at one another, before I remembered. "Isn't there a bottle of bourbon in the basement?"

"What?"

"Don't you remember? Mother bought a big bottle ages ago for our fallout shelter because her civil defense booklet said no fallout shelter would be complete without bourbon for medicinal purposes."

"You think it's still there?" Tia ran to the basement with us close behind.

She was in her high heels and old chenille bathrobe, but Davy whistled at the lacy underthings revealed in her dash down the rickety stairs. My brother navigated the descent surprisingly well for a man on crutches, with a walking brace on one leg.

Past Mother's Ping-Pong table, around Dad's makeshift woodshop, into the bowels of this old family house, we finally found the small red door to our long-ago fallout shelter. Originally it was a root cellar, then Mother's pantry for her precise bell-jar rows of canned goods. It hasn't been a real fallout shelter since the midseventies, when Mother landed her CIA job and was given her top-security, emergency instructions which are so much more impressive than holing up in one's own basement. With her visions of vast underground CIA bomb quarters, Mother lost interest in this small pantry lined with shelves of emergency food, one army cot, a wall of bottled water, and a stack of Parker Brothers games, including her favorite, Clue, and ours, Parcheesi.

"I'm amazed we all ever fit in here," Tia said as she squeezed past a shelf of gardening tools.

"We were a lot smaller," I said, joining her on the cot.

Davy made an agile pirouette on his crutches and let fall his body which bounced us on the cot like a trampoline. "Perfect landing!" he laughed.

"Well," Tia said. "If we were under nuclear attack today instead of this shotgun wedding, we'd have to leave your leg outside, Davy."

"Haven't you heard, sis?" Davy grinned as he rearranged his braced leg so it stuck out the door. "We don't have to duck and cover anymore. Communism has up and died."

"Yeah, like you did, baby brother...," Tia said. "Now, where is that bourbon...?"

We all looked around at shelves crammed with nonessentials—a set of our old World Books, a row of pesticides, even an aluminum Christmas tree, its green-foil prongs sticking out of the box.

"It's dangerous in here," Tia said as the artificial tree snagged her nylons.

"Sure ain't much of a shelter, anymore," Davy murmured.

"Never was, Davy," I said.

"Ah ha!" Tia leaned backward and came up with a dusty fifth of Jack Daniel's. "Oh, let's have us a little nip."

With a manly flourish, Davy unscrewed the old bourbon and offered me the first swig. "Age before beauty, sis," he said.

Mother once counted up that her side of the family were teetotalers for six generations; add that to my father's half-breed

Seminole bloodlines, and you get offspring who can't hold their liquor. That one gulp of fine bourbon felt like a fireball from my throat to my belly. But it was pleasurable, this burning sweetness inside.

"Here's to the bride and groom." Tia held high the bottle. "May they last this time, may they never fear one another, may our children live to bury us both."

"Kinda grim, sis." Davy shook his head.

"Considering where we're sitting," Tia remarked, "it's downright hopeful."

"You don't remember, Davy," I told him. "You were too small to understand all our civil defense drills and things like the Cuban missile crisis."

"Yeah, Davy. We were holed up in here almost all weekend with Mother, and you thought it was just a Parcheesi marathon."

"Wrong!" Davy said. "I remember. And we played dominos, not Parcheesi."

He was right. It's always startling to check one's childhood memories against those who shared the same history. That bleak weekend in 1962 when we were let out of school early because President Kennedy had just announced the blockade of missile-carrying Soviet ships bound for Cuba, Mother shooed us all like little chicks into her fallout shelter. At first it was just like hiding out, playing in a pretend fort. We played games in the dark with only a kerosene lantern to light us. We ate Campbell's soup and animal crackers, with an entire box of Reese's peanut-butter cups for dessert. We took catnaps and listened to Mother's transistor radio. All three of us kids slept curled on the cot in a kind of litter, with Mother guarding the door. Sporadically, she led us in prayers for our father, who was out of the country working with Peace Corps volunteers in Costa Rica.

By Sunday afternoon we were more fractious than frightened, more worried about Mother's attacks than the Soviets'. And right before President Kennedy announced that Khrushchev had mysteriously called back his ships from our embargo, we kids, like the Soviets and Americans, came the closest ever to World War III.

"Remember this, Syd?" With a sly grin, Tia held up an arm and showed us a tiny but deep scar on her wrist. "Our scratching, biting, no-nails-barred catfight?"

It was a vague memory. What had we fought over? It was so rare Tia and I ever got a chance for a good, old-fashioned sibling conflict; we were too busy bonding together against the common enemy, our parents.

"I remember! I remember!" Davy almost shouted for joy. He took another long gulp of the bourbon. "Sydney said, 'It was Mrs. White, in the ballroom, with the lead pipe,' but before Sydney could find out and win the game, Tia knocked everything over. Then the two of you went at it like she-devils!" Davy rocked the cot with his laughter and we rocked with him. "Oh, it was a wild brawl!" He cocked his head. "Say…who won?"

Tia and I looked at one another blankly. "Well, obviously you did," Tia said, "because I have the battle scars to prove it."

"Wait a minute," I protested. "I've got scars, too." I held up my knee which was crisscrossed by thin lines that well could have been made by fingernails.

"I did that?" Tia demanded.

"Well, maybe you did." I laughed and shook my head. "Oh, Tia, the truth is we've got scars all over our bodies, the three of us, and we don't have a clue how they got there, do we?"

"The Evil Empire…," Tia intoned and took a long drink of the bourbon. Politely, she stifled a belch. "But we were some spitfires, ourselves."

"Right," I said and took my turn at the bottle. "Born terrorists." The bourbon didn't burn now. It flowed through my body like a molten lava made of honey. "Hey, did I ever tell you about my first therapist? After I told her about our childhood and then Josh's death, she very calmly looked me in the eye and said, 'Perhaps, Sydney, we might talk about your *own* capacity for vio- lence.'" I shook my head. "Well, that pissed me off so much!"

"What did you do?" Davy asked.

"Punched her out!" I said.

"Not really?" Davy asked.

"Not really," I answered.

We all threw back our heads and howled like a little chorus of wolves. Somehow midhowl it changed to singing. We were on the third chorus of "Blue Moon" when Gabriel, Daniella, and Timo found us.

"It's time for the wedding!" Timo announced. His face seemed smaller than usual. Or maybe it was because I was squinting. With a start, I realized that I was completely drunk. It was so rare for me, for all of us to lose control, that we didn't recognize the symptoms. With Davy between us, Tia and I tried to stand up. We wavered, then fell in a giggling heap back onto the cot.

Then Davy took up another song we used to sing together as children:

I saw shining lights, but I never knew
They were you, they were you, they were you...

"Start at the beginning!" Tia laughed. "You forgot the verse."

"I don't remember..."

"I do," I said and took up the song, as they joined me in three-part harmony:

When the dance was done, when I went my way
When I tried to find rainbows far away
All the lovely lights seemed to fade from view,
They were you, they were you, they were you...

"Well, darling," Tia said as she gazed up at Gabriel, her eyes crossing. "Here's the *worst* that goes along with the *better.* Do you still want to marry me?"

"How could I miss your mother playing samba on her Southern Baptist organ?" Gabriel smiled and reached out his hands to Tia on one end and me on the other.

"Is it safe to come out?" Davy asked as Gabriel pulled us all up. We stood unsteadily, with Daniella and Timo righting us like a rickety fence.

"What about the punch, Mommy?" Daniella asked. "What are we going to spike it with now?"

"Well, what about these pesticides here?" Tia turned to me with an amused look. "Sydney, do you remember the time you and I tried to poison Mother?"

"Sure," I said. "We did it with my chemistry set."

"What happened?" Daniella asked, jumping up and down.

"Well, we put our little magic potion in Mother's coffee, all six cups during that one day. That night she threw up a lot. But in the morning she was still there. Dad said it was food poisoning."

"Do you think your father knew?" Gabriel asked. He was herding us up the stairs and into our wedding clothes—zipping Tia's long-waisted blue silk dress, fastening my matching outfit, and struggling to get Davy's bow tie straight.

"Yes," I said and suddenly felt almost sober. "Come to think of it, I'll bet he did."

"Really, Syd?" Tia stared at me wide-eyed. "Daddy knew we were little poisoners?"

"Don't you remember we both got sent to summer camp in the States shortly after that?" I reminded her.

"Boot camp," Tia nodded and laughed. "Oh, yes."

"Did the Girl Scouts offer merit badges in poisoning?" I asked. "I think we earned ours."

"But did you two ever fly up?" Davy asked.

"You forget," Tia laughed, "we're afraid to fly."

I saw Davy's gray eyes well up, but he smiled. "How could I ever forget my ground crew?" Then he put an arm around Tia and Daniella. He threw back his head and sang, "Ground Zero, oh, it ain't so blue, if I'm with you…"

IV

The wedding went off without a hitch. Mother flipped every percussion key on her organ to a calypso and samba beat. So our sashaying down the aisle suggested we were in sync rather than besotted. It is still a mystery to me why my mother, with her native rhythm, has herself always forsworn dancing. Her music makes a congregation want to jump up from their pews and move. When Davy sang "Gracias a la Vida" in Spanish, balancing between his crutches like two slim, wooden partners, the small wedding congregation swayed as one.

The sermon was short, the benediction actually upbeat. Before we knew it, we found ourselves at the reception, sipping Mother's pineapple piña colada sans spirits. There were a few arguments among my father's State Department friends over Lithuania and the diplomatic intricacies of the just-released Iranian hostage. One of my mother's CIA cronies offered a toast to Davy and Operation Just Cause, which made Davy glower and Daniella frown because her father has returned to Panama as a bush doctor and won't say when he's coming home. But overall, the reception was as tame as a church social. Mother tried to liven it up for her new video camera.

"Now do something *really* risqué!" Mother directed me and Gabriel as we stood together chatting near the punch table. "Like dance!"

"I bet she'll show this X-rated home movie to her Women's Missionary Union," I told Gabriel as he swung me into a samba. Though he had not imbibed that fifth of bourbon with us, he was slightly off-balance; or perhaps he was merely disoriented to find himself smack-dab in the middle of our family. "Is it strange for you?" I asked Gabriel. "Being with us?"

I noticed his accent was thicker as he spoke, as if when dancing his voice falls into its native rhythms—the way my southern accent returns when I have too much to drink. His dark eyes met mine with a frankness I hadn't expected. "There are some advantages to leaving your family behind in another country," he commented.

I burst out laughing. "Yes, Gabriel," I said. "Nostalgia is a great cover-up for reality."

"Use to be...," Gabriel began, and we easily shifted into a slow dance, "I think, if I can go back to Cuba, my family will be..."

"Fixed?" I suggested.

Gabriel's oddly shaped mouth turned downward even more as he shook his head and laughed. "Yes. But my family...when we are together, we fight all the time, too. Like yours."

"You know, Gabriel," I told him, "everybody in my family owns a gun, except me...and it's legal."

"In Cuba, everybody in my family owns a gun, too," Gabriel laughed. "And it's illegal."

"That's enough dancing!" Mother called. She'd turned her video camera on a table of wedding guests singing "Shuffle Off to Buffalo."

"What is this Buffaloed?" Gabriel asked.

"It's what happened to you and Tia," I said and laughed.

That evening we all lounged exhausted in our parents' rec room snacking on trail mix and caramel corn my mother had made especially for the grandchildren. Tia slouched sleepily against Gabriel on the couch. They have postponed their honeymoon until Castro's fall which, Cuban style, they anticipate momentarily. In a rare agreement between my sister and mother, Tia gave Mother a bumper sticker that reads: "Next year—in Havana!"

"So...Tia...?" Mother began, munching on her great glob of caramel corn. "What did you mean by making your wedding on Earth Day?"

"Oh...is that today?" Tia said casually. "I didn't even think about it, Mother. But I like the idea of multitudes of people celebrating a second Earth Day at the same time I'm attempting my second marriage." She turned to Gabriel with a wink. "We need all the help we can get."

"So," Mother seized upon the subject, "it *is* some kind of statement."

"No more than your deciding to wear a fuchsia dress to my wedding, Mother," Tia laughed. "Come on, Mom, let's not fight on my wedding night. Throw me a caramel corn, will you?"

For a moment, Mother wavered, then she brightened as she picked one of the biggest caramel corn balls and sent it soaring high through the air.

"Incoming!" Timo called out. He and Daniella sat side by side on the old leather hassock that Tia and I used to pretend was our princess throne. Their faces were smeared with caramel.

"Come on, kids," Dad entered the rec room carrying a tray of blue corn chips and a giant bowl of salsa. "Let's not have a food fight."

We all dove into the chips and salsa. Mother's salsa is hotter than any we've ever had in all our travels. Ever since she heard that jalapeños have seven times the vitamin C of an orange, she has concocted what we call "killer salsa" as a way of keeping her family healthy.

"*Caliente!*" Gabriel breathed as he sampled the salsa.

"These Cubans are such gringo-mouths," Tia teased. "We'll cure you of that, honey." Tia laughed as she watched her new husband down his full glass of ice-cold Russian tea.

Gabriel frowned. "Tastes like…like Tang."

"Astronauts drink it, Señor Alvarez," Daniella informed her new stepfather.

It was obvious that she liked the man, but she was also shy with him and that diffidence took the form of polite formality.

Gabriel looked over at his stepdaughter. His coloring was so similar to hers—the dark curls and deep-set black eyes—they could be father and daughter. There was something else kindred between them, aside from the fact that, according to Tia, her daughter and new husband were actually very distant cousins. The kinship was deeper than blood; it was that rarest of family bonds—understanding. "What are you going to call me, I wonder?" Gabriel addressed Daniella thoughtfully, as if the decision were all hers.

"You're not my daddy…" Daniella furrowed her small brow. Then she lit up. "What about *Primo* Gabriel? *Primo,* for short?"

"Does that mean he's the best?" Timo asked her.

"No, that's what Cubans call cousins," Daniella responded in her little lecture voice.

"Then call me that, too!" Timo insisted. "Because I'm your cousin and I'm your best cousin."

"I think those two have the makings of diplomats," my father smiled. "Now, let's get this show on the road."

"What show?" Tia yawned. "It's late, Dad. We don't want to go anywhere, just all stay here together. Soon enough we'll all have to head back to the four corners of the earth."

"Your mother has a surprise for you all." Dad disappeared and returned with a video cassette.

"Oh, noooo…," we all groaned. "Not that! Not home movies!"

"We spliced your entire childhoods—all those years of home movies—into one video," Mother said excitedly. "It was expensive, but it sure was worth it. No more silly projectors and film catching on fire."

"But that was our only hope, Mother," Tia commented. "Every time you showed those awful movies, a little more of the evidence would burn up."

"Don't be silly, Tia," Mother said and stood up. With a lightning hand, she snatched the video from Father. Then she ran to the television, popped the cassette into the VCR, grabbed the remote control, and stood solemnly in the center of the recreation room. "Dim the lights, please, Timo." Gleefully, he did. We were all plunged into darkness. "Let's have a moment of silent prayer," she blurted, before anyone could flick on a lamp. "To thank God for our family and ask His help in the days to come…"

"*What* days to come, Mother?" Tia demanded. "What are you up to now?"

Mother flicked on the television, and its eerie blue light illumined the room as if we were all underwater. Familiar faces wavered in the half-light. As the video began we were astonished to see credits that read "The MacKenzies, 1956–1990! Madeleine MacKenzie, Camerawoman and Director…"

"Oh, you'll love it, kids!" Mother could hardly contain her excitement. "I've even had them put *music* to it!"

We all sighed as images of ourselves flickered across the small screen: myself a scrawny seven-year-old in a bikini on some tropical beach. One of my hips is higher than the other from carrying my siblings. From the waves, Davy toddles out and climbs me like a jungle gym. The film stutters and jazzy strains of "Jamaica Farewell" segue us into another country, another year. Tia is scowling from behind a palm tree; she clutches a life-size doll— she called her Baby—who was her double. One day I found that doll face down in the embassy pool, an iron tied to her plastic foot. Tia did not mourn her; nor would she ever say whether it was she who sank Baby or a foreigner. Actually, we were the foreigners.

To the soundtrack of "Hobo's Lullaby," there was a shot of Davy swinging in a brightly colored hammock, thrusting himself higher and higher, his luminous eyes staring past everybody and everything. Even as a child, he scanned the sky. More images flickered, more of Mother's favorite songs. Here was a scene of us kids holding a butcher-paper banner marked "Christmas in Costa Rica!" Behind us was a wizened tree made of green foil that glared out from behind blinking bubble lights. Next shot: my father and I sit over a chessboard, stalemate showing in the wary slouch of our bodies, our tight smiles as we gaze, eyes half-lidded against the light. We are failed negotiators at a press conference, each trying not to admit defeat. The same shadows beneath our eyes, the same eyes, the same sorrow beneath the surface.

I have never been able to not see shadows beneath the surface—my vision like those infrared cameras that detect heat loss in even the most well-insulated houses. I wonder, do other people see these leaks and vulnerable cracks? Do they register the cold air seeping in, yet hide the feeling even from themselves? There is a loneliness in seeing, in sensing what is often invisible. Often it breaks my heart; and I am shaken by what I see yet cannot say. Someone once wrote, if you show a person his shadow, you also show him his light. But what if no one wants to see it? I used to have a recurring nightmare that I was summoned to a high court as a witness. But as soon as I gave my testimony, the trial changed to my own—and I was condemned. Condemned for witnessing.

On the screen I see my mother dusting her piano, her hands more tender than we ever felt them as they circle and circle the shining upright that these many years later is a player piano with scrolls of her beloved tunes. As she waxes that cherry wood there is a childlike determination and devotion, a mantra of movement: *If I do this over and over I will come out all right. This will make everything new, this will make me whole.*

Over and over, our coming together as a family to make everything whole, that's what these reunions are all about, that's what these movies yearn toward. And I suppose every home movie is the same home movie: you watch yourselves growing up like those fast-motion films of flowers opening in what seems like seconds.

Now as I watched my family's home movies, I noticed the youngest generation had already fallen asleep, and there was a low humming in the room—someone singing one of our old family lullabies. They say that children grow in their sleep. I wondered, glancing at my family, if the reason we still sing lullabies to each other is because even though we're adults, we haven't stopped growing.

Mother startled us all by cranking up the soundtrack volume of "The Anchor's Aweigh." On the screen Davy snapped to attention in his navy whites as Mother's camera zoomed along the aircraft carrier deck, adorned with sleek, gray jets.

"Well," Dad drawled, trying to make light of it. "There'll be quite a few less of those these days, now that the Cold War is over."

"Fewer jets?" Davy asked, his voice strained. "Or fewer pilots?"

"Well, both, son. They do go together."

"Not always," Davy said.

"Now, Davy…," Dad took up in his most sensible tones. He wore his neutral face, the one we imagined worked best at the negotiating table. It didn't go over big in this family.

"Maybe…," Gabriel entered the family fray for the first time. I could hear Tia holding her breath for him as he navigated the impending cross fire. "Maybe cutting defense is a good place to start, as your father says—that's where we are now. Who knows where we are going?"

"How can you say that?" Mother demanded. "You hate Castro, don't you?"

Gabriel did something that has rarely occurred to us; he simply did not respond to Mother. It was not impolite; he did acknowledge her words with a brief nod, but he did not engage her. Instead, he kept his eyes on Davy, who sat across the room from him. Between them was the liquid beam of the home movies like a no-man's-land of light.

I saw my brother hesitate and at last sink into himself. His bitterness with the military was really no more than skin-deep, and what it covered most was Davy's sense of shame—that he had failed us, that he could no longer be our first line of defense. "Yeah, who knows where we're going?" Davy echoed Gabriel and let out a withheld sigh.

"We never do know, kiddo," Tia crossed over to sit next to Davy. She wrapped her arms around him and rocked him as if he were still her baby, still the boy Tia and I carried around on our small hips. "We all—everyone in the world—we just blunder along."

There was a long silence, during which we at last turned back to the screen. The sight of her startled us—after all, she was not family, no matter how intimate we were with her life, her sorrows.

"Turn it up!" Tia called. "Turn it up!"

"How did *she* get in here?" my Dad asked, bewildered.

"Oh, Sam!" Mother said happily. "It was a surprise. They can do anything these days with video. I thought it was a good way to end."

On the startlingly black-and-white screen was a smaller-than-life Judy Garland wearing her tattered bum's outfit—oversize tails with haphazard patches. A charcoal beard stubbled her chin, her eyes drooped low, she ran an abstracted hand across her short hair. She looked like a worn, but well-meaning, gamin gamely performing for a backstreet crowd.

Ohhhh, beautiful for spacious skies,
For amber waves of graaaiiin.
For purple mountain majesties,
Above the fruited plaaaaiin...

She took a deep breath and threw herself into the chorus, throwing open her arms as if she were leaping into a void, but someone would catch her.

Americaa! Americaaa!

"I wanna go home!" Tia sang. She clicked her house slippers and the kids joined in. "I wanna go home!"

"The old girl's drunk as a skunk." Davy nodded toward the screen.

"Now..." Mother turned up the volume as high as it would go. Though it blasted us, none of us covered our ears. "Now, that's a slow song that should stay slow!" Mother yelled.

And crown thy good
with brotherhood
from sea...to...shiiining...seeeeea!

The song ended with a bum's bow as Judy flopped over herself, then stood up straight, hands open to the clamoring crowd. Then she bent on one knee and reached out to the hands seeking hers. There was a stutter of the tape and suddenly all was silence, then the white noise of the UHF signaled the end of our home movie.

"I have an announcement!" Mother said, before anyone could turn on the lights. On the screen a gritty static buzzed like after a station plays the national anthem and then goes off the air. Mother punched the remote control. She turned off the sound but not the white blur.

No one seemed to mind the ashen white light that shone out on all our faces like a little volcanic blizzard. Gathered as we were in the rec room, it was even comforting to have such soft illumination. No one stood out; we all blurred together.

"Well...?" Tia finally asked. "What is it, Mother? Let me guess, you're pregnant."

Mother laughed gaily. "I'll take *that* as a compliment, Tia." Mother shifted from foot to foot. As she did so, standing in the middle of us, I realized with a little start, like electricity up my spine, that this hesitation was new for Mother. I'd never seen her reflective—not one moment in my life. "Weelll," she said and again fell silent.

We were all stunned by her shyness. It was so strange.

"Are you sick or something, Mother?" Tia demanded. There was an edge of alarm to my sister's voice.

"Tell us, Mom," Davy soothed.

"*Dígame,* Nana!" Daniella piped up.

"All right, all right!" Mother snapped with her old pizzazz, and we breathed a collective sigh of relief. "It's nothing, just that...well, I've given up."

"Given up what?" we clamored.

"Given up fighting you kids single-handedly. I've found myself an ally...a good Christian counselor,..." Here she cast a baleful glance at us all, then rushed on, "and she understands me perfectly." She paused, then sprung it on us. "In fact, Dr. Carlyle says it's not me. It's all of you!"

"Oh, perfect, Mother!" Tia said. "Does this shrink work for the CIA as well as God?"

"No," Mother said firmly. "She's an outsider—that's what we need in this family, an outsider." She paused and then said graciously, "I don't mean to slight you, Gabriel, but now that you're part of us, you're also part of the problem."

"What's that old Peace Corps saying?" I asked. I couldn't help but laugh. "If you're not part of the solution...you're part of the problem?"

"I'm just doing what you kids asked," Mother protested. "I'm doing my part to end the boycott. Aren't you...well, aren't you all glad?"

"Yes, dear," Dad said quickly. "They're all very pleased."

"I bet you're telling her what a rotten childhood you had, Mother." Tia started laughing, too, in spite of herself. "Or how your kids make your life miserable."

"Well," Mother tossed her head, "I have mentioned a few incidents."

"Turnabout is fair play," I said. "Are you going to embargo us now, Mother?"

"Oh, no," Mother said. "I want you with me. In fact, before you all head back to your homes tomorrow, I've set up a little meeting with Dr. Carlyle—you know, kind of a round-table session." She looked around at us, but we were too stunned to speak. "You know, like Sam does when he sits down with all those other ambassadors from every little country you can think of."

"Well, I'm not going!" Davy spoke up. "I've had enough psychiatrists to last me a lifetime."

"No one says you have to go, son," my father said. He leaned forward and I saw his face was calm, smiling. He was in his element.

"I thought it would be fun," Mother said, her pout evident in the shadows. "Something we could all do together as a family."

"Mother," Tia sighed, "therapy is not a picnic. Ask Sydney."

The spotlight was on me, but I didn't know what to say. In my own practice, whenever someone gets to a point when they come right up against some barrier or black hole or memory that is too hot to handle at the moment, I'll suggest they set it aside until they can face it, until they can feel it without exploding inside. Over the years, I've come to imagine all the things we can't face, all the fears or memories we can't handle as so much radioactive material. We stockpile it, we bury it, toxic though it may be; we hope we have years and years to figure it all out. I've read somewhere that the half-life of plutonium is 24,000 years, which means that's how long it takes to break down half of our poisonous wastes. There are even people now whose job is to devise some kind of symbols or hieroglyphics to warn future generations, those families twenty-four millennia from now, that what we've buried under their earth is still dangerously active. Our radioactivity can touch them, long after we are gone.

"I'll go with you," I said slowly, considering. "I'll go with you, this once."

"All right, all right, we'll all go," Davy muttered. "But then, Mother, you're on your own."

"Oh," Mother said and clapped her hands happily. "The Cold War really *is* over, isn't it?"

We all looked around at each other; we might as well have exchanged family faces, we looked so alike at that moment. We might as well have been naked, since we have never been so unsure, so small, so unskilled. For what we are going to do we have no training, no practice at surviving. In the soft, unfocused light falling from the blank screen, we all glow in the dark.